For Connor, Cooper, & Samantha

A FORGERY HIDDEN BY A MURDER DISGUISED AS A THEFT

THE SQUIRE THIEF

KIRSTEN SMITH NAVIN

CHROMATIC BLACK PRESS

The woman shoos the two boys through the back door and sternly tells them to play outside while the grown-ups talk. The door bangs closed behind them, and the children stand in awkward silence, eyeing each other. It's their first time meeting.

The older boy, Andy, breaks the stillness by leaping onto the knee-high wall that surrounds the patio. Beyond it lies a meticulously manicured lawn, unmarred by any evidence that a child lives there. He balances on one leg, the other reaching high into the air behind him, his body horizontal to the ground—as best as he can manage—arms outstretched to the sides. "Look at me, I'm Superman."

There's a strong family resemblance; the boys could easily be mistaken for brothers. The younger one, Hank, cradles a box close to his body and glances around, unsure whether to join his cousin on the wall.

Andy jumps down, no longer pretending to be Superman, and now mimics a tightrope walker. His arms remain outstretched, his feet tracing a crack in the cement patio. "I bet my house is bigger than yours."

"We live in an apartment, with a park and playground across the street," Hank says.

Andy's eyes lock on the box in his cousin's arms. "What's that?"

Hank stands straighter, puffing out his small chest with pride. "A prize for being the best in my class at art."

"Let me see."

"I don't know—it's special." Hank hugs the box tighter and turns away from his cousin.

"Fine, I don't care. Art's dumb anyway."

"It's not dumb. I'm going to be a great artist when I grow up."

"Well, I'm going to be a boxer." Andy clenches his fist and swings with all his might, punching the younger boy in the arm.

"Owwww!" Hank releases one hand from the box and vigorously rubs his upper arm. The older boy springs into action, snatching the container. He trots a short distance away, opens the box, and takes out a small tube.

"What are these? They look like baby toothpaste."

"They're artist's paints. Give them back." He's forgotten about the pain in his arm and rushes to close the gap between them, hoping to grab his prize back.

"I've never seen paint in a tube before."

Andy lifts it to eye level, examining the tube closely. "Crimson? What color is that?" Without waiting for an answer, he drops it on the ground and stomps. Bright red paint burps out. Hank's mouth drops open; he's too stunned to speak. Andy erupts in laughter, then grabs another tube, dangling it between his thumb and forefinger.

"Stop it!" Hank cries.

Andy wiggles the paint at his cousin. "This one's ultramarine."

"Noooo!"

Tears stream down Hank's cheeks as another tube from his precious set gets squashed, splattering the patio blue. Fueled by his cousin's misery, the older boy dumps the box and jumps on the remaining colors, cackling the entire time. The patio soon resembles a Jackson Pollock painting.

Hank collapses to his knees, sobbing uncontrollably. The laughing and jumping abruptly stop. As Hank gasps for breath, he hears the older boy say, "He made me."

A sharp thwack to Hank's head sends the young artist tumbling onto his side. Instinctively, he throws up his arms to protect his head from further assault. A woman towers over him, her face as red as the crimson paint.

Hank tries to shrink from her grasp as she grabs a fistful of his hair and yanks him to his knees. Carefully avoiding stepping in any stray paint, she forces his face down into the colorful mess, like a dog having its nose rubbed in its own waste. Her voice booms in his small ears.

"You horrid little monster! You will clean up every last speck!"

The older boy stifles a giggle. The woman turns her head in a bird-like manner, looking over her shoulder without moving her body. Her voice softens.

"Oh darling, did he get paint on your shoes?"

Andy bobs his head enthusiastically.

She snaps her head back to face the crying boy. "You'll have to clean and polish those."

Releasing her grip, Hank crumples to the ground, shaking with fear. His head throbs and his knees burn from being dragged across the rough cement. But the worst pain, by far, is the sight of his crushed paint tubes. Hank is heartbroken. Then—a glint of sunlight reflects off something metallic. One tube skittered away, having escaped the jumping onslaught. Despite the pounding in his skull and the sting in his knees, Hank dares to hope—maybe part of his treasure will survive.

The woman realizes something has caught the boy's attention. She follows his gaze to the intact paint tube. With deliberate calm, she steps away from Hank and toward the glinting tube.

Hank's voice trembles, "I want my mom."

Unmoved by his plea, the woman places her heel behind the tube, the ball of her foot at a menacing angle. She narrows her eyes and pinches her face together in a grimace, reminding Hank of how his mother would scrunch her face when pretending to be an evil witch in his bedtime stories.

"Your mother's gone. You'll be staying here now."

She flattens the last tube. An oozing blob of white spurts out.

He stares at the crushed mess of paint and metal, struggling to understand what the woman just said. Questions explode in his head, but he's unable to speak. Mom left? Why didn't she take me? When's she coming back?

"What do you say when someone generously opens their home to you?"

Hank continues to stare at the flattened tube; fat tears rain down his cheeks.

The woman walks back to where Hank is kneeling. She looms over the boy, punctuating each word with a tap of her foot, "Well, what ... do ... you ... say?"

Terrified of another strike, he forces himself to respond, "Thank you, Aunt Patricia."

CHAPTER 1

A guttural cry breaks the night's stillness. The Squire freezes in place while his heart races like a chased rabbit's. He breathes in, counts to seven, and releases his breath, steadying himself. Then he closes his eyes and focuses his attention on the sound. The low moan repeats, followed by rustling from the other side of the hedge. He is several yards from the door, but he can't go back into the house he just "borrowed" from, so instead he shifts his position into the shadow of a nearby tree.

He always takes precautions on these excursions, and tonight was no different—before setting out he confirmed the family doesn't own a dog. He debates what else the sound could be: a raccoon, fox, or even a white-tailed deer (unusual but not unheard of on the north shore of Long Island, New York). The beast sounds large—certainly not just a squirrel scurrying around.

A new, high-pitched sound cuts through the night, and he instantly knows the source—the most dangerous kind of animal. A tingling sensation runs down his spine as he fights the primal urge to flee. His hands suddenly feel clammy, and he rubs his palms on his pants leg. The Squire scans the area in search of escape options.

The sound; a giggle. The dangerous animal: a woman, or in this case, a couple. Hopefully, their fascination with each other will keep them preoccupied.

Had the owners returned early? Doubtful. More likely, their son is home on break from college. The vice president of North Shore Bank would not be making love outside on the lawn furniture.

The Squire is familiar with the property and knows the quickest way out means crossing the flagstone patio. Unfortunately, the pair of lovers have spoiled that option.

He reassesses his route and heads toward the neighbor's property, away from the couple. This course will take longer and leave him exposed in the open, but he's confident his dark clothes will provide sufficient cover. The Squire moves with the deliberate steps of a hunter, his sights set on the evergreens that line the yard. The neatly trimmed hemlocks look less like trees and more like a grand green drapery, separating neighbors. Escape lies just beyond that curtain.

The air is silent. Has he moved far enough away so that he can no longer hear the couple, or have they finished their amorous entanglement and might now notice a man standing in the middle of the yard? He crouches and waits.

"Woo-hoo!" the son yells, followed by a loud splash.

There's talking, but from this distance the words are indistinguishable. A second splash is his signal. Taking advantage of the couple's new activity, he sprints toward the tree line.

While on these outings, he avoids walking along the roadside; someone on these narrow winding streets at this hour would draw undue attention, or risk getting hit by a resident who has had too many cocktails at the country club. Instead, he crosses through adjoining yards, keeping hidden from any passersby.

The Squire has a long history with the area, and that provides him with unique knowledge about how to avoid estates with security cameras or dogs. He knows the secret spots to stash a car so that it remains undetected by local police patrols. But he rarely drives on these excursions. A car multiplies the chances of being caught—a flat tire, a backfiring muffler, or a dead battery are all risks he can't afford. So he prefers to dart between shadows and make his escape into the woods. Walking also keeps him true to his code: take only what he needs and what he can comfortably carry.

A car approaches. Even though he's yards from the street, the Squire instinctively crouches behind an old stone wall. Once it passes, he looks for a safe place to step. Obstacles he used to leap over in his youth, he now gingerly treads around.

He listens for a moment before stepping onto the blacktop, then sprints across, cautiously avoiding the soft, glowing circles cast by the streetlamps. Slipping into a small patch of woods, he follows the path until he reaches his landmark—a shagbark hickory tree. Its unique, peeling bark makes it easy to distinguish even in the dark. The Squire brushes his fingers over the rough surface. From here, at his usual pace, the Locust Valley train station is about thirty minutes away. He leans against the hickory to rest.

The close call with the couple still has him on edge. Memories of his first "borrowing" excursion come flooding back. He had checked and double-checked all the details. He knew the family was away, knew they didn't have an alarm system, and knew exactly where the item was. Yet, despite all those preparations, his hands shook, and his heart pounded. He hated everything about the experience. But he was desperate. She needed help. One or two of these borrowings should have been enough, and that would have been that. But since then, it's only gotten worse—ebbing at times but never resolving—forcing him out again and again. How many trips have I made now—twenty? Thirty? Does it even matter? It works, and for her, I'll do whatever it takes. Somewhere along the line, his jitters faded away.

Tonight's scare reminds him he can't afford to let his guard down.

In all aspects of his life but one, he has always considered himself an honest man. He works hard, met a girl, got married; by now, he should have a peaceful life filled with children and grandchildren. He rationalizes his actions. He takes from those who can easily afford the loss, and only takes items neglected by their owners. Many of his clients still haven't realized that anything is missing—he calls them "clients" to soften the reality of what they truly are—victims. But no matter the semantics, his justifications fail; the truth is, he's a common thief, far removed from the image of an honest man—and the shame haunts him.

They call him "The Squire" in the papers. Reporters tested a few different nicknames, looking for something catchy—like Silver Bandit, or even Robin Hood. But it was the Squire that the public embraced. As aliases go, it isn't bad. The Squire even has a noble ring to it, and at least his intentions are noble—even if his actions are not.

A plump full moon hangs almost directly above him. Earlier it had been playing peek-a-boo with the clouds, but now it shines unobstructed. He lifts his face toward the moonlight, asking for strength and grace. He's tired—down-to-his-bones tired. The burden he carries is beyond physical.

A train whistle trumpets in the distance. It's a comforting sound, and he closes his eyes. Some of his most treasured memories involve trains. "If you're quiet enough, you can hear a train whistle from anywhere on Long Island"—a saying from his childhood, and after all these years, his old man's words have always proved true. He lingers a few more minutes before setting off again.

"**O**ld Brookville Police, state your emergency," the dispatch officer says pleasantly.

The Old Brookville Police Department covers five villages: Brookville, Old Brookville, Upper Brookville, Matinecock, and Muttontown (the latter named for the sheep farms that once populated the area). At 21 square miles, it's the second-largest police force in Nassau County, New York. The district consists of sprawling estates and businesses that cater to the wealthy—country clubs, private schools, equestrian farms, and a small selection of high-end retail shops—all nurturing the Gold Coast way of life on Long Island's North Shore. The area is considered idyllic.

Residents call 911 for life-threatening emergencies, which are then routed to the appropriate agencies. For everything else, they call the Old Brookville station directly via its local number.

Many of the residents, especially the older, long-established families, view the police department as their own private security service, and often request help for the most mundane incidents. These calls are derogatorily referred to as "CCS calls" by some officers—CCS meaning "Country Club Set." The complaints are considered trivial by all involved, except of course by the caller.

"Vital" issues, such as the neighbor's dog trespassing (or doing something even more unseemly) on their property, or landscapers dramatically pruning their shrubs, are typical complaints. While none of these events truly require a police presence, department policy is that an officer responds to every request.

Dorothy 'Dottie' Garvey is a frequent caller, infamous for the outrageous demands she makes of the police. One such "emergency" involved the high crime of a squirrel eating from her bird feeder. When the responding officer merely chased the furry-tailed creature away, she berated the young policeman, insisting he should have shot it.

"It's a thief. Isn't that what you people do?" she said, slightly slurring the words.

Mrs. Garvey enjoys four (or more) extra-dry martinis when out for lunch, leading to arguments with the server, her husband, or the neighbors. New officers always draw the calls to the Garvey home. Putting up with arrogant and demanding locals is one concession officers accept while serving at the Old Brookville precinct. On the upside, the area is wealthy and predominantly residential, thereby resulting in very few instances of violent crime. Most of the officers are family men and women; those wanting excitement and big collars gravitate toward New York City.

Of course, not every call is quite so minor, so Sergeant Eileen Stone is unfazed when she hears, "There's been a break-in at Glenwood. Please send someone right away." The caller abruptly hangs up without providing additional details.

Sergeant Stone enters the squad room and glances around. A few officers are at their desks attending to the routine, unglamorous tasks of police work; one detective is on the telephone, and two others are typing. She addresses the most senior man in the room. "Hackett, there's been a break-in at Glenwood. Take Ryan with you."

Hackett stands up with a smile. Lieutenant Denis Hackett has a face well suited for his name—angular features with a sharp notch in the bridge of his nose, as if carved by an ax. Ambitious, with an eye on becoming chief, or venturing into politics, Lieutenant Hackett is always on the lookout to get a leg up. Taking a call from Glenwood is just the thing he hopes to parlay into a future recommendation. His smile fades when the eager young patrolman stands to follow him.

The black Ford Police Interceptor Utility (PIU) speeds out of the station parking lot. Hackett makes a fast left turn onto Wolver Hollow Road, fishtailing as he goes.

"How'd you know where to go? Sergeant Stone said 'Glenwood,' no street address," Ryan asks.

"Yeah, the Blues name their houses. Most pick something from old English castles, Moorefield or Dovenby Hall, like that. Story goes old Isaac Vos went out to the glen and cut down the trees himself to build his home; that's why it's Glen-Wood. Get it? I should call my place Casa Dung Heap since the ex took everything when she left." Hackett guffaws at his own joke.

"Blues?"

"You know blue bloods—the upper crust, aristocracy, old money. Didn't they teach you this stuff at college? Don't worry, rookie; once you've been around for a while, you'll get the hang of it and know where to go."

Officer Ryan watches out the side window, taking mental notes of the route. After a series of turns, the patrol car passes several sprawling estates and a horse farm before finally swinging onto a cobblestone driveway. A small sign reading "Glenwood" peeks above the leafy pachysandra, with "1230 Fox Run Road" inscribed below.

Glenwood is the estate of the Vos family, a philanthropic dynasty that shuns the limelight, as opposed to more famous givers. It's believed that Isaac Vos was a member of General George Washington's spy ring during the Revolution, since his wife, Ruth, was a cousin of Robert Townsend (a known member of Washington's spy network, code name Culper Jr.). Descendants of Isaac Vos have resided in Old Brookville for generations; the current owner of Glenwood is Caleb Vos, direct heir of Isaac and President and CEO of Vos Technologies.

As they drive past the expansive front lawn, Hackett lets out a low whistle. "The Jets could hold training camp here."

Hackett parks the vehicle. Eager to impress, he leaps out of the car and takes the stairs two at a time, hoping Caleb Vos is home and he can press some flesh. Officer Ryan trails behind, catching up just as Hackett rings the bell. The door opens, and a petite older woman with silver-streaked hair greets them. She's wearing a charcoal-gray skirt, a pale lavender blouse, and a double strand of pearls draped around her neck.

Ugh, pearls; doesn't she know they're just oyster spit? Hackett's hand drifts to the back of his neck, rubbing away a sudden knot of tension.

"I'm Katherine Tierney. I'm the one who telephoned. Follow me." She sweeps through the foyer, not looking back to confirm whether they are behind her. The officers step around a table with a massive bouquet of fresh flowers. A pair of small Impressionist oil paintings hangs on the wall opposite the front door.

Hackett ignores the pictures, preferring the ostentatious homes of the nouveau riche, dripping with gold, crystal, and marble. "If you have it, flaunt it," is his motto. He's dumbfounded that some of the oldest and most revered families in Brookville live as if they're broke—wearing off-the-rack shirts long after the cuffs have frayed, lighting a room with a single 40-watt bulb, and not bothering to invest in a simple door-mounted security camera. Rich people acting cheap. Hackett huffs at the thought. At least Glenwood is brightly lit.

Miss Tierney continues down the hall and into a spacious dining room. The table, large enough for sixteen, has three crystal vases, each filled with another lush bouquet similar to the flowers they just passed in the foyer.

Precinct policy is to decline offerings when out on emergency dispatches. Hackett deems Miss Tierney a low-level threat and waits for the older woman to adhere to societal protocol and offer coffee. He slowly scans the room, his eyes returning to Miss Tierney, who has an expectant look on her face. Clearly, refreshments are not forthcoming. Hackett begrudgingly begins his questioning.

"Is Mr. Vos at home?"

"No, the family is in Sonoma. They spend the summer on the West Coast and return in September."

"What's your relationship with the Voses?"

"I'm Glenwood's secretary. I manage the estate, supervise the staff, and handle Mr. and Mrs. Voses' personal affairs, and coordinate any events that may take place here at Glenwood."

"And how long have you worked for the Voses?"

"Almost sixty years."

Hackett looks up from his notebook; the silver strands in her hair and pearls signal old to him, but not that old. "Who knew the Voses would be away so long?"

"Family and some friends. There's also the regular Glenwood staff, though they take advantage of the summer hiatus. They're all away. I'm the only one who remains on site."

"Anyone else?"

"Shouldn't we be addressing the reason I called?"

"Just answer the questions."

"Alison King is the office manager at Vos Technologies. She can give you a list of specific people, including Mrs. Vos' staff. There is also Andrew Sutton, their attorney."

Hackett's eyes widen, and his jaw muscles slacken, but he catches himself before his mouth falls open. "Mrs. Vos works?" In his experience, very few of the country club elite work, and certainly none of their wives.

"Yes, of course she works. Mrs. Vos is in charge of marketing at Vos Technologies."

"Okay, Mrs. Tierney, why'd you call? What was taken?"

"It's 'Miss,' and... nothing."

"What do you mean, nothing? You said there was a robbery."

"I said there was a break-in. As far as I can tell, nothing is missing, but the room has been disturbed."

Now we're getting somewhere. "Which room? Take us there." Hackett starts for the doorway.

Miss Tierney does not move. She crosses her arms in front of her chest and stares at Hackett. Her face wears the expression of a professor waiting for a distracted student to answer an obvious question.

Hackett still has "almost sixty years" ringing in his head and wonders if the older woman is having a senior moment. He's about to repeat the question when Miss Tierney responds.

"This room, the dining room." Her tone takes on a clipped harshness.

The room is immaculate; the sideboard has an array of silver platters on display, along with another crystal vase containing even more flowers. An abstract painting hangs on one wall, another faces it from the opposite side of the room. To Hackett, the room doesn't appear as if anything has been disturbed; his eyes linger on Miss Tierney's gray hair as he starts mentally formulating a reason to cut and run. But he reminds himself that she's Caleb Vos' private secretary and tries again.

"If nothing's missing and there are no discernible signs of a break-in, why'd you call us?"

"The flowers," she waves her arm toward the table. "Somebody moved the flowers. I always set them to divide the dining table equally in quarters."

"Maybe the maid moved them when she was dusting." The right side of Hackett's lip curls into a sneer. He watches his underling bend to get a level view of the table. Ryan positions himself directly in front of the middle vase, glancing left, then right. Hackett lets out a short snort. If the kid breaks out a measuring tape, he's walking back to the station.

"I told you, I'm the only one here. I replaced the flowers in this room yesterday morning, and the vases were positioned equidistant from each other."

Disappointed, first because Caleb Vos is away, denying him a face-to-face, and second because Miss Tierney is not the cute French maid he secretly hoped would answer the door, Hackett can't conceal the annoyance in his voice. "Looks like you mis-measured this time."

Ryan stands upright, snapping his head toward the lieutenant, stunned that the senior officer would be so curt.

Hackett opens his notebook, buying himself some time before trying again. Unfortunately, his second attempt sounds equally condescending.

"You've been staying in this big house all alone for quite a while, Mrs. Tierney; I'm sure your mind is playing tricks on you. We'll write a report, but nothing will come of it. You can't account for any stolen items, and to the professionally trained eye, everything looks fine. When Mr. Vos gets home, have him contact me should he find anything amiss."

Miss Tierney's eyes narrow and her lips purse. She is accustomed to people doing as she says. "I told you—it's Miss. There's also a broken herb pot on the patio, that's an obvious disturbance."

Hackett lets out an exasperated huff. "Probably the dog."

"The Voses don't own a dog."

"The neighbor's dog then."

"They don't own a dog either."

"Well, someone in this town owns a damn dog." Hackett catches Ryan's eye and jerks his head toward the door.

"Wouldn't you want to dust for fingerprints?" Miss Tierney blurts, uncomfortable with someone so easily dismissing her. The lieutenant grins. "That won't be necessary. Besides, it makes an awful mess, and the maid's away, isn't she?" He strides down the hallway calling over his shoulder, "C'mon, rookie." Behind him, he hears the young officer trying to appease the woman. Rookies, they're like puppies, always trying to please. What a waste of time.

"It was nice meeting you, Miss Tierney. If you do discover that anything's missing, please don't hesitate to call us back."

"Thank you, officer," she says and escorts him to the door.

Miss Tierney gazes through one of the antique glass sidelights flanking the front door. Printed on the side of the black car is "Old Brookville Police"; the large white letters slant back toward the rear, presumably to convey speed. As they drive away, the shape of the car wiggles and warps, heightening her sense of unease. Once they've disappeared from sight, she returns to the dining room, scanning the area for anything else that may be out of place. She places her hands on her hips and lets out a quick huff, annoyed by Hackett discounting her concerns. "It's just not right," Miss Tierney mutters, unsure if she means how the room looks or how the lieutenant treated her.

ieutenant Whitney stands on the front doorstep, consoling the older woman. She clings to him, sobbing into his chest. Her tears soak through his uniform shirt. Mrs. Shundi correctly guessed the reason for his visit and broke down immediately.

The procedure for delivering a death notification is to say you have important news and ask to be let inside. It is one of the, if not the, most difficult responsibilities of a police officer. He has had to deliver the devastating news that a loved one has died more times than he would have liked to over the course of his career. All his years on the force have taught him that everyone reacts differently, so be prepared for anything—tears, screams, silence; one woman even threw plates at him. He helps Mrs. Shundi inside, calls her brother and minister, and stays with the new widow until they arrive.

Death notifications always leave him drained. At least Mr. Shundi was an older man. Telling a parent their child is gone—that's the hardest part. Whitney knows. His greatest fear is losing his own daughter.

A senior officer with the Old Brookville Police Department, Lieutenant Richard "Rick" Whitney joined the force over twenty years ago after completing a stint in the army. Since then, he's worked his way up through the ranks from patrolman to sergeant to lieutenant. He's in his mid-forties but still considers himself to be in decent shape, even though he runs less and less, and plays golf more and more.

While in the army, Whitney got punched in the face during a fight with an AWOL private, resulting in a broken nose. Despite this imperfection, he's often told he resembles a certain Hollywood actor—a comparison he doesn't appreciate. On-screen, his doppelganger is suave and daring, charming both men and women. Off-screen, however, the actor is known for being cheap, crude, and, worst of all, for neglecting a young son from a previous relationship. This disregard strikes a raw nerve in Whitney;

when he was young, his father went out, supposedly to buy ice cream for Whitney's birthday cake, but he never returned.

At the time, neighbors told him, "You're the man of the house now." Looking back, he realizes that while well-intended, their comments placed an awful burden on a child already weighed down by shame and guilt. He vowed never to be the kind of man who would abandon his family.

Once back at the station house, Whitney heads to the lounge for a cup of coffee. Hackett is there, rummaging through a bag stamped with the bright red logo of a local bakery. He lifts a bagel, turning it over in his hands, inspects another with a sniff before moving on to the next. Whitney wrinkles his nose in disgust. Finally, Hackett selects one with poppy seeds. He crams a third of the bagel into his mouth while poking Whitney in the chest.

"Your girlfriend left mascara on your shirt, Whit."

Whitney's jaw tightens. When younger officers are present, he'll chide Hackett; jokes about the dead and their grieving families are disrespectful even within the confines of the station house. If word gets back—which has happened—the insult is devastating. Whitney remains silent; it's only the two of them in the kitchenette, and he's not in the mood to spar with the other lieutenant.

As soon as Hackett leaves the room, Whitney gathers the bag of baked goods and tosses it into the trash before heading to his office. There's no point in letting other members of the department pick up whatever stray germs Hackett left behind.

An unspoken competition has developed between the two, at least on Hackett's part, after both men expressed interest regarding the chief position. The current chief, Roger Eaves, hasn't formally announced a stepping-down date for himself; however, he and his wife recently purchased a condo in a North Carolina retirement community.

The role of chief is for the most part an administrative one; qualified candidates are interviewed, and an appointment is made. Hackett, however, operates under the misguided notion that celebrity plays a heavy hand in the process, and he actively pursues the more high-profile assignments, hoping to get his name in the papers. He's also started a soft campaign to woo over the beat officers, whom he previously treated as servants—as if popular vote determines the chief appointment.

Meanwhile, Whitney handles the vital, but less exciting, elements of the job. He's tasked with duty assignments, coordinating time-off requests, and serving as the liaison with other agencies, all while still investigating cases. He's conflicted about the role of chief—sure, the bump in pay would be great, but the politics of the position, having to answer to five different mayors from five different towns, is a headache he isn't looking forward to.

"Lieutenant?"

A clerk leans in through the doorway of his office.

"Yes, Lois."

"It's your wife, line three."

Isadora divorced him fourteen years ago. After eight years of marriage, she couldn't stop being his wife fast enough, moving out right away and dropping his name just as quickly. But now, whenever she calls the station, she is once again his 'wife,' and makes a point of announcing herself as such to the switchboard operator.

"Izzy, how ya doing?"

His voice takes on a cheerful intonation as he makes a dig at his former spouse. During their marriage, Whitney tried to get her to give up her childhood nickname, "Izzy." But whenever he told her she had a beautiful name, or called her Isadora, he was the recipient of an icy stare. After she left and established herself as a professional photographer, she embraced the name Isadora. And so, Whitney started calling her Izzy.

She must want something bad, since his use of her nickname slides by without comment.

"I have a three-week assignment for *Vogue Italia* next month, shooting in Rome, Milan, and Florence. I want Laurel to come with me," Isadora says.

"What about school?" Whitney asks.

Their daughter, Laurel, should have finished college by now. Whitney did not sign up to support a perpetual student. Laurel is on track to graduate the following year, an event he's looking forward to.

"It's a few weeks; I'm sure she can make up the work. Plus, a change of scenery before she gets pulled into someone else's orbit would be a good thing."

"So, there's trouble in paradise with what's-his-name? Did you two plan this out already?"

"I've been asking for a while; she kept refusing until today. I thought you could nudge her a little."

"To drop out of school and traipse around Italy with you?"

Lois reappears in his doorway; Whitney nods in acknowledgment and holds up an index finger.

"Don't be ridiculous," Isadora says. "Of course I don't want her to drop out. Hopefully, seeing the greatest art in the world will inspire her to finish and not get swept up by the next guy she meets on the quad."

"Yeah, yeah, OK. I'll talk to her."

"Thanks, Ricky. *Ciao!*"

He places the handset in its cradle and nods to the clerk.

"Chief wants to see you," Lois says.

The day just keeps getting better and better. Whitney makes his way down the hall to his boss' office.

Chief Eaves motions for Whitney to sit. "Do you know Caleb Vos?"

"We've met."

"I got a call from him. Seems his private secretary called about a burglary. Hackett checked it out. He thinks she's imagining things, and with typical Hackett charm, ruffled her feathers when he was at Glenwood. Vos asked me, as a personal favor, to look into her claim. So, I'm sending you."

Whitney raises an eyebrow.

"I'm not going out every time a resident has a problem," Eaves says. "It's enough that the mayors already think I should be at their beck and call. You have better people skills than Hackett. Get his notes and head over to Glenwood right away. I think Denis brought the new kid; bring him with you on the follow-up."

Whitney rises and heads for the squad room, shaking his head. Smoothing out Hackett's impulsive messes had quietly become part of his job description. The two officers jockeyed for position as they rose through the ranks. From his perspective, handling the administrative duties was a fair trade-off—having a set schedule made raising a daughter on his own slightly more manageable.

Hackett is at his desk, typing out a report with his two-finger method—inefficient, but it gets the job done.

"Chief wants me to get your notes on Glenwood."

"You pulled follow-up on that loon? She's batty, that one. Nothing's missing, and there's no sign of a break-in," Hackett says, not looking up from his screen.

Officer Ryan interjects, "Maybe the Squire is back."

"Listen to the rookie, thinks he's Sherlock bloody Holmes." Hackett rolls his eyes and tosses a small spiral-bound notebook.

Whitney glances at the notes; Hackett's chicken scratch is marginally legible. "Have you typed this up yet?"

"Why bother?" Hackett shrugs.

"Procedure. And I don't think Eileen would appreciate being referred to as Sergeant Sweet Face."

"All the more reason not to bother typing it."

"Ryan, come with me," Whitney says as he heads for the door.

Whitney pulls out of the parking lot, heading in the same direction Hackett did the day before, but without the fishtail maneuver. Whitney asks Officer Ryan a few questions about his background and goals during the drive, then turns to the Glenwood incident. Ryan quickly realizes the two lieutenants have vastly different approaches to police work.

"What do you know about the Squire cases? The last theft was well before you started."

"I read about it in the papers, and some officers still talk about him. The Squire is intriguing: always antique silver, always weird, unusual things like grape shears, asparagus tongs, and sugar casters. I had to look up sugar casters; who knew people used to sprinkle sugar on their food like they do with salt and pepper?"

Whitney glances at Ryan—the new kid does his homework.

"As jobs go, it's pretty clever—people rarely miss an item they never use." Whitney pauses his comment as he waits for a horse trailer to pass before turning onto the driveway for Glenwood. "Those neglected pieces are just lying around. The Squire could have been at this for even longer than we think."

"Then why does he leave notes behind, calling attention to himself?" Ryan asks.

"Why indeed? Does anything about Glenwood make you suspect the Squire?"

"A few things: There's no sign of a disturbance, and it appears as if nothing's missing. But Lieutenant Hackett is wrong about Miss Tierney; she's not a doddering old lady jumping at shadows. She's sharp. I don't think she's imagining this."

"Let's go find out." Whitney gets out and walks around to the back of the police car and opens the trunk. "You can operate the camera, right?"

"Sir?"

"You know how to document the scene using the station's camera?"

"Yes, sir," replies Ryan in a manner more confident than he feels.

"Good, bring this along." Whitney hands Ryan a bright yellow hard camera case.

Large police districts, such as the Nassau County Police, have an in-house forensic team to document accidents and crime scenes. As a small police force, Old Brookville relies on its patrolmen to photograph routine investigations.

They walk up the pathway together. Miss Tierney opens the door even before Whitney has a chance to knock.

"Hello, Mrs. Tierney. I'm Lieutenant Richard Whitney and Officer Ryan you've already met."

"It's Miss."

"My apologies, Miss Tierney. Thank you for seeing us. I have a few follow-up questions; we won't take up too much of your time."

"'Tis no trouble at all," she says with practiced calm as she leads them down the hall to the dining room. I'm surprised you are even here. Your man seemed to believe there was no credence to my concerns. I suspect he thinks it's all in my mind."

Whitney notes the steady rhythm of her voice, the faint lilt of an Irish accent—softened by time, but still unmistakable. "Well, we want to be thorough. Is this the room?" Whitney asks.

Miss Tierney nods.

"Has anything been touched since Lieutenant Hackett was here?"

"Everything is exactly the same."

"Would it be alright for Officer Ryan to take some photographs?"

"Yes, of course."

Whitney turns toward Ryan. "When you're done here, get the outside."

Ryan nods, sets the camera case on the floor, and unsnaps it. Whitney asks Miss Tierney if there's somewhere they can sit and talk while Ryan works. She pauses for a moment, gauging this new lieutenant's sincerity. "All right so, follow me."

The young officer sighs and relaxes his posture as soon as Whitney leaves the room. When first hired, he attended a training session about crime scene documentation, but he hasn't used the camera since then.

Lieutenant Whitney has a by-the-book reputation, insisting on proper procedure and being a stickler regarding grammar in reports. He's also known for being fair and even-keeled—unlike Lieutenant Hackett, who plays favorites and holds grudges. As the newest member of the force,

Ryan can't help but feel intimidated by Whitney's command presence and wants to make a good impression, or to at least not screw up. After thumbing through the manual, he feels ready to photograph the scene. Ryan also checks the battery life on his phone with the intent of taking duplicate shots as backup.

Miss Tierney leads Whitney to a huge, state-of-the-art kitchen. Glenwood hosts many notable events, so he expected a sizable kitchen, but this is even more impressive than he imagined. Laurel likes to watch the Food Channel when she's home, which means Whitney also watches a lot of cooking shows. This kitchen rivals any he's seen on television. Despite the size and all the gleaming stainless steel, there's a homey quality to the space. Along the outer wall is a breakfast nook: large windows surround the table, allowing for sweeping views of the property. Miss Tierney motions for him to sit and asks if he'd like a cup of coffee.

While procedure says not to accept food or drink during an emergency call, sometimes the situation calls for bending the rules. Whitney's mission is to rebuild Miss Tierney's trust in the department—and, by extension, please her influential employer. Politeness matters here. And since she didn't poison Hackett during his visit, Whitney agrees to coffee.

Miss Tierney busies herself boiling water and setting up a French press. The coffee grinder pulses—a process that will take a few minutes—so Whitney uses the time to scan the backyard. A specially mowed, amoeba-shaped patch of grass forms a practice putting green. Caleb Vos spared no expense on it's discernible, sloped surface (a stark contrast to the tabletop-flat greens at the public courses Whitney usually plays). Several bunkers surround the space, adding further challenge to the practice area.

He's still admiring the green when Miss Tierney says, "That's modeled after the seventh hole at Shinnecock Hills Golf Club, I believe."

She places a tray on the table and offloads its contents: three coffee cups, a small pitcher of milk with matching sugar bowl, and a plate of cookies. "The madeleines are homemade, try them."

The rich aroma of the coffee is stimulating on its own, and Whitney is eager for the jolt of more caffeine. He reaches for the milk and realizes that it's cream. Whitney thinks back to the last time he had real cream with his coffee—one of Isadora's indulgences was to have cream in the house, so it must have been back when they were married. Miss Tierney slides into the seat opposite the lieutenant. He offers the plate of cookies to her before taking one himself.

"Delicious. Did you make these?" Whitney asks.

"Oh no. Teresa—she's the cook—she knows how much I like her madeleines and baked me a batch before going to visit her son in Boston."

He asks Miss Tierney to repeat everything she told Lieutenant Hackett. Whitney listens, occasionally jotting notes. "And have you noticed anything missing at all? Maybe something small, seemingly unimportant?"

Miss Tierney glances out the window. Ryan is outside, taking pictures of the back patio. She purses her lips tightly together. Her hands clasp and fingers intertwine with the left thumb on top. Whitney watches as she straightens her fingers and re-clasps her hands, this time with the right thumb on top. Miss Tierney repeats the process, stopping only when she turns her gaze back to Whitney.

"I don't want to get anyone in trouble for a prank," her voice trails off.

"You called the police; didn't you think someone would get in trouble? Who would pull a prank, and why?"

"Mrs. Eliza Vos, Caleb's mother, had special needs and wanted Glenwood to be presented in a certain way. It was my responsibility to ensure that. Caleb respects those traditions. My standards are high, exacting even, especially when it comes to the upkeep of Glenwood. Some of the staff think I'm too hard on them."

"Are you?"

She leans in toward the table, her voice a whisper. "They call me 'The General.'"

Whitney raises his eyebrows and stifles a smile. He has a hard time envisioning the petite woman in front of him as a harsh taskmaster. A tapping noise from the back door draws their attention, and Miss Tierney gets up to let in Officer Ryan.

"Did you find any evidence of a break-in?" Whitney asks as Ryan joins them at the table.

"No, the windows and doors are all secure, and none of them appear tampered with." Officer Ryan sits next to Whitney, sips his coffee and reaches for a cookie. He makes an appreciative mmmm sound, signaling his approval of Sophia's baking. "Oh, and there's a cracked flowerpot lying on its side."

"I mentioned that to your man; he dismissed it as being toppled by a stray dog," Miss Tierney says.

Ryan busies himself adjusting the sweetness of his coffee. The spoon makes rhythmic clinks against the cup. Whitney waits for the noise to stop and stares at Ryan, hoping he'll catch the hint.

"Miss Tierney was about to describe an item that's missing. Go on, please," Whitney says.

"It's my own cup and saucer that are missing. One of the few things I brought with me when I came to America."

"Would you describe them, please?" Whitney asks.

"The teacup is very old and looks like a clamshell sitting on three tiny seashell feet with a handle of twisted seaweed. The outside is white with faded flowers, and the inside is pale blue. The saucer matches the cup."

"Is it possible someone else used it? Or that it got mixed in with the other tableware?"

"It wouldn't be mistaken. It's Belleek—Irish porcelain—and doesn't match the Vos' china. Everyone knows it's mine."

"Vintage Belleek must be worth a pretty penny, but it doesn't fit the pattern," Ryan says.

"Pattern? What pattern?" Miss Tierney asks.

Whitney shoots him a look; he doesn't want to reveal any information that may muddy their investigation. All they need at the station is for a new rash of supposed Squire burglaries. He responds as vaguely as possible.

"There had been a few burglaries in the area. The last we know of was several years ago. The thief took small items. Is your set valuable?"

Miss Tierney shakes her head as a bittersweet memory rises up. She intertwines her fingers again.

"Only sentimental. 'Twas my mother's—her prized possession. She sipped her tea from it every day. When she fell ill—bed bound, too weak most days to even sit up. My little sister and I painted yellow flowers on it to make her happy. But the paint wouldn't come off, and I thought for sure I'd get the strap when Da came home. He was raging—but she stopped him. That night, he said, 'You made your Ma happy; for that, you are a blessing,' and hugged me. The only time he showed any affection. She held on for a few more years. At one point, we even thought she might recover, but, well... as I said, just sentimental value."

Miss Tierney looks down at her entwined fingers, a slight flush tinges her cheeks. She quickly unclasps her hands and moves them out of sight onto her lap.

"And those are the only two items that you've noticed missing since yesterday?" Whitney asks.

"Oh no, my cup and saucer have been gone for six months, maybe more now. Do you think the same person who took my cup came back and moved the flowers?"

"Do you think it's the same person?"

"I don't know." She looks out the window, formulating her words. "When I noticed my cup and saucer were gone, I figured it was a prank and that eventually they'd turn up. The flowers are different, and even though nothing's missing, it just feels like something is wrong—almost menacing. I know that doesn't make much sense."

"Is there anyone on the staff that you think might have taken your cup as a prank?" His tone is neutral, but probing.

"Not off the top of my head, none of the current staff, but we hire temps for special events. What was taken from the other homes?"

"Silver," Ryan says, this time acutely aware of Whitney's piercing gaze. Realizing his error, he looks down at his shoes in embarrassment. Whitney pivots; there's no point in being evasive about the Squire crimes now. He taps a finger against the cream pitcher, steadying the conversation. "Do the Voses have an extensive silver service? Antiques, perhaps?"

"Most of their collection is from the late 1800s to early 1900s along with a few pieces from colonial times."

"I saw a few pieces on display in the dining room. Is there more?"

"In the butler's pantry. Let me show you."

Miss Tierney leads the two policemen to a pantry the size of a large walk-in closet. Custom built-in cabinets line opposite walls. On one side, the cabinets extend from floor to ceiling. On the other is a waist-high cabinet topped by a marble slab, creating a workspace. The far end has a stained-glass window, an odd extravagance for a pantry. Opening one pair of doors to check the contents, Miss Tierney sighs, "I almost hoped something was missing; then I wouldn't sound so silly."

The trio return to the kitchen. On their way, Whitney asks, "Do you have an inventory of the pantry items?"

"For most of the items, yes, of course."

"When you have the time, check everything and let us know if you find any discrepancies."

"I remember reading about those robberies; the 'silver bandit'. He had another name too, something unusual, but also regal sounding—the Squire. Would you say he's at it again, so?" Miss Tierney asks.

This is exactly the kind of speculation Whitney was hoping to avoid. He wonders if she'll still provide an honest accounting now.

"Hard to say. The only missing items are your cup and saucer, which you said yourself you think is the result of a prank. Honestly, there isn't much to go on. That said, I would like to get the inventory confirmed, as well as a list of employees—both staff and temps. Here's my card; I'm writing my cell number on the back. Please call me directly once you've gathered all the information. I think that's all for the time being."

Miss Tierney takes the card and stares at the handwritten phone number.

"Thank you, Lieutenant Whitney. And it was nice to see you again, Officer Ryan. I'll show you out."

But Miss Tierney doesn't move; instead, she's fixated on the card.

"Is there something else, Miss Tierney?" Whitney asks. "Miss Tierney?"

"Well, yes." She looks up at him. "There was a note."

"A note!" Ryan is about to say more, but remembering his earlier blunder lets his outburst hang in the air with no further comment.

"What about the note?" Whitney asks.

"I'd forgotten all about it. The day my cup and saucer went missing, there was a note left in its place. I suppose that's why I thought it was a prank."

"Do you still have it?"

"It's in my desk drawer. I'll be right back."

She returns a little out of breath and hands a note card to Whitney.

In a combination of printed and cursive letters, it reads:

> Your shell is enchanting, and I am sorry to take it from ye,
> but I know one who will draw great joy in drinking from
> the Irish Sea, and so I must set your lovely free.

"Sure, it's a joke, isn't it?" Miss Tierney asks.

"I'm not sure. It is interesting, though," Whitney says. "May I hold on to this for a while? And if it's alright, I'd like to leave through the back door and walk around to the front."

Miss Tierney holds the door ajar as the policemen pass. The lieutenant points to the toppled flowerpot, then to the house. Officer Ryan crouches low to photograph the pot with its mangled herbs. Her shoulders relax— she feels better now than she did after that rude Lieutenant Hackett's visit. She closes the door and heads back to tidy the kitchen. Yet the same unsettled impression from earlier still lingers.

CHAPTER 4

Officer Ryan can barely conceal his excitement during the ride back to the station house. Working on a notable case like the Squire is a fortunate break for a rookie. "Do you think the Squire is really back?"

"Can't say yet," Whitney replies. "And don't get in the habit of accepting food or drink on calls—this was a one-off."

"Yes, sir. But the Squire... there was a note—that cinches it, doesn't it?"

"Or someone's copying him. Let's not get ahead of ourselves. The Squire is certainly a colorful character. Could be a maid broke the cup and left the note to cover it up. Let's keep this in-house; the last thing we need is for the station to be inundated by calls about the Squire. Can you make me prints of the pictures you took? I know they're uploaded to the system, but I still like to see prints. I don't need everything—ten should do it."

Whitney pulls the PIU into a parking spot marked "Reserved for Official Vehicles."

"I'll put a rush on it and get them to you before you go home tonight." Ryan races into the station house.

Lieutenant Whitney ambles along after him. He enters the evidence storage room. Recent cases are in a digital system, but it took a long time for the powers that be to invest in modern technology. Older cases, like the Squire, are still on paper. After locating the file, he heads to his desk.

Chief Eaves steps into the lieutenant's office. "How'd it go at Glenwood?"

"Fine. We also learned a personal item of hers went missing six months ago. So, there's a moved vase and a missing coffee cup. The most likely explanation is it's a practical joke."

"And the other possibility?" Eaves asks.

Whitney holds up the file he pulled from the archives.

"The Squire. Are you sure?"

"No, but there are similarities."

"Okay, so when Caleb Vos calls, I can say I have a team investigating," Eaves says.

"A team?" Whitney cocks his head to one side.

"You, Hackett, and Ryan. Three of my men have been out to Glenwood so far; that should put his mind at ease."

The chief's adeptness at political spin both impresses and concerns Whitney. How will he handle that aspect of the job if he moves into the top spot?

"I've got a couple of small leads. I'll let you know if anything pans out."

"Good." Chief Eaves starts toward the door. Turning back, he asks, "How you hitting them these days, Whit?"

"Not bad."

"The Brookville mayor invited me to play at the Wolver Hollow Golf Club with him. You still friends with the pro at Oyster Bay? Can you get him to fit me in this week? I need to straighten out my slice."

"I'll give him a call."

"Thanks, and don't stay too late with the Squire."

Whitney heads to the break room for a snack but, recalling Hackett's gross fondling of the bagels that morning, wonders what else he may have touched. He turns back toward his office, thinking he doesn't need the empty calories anyway.

At his desk, he goes through the papers listing the stolen property attributed to the Squire: mustard ladles, chip servers, lemon forks, fish knives. His mind drifts—observing proper etiquette in the gilded age must have been like navigating a minefield. Would someone be shunned for using an olive pick to take a pat of butter? What kind of punishment goes with the faux pas of carving the Thanksgiving turkey with a fish knife?

Between his flights of fancy and the gurgling in his stomach, Whitney realizes it's time to go home. He glances at the clock: 6:47 p.m.—losing track of time is easy when chasing the Squire. His office phone rings, and after a brief hesitation, he picks up the handset.

"Yes?"

"Call for you, Lieu. Some lawyer named Sutton."

"Put him through."

"Good evening, Lieutenant. I'm Andrew Sutton, attorney for Caleb Vos. I understand you've been questioning Miss Tierney without her attorney present."

"Mr. Sutton, you said you're Mr. Vos' attorney. Do you also represent Miss Tierney?"

"I represent the whole of Glenwood. And want to know why I wasn't contacted regarding this interrogation."

"There must be some confusion here. I went to Glenwood as a follow-up on another officer's initial investigation. Miss Tierney is not a suspect and wasn't questioned as such."

"Yes, but as I understand from Lieutenant Hackett, there was no crime. By what authority are you harassing my client?"

Whitney takes a deep breath before responding. "Mr. Sutton, I am not at liberty to discuss an open investigation with an unsubstantiated third party over the telephone. I have other work I must attend to. Good night." He disconnects the call.

Jackass. Must be desperate for billable hours.

CHAPTER 5

L ong Island, New York, a narrow stretch of land east of New York City
extending 118 miles into the Atlantic Ocean, is known for its beautiful
beaches, bumper-to-bumper expressway traffic, and a distinctive
accent that includes 'caw-fee,' 'tawlk,' and 'regulah.'

The North Shore began as farmland. After the Great Depression, the
area became a popular destination for wealthy New Yorkers to build their
country estates—a nearby respite from the hustle and bustle of city life.
During this time, hundreds of mansions were constructed, transforming
the once fertile farmland into replicas of European country estates. This
area, which includes the Old Brookville Police District, soon became
known as the "Gold Coast."

Nearly a century later, to accommodate more suburban housing, the
expansive estates were subdivided. Yet, the homes remain large and
continue to attract the elite. Though, instead of New York industrialists,
the residents are now celebrities: a national news anchorman, a best-
selling novelist specializing in espionage thrillers, and a Broadway
producer with his songstress wife. Plus, many current and retired
professional athletes live in the Brookville area due in part to its proximity
to Madison Square Garden, Citi Field, and the National Tennis Center.

Whitney drives ten minutes from Old Brookville to his home in East
Norwich, covering approximately five miles door-to-door. In that short
distance, the average house price drops by about 1.7 million, and lot sizes
shrink from an expansive three acres to a cozy 10,075 square feet. No
one in the department earns enough to buy a home in the Brookvilles.
Most of the senior officers live in suburban towns surrounding the Old
Brookville district: Oyster Bay, Sea Cliff, Bayville, and Jericho are the most
popular locales. The younger patrolmen opt for apartments in the nearby
City of Glen Cove.

He parks on the street in front of his house. Glancing at his yard as he walks along the brick pathway, Whitney evaluates whether or not the grass needs a trim. He enters to find his daughter, Laurel, lounging on the sofa watching a cooking show. Maybe she's met someone from Le Cordon Bleu school and plans to transfer—not another change. A sigh escapes as he takes off his jacket.

There it is—the crux of Laurel's problem: She's a smart girl who, frustratingly for her father, lacks the self-confidence to pursue her own future. When first applying to college, she planned on going with her then-boyfriend. They broke up—as most high school sweethearts do—and thankfully she applied to a few backup schools. Whitney was happy when Laurel decided to live at home and attend Post College, but now he's concerned about her lengthy student career. Laurel has studied communications, literature, history, and now fine arts. Each field she delved into was to follow a boy. Her grades were always excellent; she threw herself into each major passionately, but when the romance fizzled, so did her interest. Hence the multitude of majors.

"You watch enough of these shows; shouldn't a gourmet dinner be on the table waiting for me?" he asks.

"Ha-ha, very funny. I picked up a few things from the store. I'll start now that you're home," Laurel says.

"That would be great, but first I have some work to finish up."

"No prob, I'll call you when it's ready."

Whitney settles into his home office. Puzzled by the events at Glenwood, he starts by looking up vintage Belleek online. Why would the Squire take the cup and saucer? Pristine, the pair is worth two-hundred fifty dollars; marred, they're worthless. He hasn't heard back from Miss Tierney regarding the inventory yet, even though he's sure she started counting the silver as soon as he and Ryan left. And what about the flowers? She seems more upset about a misaligned vase than her actual missing cup, which she claims has great sentimental value.

Ryan's photos from Glenwood are fanned out on the floor. Whitney circles the display, hoping a new angle will provide fresh insight. It does not. When Laurel calls from the other room, he leaves the photos behind and joins her for dinner.

At each place setting is a bowl of rigatoni pasta with chunks of grilled chicken, chopped tomatoes, olives, and onions. Two green salads sit alongside the main meal. Whitney grates some fresh Parmesan cheese over his dish. "So, is there a special reason for this meal?"

"I thought you liked this dish."

"I do. I mean, it's Italian."

"You talked to Mom."

"I talked to Mom."

"Really?" Laurel brightens. "Then I can go? Mom has never asked me to join her on a travel assignment before. It's a great opportunity."

"To do what, carry her film canisters?"

Laurel rolls her eyes. "It's all digital now, no more film canisters."

"No, seriously—how is this a good opportunity for you?"

"Really? You're going to make me argue my case for this?" Laurel says, crossing her arms and leaning back.

Whitney nods while pouring vinaigrette dressing on his salad.

"Okay then, first there's the chance to experience a different culture— their language, food, scenery; you always say there's a big world out there beyond the Whitestone Bridge. Second, do I really need to go into how important it is for an art student to see great works of art up close and personal, not just from books or the Internet? Da Vinci, Michelangelo, Botticelli, Titian. And finally, there's the mother-daughter bonding time."

"Sorry, no go. You had me until that last one."

Laurel grins. "Thanks, Dad. And I've already spoken to my advisor. I'll need to make up some of the studio time and write a paper, but I can keep my full course load. So, I'm still on track for graduation."

"What about 'Sculptor Boy'?" Whitney asks. He never calls her boyfriends by name, instead referring to them by the subject they're studying. With this one, things never seemed on firm footing—on-again, off-again—and Whitney has been especially unimpressed. A sculptor? How will he support a family?

"Birk? He's caught up in his senior show, and I think some time apart would be a good thing."

"Oh," Whitney says as nonchalantly as he can while helping himself to more chicken and pasta. Meanwhile, the triumphant strains of Beethoven's *Ode to Joy* play in his head.

"What?"

"Nothing, I just think you're right. This trip will be good for you."

They finish dinner, and Whitney returns to the photographs. He's staring at the display, not focusing on any one picture in particular. Sensing a presence, he looks up to see Laurel in the doorway.

"What are you working on?" she asks.

"A new case, a suspected burglary, but there's no sign of forced entry and nothing's missing. The only clues are a moved vase and a knocked-over flowerpot by the back door."

"The Squire?" Laurel asks.

"Maybe, but not for certain."

Laurel sits next to her father, and the two study the pictures. He tugs on a section of her hair dyed neon pink. "When are you getting rid of this?"

"I like it."

"Who's going to hire someone with pink hair?"

"I'm an artist, Dad. I don't think anyone will hold it against me. Besides, my hair is pretty tame compared to others."

"There you go. By having normal-colored hair, you'll stand out from all the other artsy types."

Laurel sighs and arranges herself in a thinking posture, one leg crossed over the other, elbows resting on her knee as she cradles her chin in both hands. She studies the pictures. The array of photos doesn't look like a typical crime scene; most of the images feature flowers on a dining room table, with a few showing a patio. The only thing out of place is a cracked flowerpot lying on its side. She tilts her head quizzically, first one way and then the other. Finally, she asks "Why is the Thorpe upside down?"

"I beg your pardon, the what?"

She points to a photo of a crystal vase, an abstract painting displayed in the background. "That painting—it's a Kenneth Thorpe, and it's hanging upside down. Whose house is it? I mean, if they can afford a Thorpe, they really ought to know better."

Whitney picks up the photo she pointed at. He's not familiar with the name Kenneth Thorpe. The painting is black and white, and to him, the broad brushstrokes resemble the chaotic scribbles of a very drunk person trying to write an algebraic equation using Roman numerals and tally marks.

"How can you tell?"

Laurel launches into a monologue about the painting's composition, the use of positive and negative space, the emphasis on spontaneous creativity, how the monochrome palette avoids any preconceptions of implied meaning, and how the dynamic brushstrokes reveal the artist's inner turmoil. As her father's eyes glaze over, she grins.

"Aren't you glad you're paying for me to go to art school?"

"I don't know yet—what was all that you just said?"

Laurel giggles. "The signature's in the wrong spot."

"What?"

He picks up the picture she first pointed to and holds it close to his face. "There's no name on this."

"His mother was blind, so instead of signing his name, Kenneth Thorpe would use paint dabs to create his initials, KT, in Braille. He used the same color paint as the background, so it could be felt, but wasn't so obvious as to distract from the rest of the painting. He always signed on the bottom left of the canvas. But look at the photo; you can just make out the dots here in the upper right corner."

She points to that corner of the photo. Whitney squints, trying to discern the faint smudges, but if you're not looking for them, they're easy to miss. He compares it to the other photos, but the "signature" is just as hard to see in those—first because the dots are supposed to be subtle, and second because the painting isn't the focus of the photos.

"How sure are you about this?"

"Very. Well, pretty sure. Wait, a sec."

Laurel darts from the room and returns with a thick art book. She flips through the pages, sending a small breeze toward him. When she finds the page she's looking for, she holds out the book for her father to see. Whitney scans the page searching for the dots at the bottom of the painting.

"Here." As if reading his mind, Laurel turns the page. The next image shows an enlargement of the Braille dots—there's no mistaking the signature paint dabs up close.

"Who's the owner? Do you think they hung the painting wrong?"

"I think that's unlikely. What are you doing tomorrow?" Whitney asks.

"Nothing. Maybe shopping for the trip."

"Want to come with me to see the painting in person?"

"Sure."

CHAPTER 6

A t precisely 9:00 the next morning, Whitney's cell phone rings. He's been anticipating the call, even though the number is unfamiliar. "This is Richard Whitney."

"Good morning, Lieutenant. This is Katherine Tierney. I finished the inventory of the silver, and two pieces are missing."

"When was the last time you saw them?"

"This past Christmas. But not since then."

"Miss Tierney, my investigation has brought up a few more questions. Would it be alright for me to come by today to discuss it in person?"

"Of course, I have time available this morning."

"I'll be there within the hour."

"Very well, see you then."

The aroma of fresh coffee lures Whitney into the kitchen. Laurel pours coffee into two mugs, handing one to him. As he's about to take his first sip, he stops the cup midway to his mouth, scrutinizing her outfit. He frowns as he takes in her shabby attire—clothes Laurel affectionately calls her "studio uniform"—jeans torn at the knees with colorful paint splotches (the result of wiping brushes on her thighs), paired with a Post College T-shirt.

"Would you please put on something presentable?"

Laurel looks down at the clothes she's wearing, shrugs her shoulders, pulls her elbows in, and turns her palms up. "What? I thought we were just going to the station."

"No, and I wouldn't want you wearing that to the station house, either. You look like a rag-a-muffin."

Laurel smiles, amused by her father's old-fashioned phraseology. She notices he's wearing slacks, a crisp button-down shirt, and a blazer, instead of his usual weekend wear—jeans and a polo shirt.

"Okay, Dad. I'll be back before you finish your coffee," she says and kisses him lightly on the cheek.

When she returns, she's wearing tan Capri pants paired with a blue-and-white striped French sailor shirt. Her hair is pulled into a loose bun at the nape of her neck, the pink streak tucked away. Whitney glances at her, the change not lost on him.

"Better?" Laurel asks.

"I suppose. Let's go."

During the drive, Whitney explains to Laurel where they are going and why. Miss Tierney tends the flowers in front of the house as he parks the car. As he and Laurel head up the path, he waves. "This is my daughter, Laurel. She noticed something unusual, and I hope it's okay I brought her along."

Glenwood's manager greets them with a smile and removes her gardening gloves before extending her hand. "A pleasure to meet you, my dear. Are you planning on entering law enforcement like your father?"

"Oh, no," Laurel says, shaking the woman's hand. "I'm an artist—or at least that's what I'm working on. I go to Post College."

Miss Tierney folds her gloves and lays them on top of the pruning shears in the cutting basket, then leads them through the house to the butler's pantry. The stained-glass window captures Laurel's attention. "Oh, that's beautiful," she gushes. "Is it a real Tiffany?"

"Yes, Mr. Tiffany gifted it to Mr. Vos' grandfather, Gabriel Vos, and personally oversaw its installation here at Glenwood."

Laurel's eyes widen. "A Tiffany window, and they keep it in the pantry?"

"When the kitchen was being remodeled, the family insisted that the window remain exactly where Mr. Tiffany placed it." Miss Tierney leans toward Laurel lowering her voice, "And Mrs. Vos' personal office is on the other side of that wall."

"The missing pieces?" Whitney prompts.

Miss Tierney opens one of the upper cabinets and motions to an empty space on the first shelf. "There should be two tastevins, another gift from Mr. Tiffany."

"What's a tastevin?" Laurel asks.

"It's a small wine sampling cup used by sommeliers, typically worn around their necks like a piece of jewelry. One was made in France in the early 1800s, the other was a prototype Tiffany design. I pulled the photographs and appraisals from our insurance records."

She picks up a manila folder and hands it to Whitney. "The French cup is valued at $2,500, and the Tiffany design is worth $3,200."

Whitney looks over the photos. The antique cup is shallow with fluted sides and a coin fastened to the bottom. The second photo shows the other tastevin—the flowing Art Nouveau style associated with Tiffany designs is unmistakable. It, too, has a coin affixed to the bottom, dated 1795.

"What's the meaning behind the coins?" Whitney asks.

"I believe the French added them as decoration. Mr. Tiffany continued the tradition, only he chose an early American silver dollar to honor Gabriel's revolutionary forefathers."

"May I take the photos? I'll make copies and have the originals returned." Miss Tierney nods.

Whitney checks his notebook. "You said on the phone that the last time you saw the cups was at Christmas?"

"Yes, it's a Vos family tradition to sample the wines with the tastevins during the holiday."

"Have they been used any other time since then?"

She shakes her head in a small yet quick motion.

"Then the tastevins could have been taken any time in the past nine months," Whitney says.

"Weren't they taken at the same time as when the flowers were moved?"

"The two aren't necessarily connected."

"Oh," Miss Tierney says, staring down at her feet. She clasps her hands together and alternates placing her left thumb and then her right on top. Her brow furrows, and her lips tighten as she thinks about the possibility that multiple strangers had been inside Glenwood. How could this have happened?

As they walk back to the kitchen, Whitney asks, "Do you have insurance photos of everything?"

"No, not everything. Certainly not every individual piece of silver. But the tastevins, being so unique, we do have photographs."

"What about the art that the Voses own? Do you have photos of those?"

"Yes, of course."

"Would you mind getting any pictures you have of the Kenneth Thorpe in the dining room?"

"What does that have to do with this?"

"Please, Miss Tierney, it could be important."

"I'll have to go through the files. It could take a few minutes."

"We'll wait here," Whitney says, indicating the table where he and Miss

Tierney shared coffee and madeleines the day before. Whitney figures the wait will be brief, knowing she'd already gone through the Vos' files the night before.

She returns a few minutes later with another manila folder in hand.

"Here it is," she says. "We have a picture taken by the SoHo Gallery, where the painting was purchased, and a few pictures of it hanging in the dining room."

"Perfect." Whitney lays the photographs on the table and scans the array. There's no mistaking Kenneth Thorpe's signature dots on the official gallery print. While the paint dabs are more subtle in the other photographs, it's plain to see that Caleb Vos did not accidentally hang the painting upside down. Whitney taps the bottom left of the painting in the gallery photograph.

Perplexed regarding the connection to the silver tastevins, Miss Tierney shakes her head slowly. "I'm not following. Why you're interested in that painting, then?"

Whitney scoops up the pictures and hands them to Laurel. "Let's go find out. Miss Tierney, would you lead the way?"

Except for fresh flowers in two of the vases on the table, the dining room looks essentially the same as it did the day before. The third vase remains out of position, its flowers wilting, several petals littering the table. Whitney senses it goes against Miss Tierney's nature to leave something out of place.

She eyes him as he looks at the table. "I thought it best to leave the vase as is until the matter is resolved."

Whitney removes a pair of latex gloves from his pocket and stretches them over his hands. "Laurel, please show the photographs to Miss Tierney again."

Looking down at the prints in Laurel's hands, then up at the painting on the wall, Miss Tierney says with a gasp. "Why, it's upside down!"

"May I take it down?" Whitney asks.

She nods, quickly adding, "Please be careful."

As he approaches, Whitney notices a faint odor and takes a couple of inquiring sniffs. He gently raises the painting and pulls it away from the wall. Then he turns toward the table, holding it horizontally as if about to lay it on top, mindful not to let it touch the highly polished surface. The vase sits a safe distance from the painting's edge, suggesting it was moved to make room for the artwork but never returned to its original position.

Whitney places the painting back on the wall, adjusting it until it hangs straight. As he releases the art, Whitney feels a slight tacky adhesion between the gloves and the canvas.

"Another prank?" Miss Tierney asks. "The flowers caught my attention, but I didn't notice the painting."

"No, not a prank. Looks like we have a forgery. I'll call for the lab guys to come down." He unpeels the gloves from his hands and places them into a small plastic bag. Then he calls the station house. "Stone, it's Whitney. Call Nassau Police and have them send a Crime Scene team here to Glenwood. Looks like we have a burglary, after all. Oh, and Eileen, make sure you give them the street address."

Whitney stares at the painting, people get so used to their surroundings, they overlook small differences. Miss Tierney's "change blindness" is understandable, especially given that the painting is an abstract. Curious that she noticed the vase out of position immediately. These three separate and peculiar incidents at Glenwood can't be a coincidence.

Laurel joins him by the painting, sniffing. "Guess the flowers masked the odor. It's faint, but I can still smell the linseed oil." Whitney takes out his notepad. While he's busy writing, Laurel meanders around the room stopping in front of the other abstract painting and sniffs. She turns around to find her father watching with an amused smirk on his face.

"I was just checking," Laurel says.

"I see, and your conclusion, detective?"

"Well, the paint isn't fresh, if that's what you're asking."

"You know, it's not too late to apply to the academy."

Laurel scrunches up her face at him in mock annoyance and sticks out her tongue. Her father has always been supportive of her choices— that is until her most recent decision to study fine art. Then he suggested she apply to the police academy; at least that would provide more employment opportunities.

A lilting chime interrupts their banter.

"That was quick," Whitney says.

Miss Tierney goes to the door and returns with Officer Ryan.

Whitney looks at him, puzzled. "I told Stone to send CSU."

"She did. I mean, she called Nassau. They're sending a unit," Ryan says.

"And you are here because? ..."

"Oh, Lieutenant Hackett said it would be a good experience for me to watch the Crime Scene Unit, so he sent me over."

Ditching the kid so he can see his bookie, most likely. Whitney dislikes Hackett's regular betting on whatever sport is in season, but it's not his call to make. The chief overlooks these extracurricular activities—probably hoping to finish his last few years before retirement without controversy.

"Did Miss Tierney discover anything missing besides her coffee cup, that is?" Ryan asks.

"A couple of pieces of silver are missing, but the big crime is forgery. One of the paintings has been replaced by a duplicate." Whitney waves his hand at the Thorpe painting.

"Really? How'd you figure that out?"

"Actually, it was ..." Whitney tilts his head, signaling for Laurel to join them. When she approaches, he slips an arm around her shoulders. "This is my daughter. Laurel, this is Ryan. Ryan, this is my little baby, Laurel."

Laurel squirms uncomfortably in her father's embrace and blushes slightly at being referred to as a baby. She extends her hand to Ryan, who hesitates for a moment, staring at her, before shaking it.

"Nice to meet you, Laurel."

"We came to investigate after Laurel noticed something was off in the photos you took. That's how we discovered the painting is fake." Whitney releases Laurel from his embrace and hands her his keys. "Why don't you go shopping for your trip? I want to stick around until the CSU team gets here. I'll have Ryan bring me back to the station, and you can pick me up later."

"I don't mind staying," Laurel says.

"No, you go. Pick me up around six."

"Okay." She gives her father a quick kiss on the cheek and starts down the hall, calling over her shoulder, "Bye, Ryan."

"She's something, isn't she?" Whitney says.

"Who?"

"Laurel. Have you had any coffee yet, Ryan? You seem out of it."

"Yes, sir—actually, no, sir. I thought your daughter was younger, school-aged."

"She is school-aged. She goes to Post."

"No, I mean ... never mind."

"Have you ever been on scene with CSU before?"

"Not yet," Ryan replies.

"It's interesting when they find something; otherwise, it's like watching paint dry. Still, it's good to have the experience under your belt."

The CSU team arrives and begins working. They find several latent fingerprints in the dining room, but none on the vase, nor are there any on the fake Thorpe painting. They also find soil samples and a few stray hairs on the floor. Whitney doesn't relish the idea of asking Mr. and Mrs. Vos to come down to the station to be fingerprinted, even if it is just to exclude their prints. With them being away most of the summer, hopefully it won't be necessary.

As Ryan drives them back, Whitney wonders if there's any way to keep these crimes quiet until they have a better handle on them. Three thefts at one location—highly unusual for the Squire. But there's no way they can keep a lid on this, not in Old Brookville, not with a juicy tidbit about Glenwood.

CHAPTER 7

Katherine Tierney runs Glenwood with military precision. Her expectations for the staff are high—those who meet them thrive, while those who don't are shown the door. Behind her back, the staff call her "The General," because of her no-nonsense approach.

Miss Tierney never married, though rumors of a long-term affair with Jonah Vos followed her, even long after his passing.

During her early tenure as secretary at Glenwood, a few of the male staff members tried to ingratiate themselves with Mr. Vos, suggesting that a man should manage the estate, adding that it's unseemly for a woman to hold such a prominent position, given the political and business leaders who frequently visit Glenwood. Mr. Vos would respond by saying he would consider their proposal, but within a week, their employment would be terminated. Their severance always included a generous bonus and a glowing letter of recommendation. It soon became apparent to the local domestic community that nothing would shake Katherine Tierney from her perch at Glenwood.

One time, a maid not-so-subtly hinted that an affair must be taking place. Mrs. Vos got up and swiftly fled the room, giving the girl a misguided sense of victory. However, within the hour, the maid was standing at the train station dazed, without bonus or recommendation.

The reason behind the devotion between the Vos family and Katherine Tierney is touching, but not nearly as salacious as the rumors suggest.

Katherine was a teenager when she left her home in Ireland. Her mother had passed away. Her father divided his time between his job and the local pub, practically ignoring his two daughters. A Catholic Church in Ireland, in partnership with an American diocese, arranged for young Irish women to be placed as domestic help at wealthy estates. The women would receive a stipend, two-thirds of which went to the church as repayment for their travel, etc., and the remaining third would be theirs. It was a meager amount, but as live-in help, their financial needs were minimal. The contract required the women to remain with their sponsored family for five years.

Katherine's parish priest, Father Timothy, recommended she take advantage of this opportunity. The money she would earn could then go toward paying for her younger sister, Maeve, to stay at the convent. Father Timothy explained that it was the best solution: Her father was in no condition to raise a young girl by himself, and her sister would be safe with the nuns and receive a proper education. If Katherine stayed, she wouldn't be able to both work and raise Maeve.

Less than a month after arriving in the United States, Katherine had her first interview for a nanny position. Mrs. Eliza Vos wore a long powder-blue coat, trimmed at the collar with white fur, and a matching fur pillbox hat. Despite being midway through her pregnancy, the woman looked glamorous. She kept her coat on during her entire time at the church, perhaps in reverence to the nuns, but Katherine could tell that the hemline of her dress landed above her knee. Even though she was the youngest of the girls interviewed, Katherine must have made an impression. The nun told her to pack right away—she would be leaving immediately. Her goodbyes were brief—she hadn't had time to make any close friends.

When Katherine arrived at the car, the sky was gray, and snow was falling. The chauffeur sneered at her as Katherine handed him her small travel case. She assumed his sour countenance was because of the weather—until he spoke. "Sit up front, bogtrotter, and keep your distance."

The three of them rode off, the only sound a steady whoosh of the windshield wipers. The chauffeur's slur rattled her. When she had packed her things, she looked forward to her new job, but now she didn't know what to expect. She interlaced her fingers, left thumb on top, then subtly switched to right thumb on top, so absorbed in the motion that she ignored the threatening storm.

The chauffeur made a loud gasp, causing Katherine to stop fiddling with her fingers. She looked up to see what appeared to be a white wall barreling straight for them—a snow squall.

In a flash, whiteness engulfed them. Katherine gripped the door with one hand and pressed the other against the dashboard, bracing herself for impact. A sharp thwack startled everyone as the car crashed into a tree branch. Katherine could tell by the jarring bumpiness that the car had gone off the road.

Branches pummeled the car. Their continuous onslaught shattered a window. Snow and small, pebbly fragments of glass sprayed across the passengers. They finally broke free from the trees but still couldn't see more than a foot ahead of them. The driver slammed on the brakes, and the car spun dizzily in circles. "We're on the mill pond!" he cried.

The spinning gradually slowed, and the vehicle came to rest. The driver leaped from the car, his arms pinwheeling as he worked to gain his footing on the ice. A loud cracking sound came from under the car and the chauffeur ran off.

Katherine called after him, but he kept running, never glancing back. She checked on Mrs. Vos, who had a gash on her head and was unconscious. Katherine stared through the falling snow, searching for the chauffeur. A queasy feeling spread through her stomach as she watched his small silhouette disappear into the storm.

She sprang into action, pushing down the rising panic as she searched the trunk for something to help. There wasn't much: a blanket, an empty picnic basket, and a set of golf clubs.

Katherine laid the blanket flat on the snow and tied one corner around the wooden head of a golf club. She did the same with a second club. The cold, wet flakes numbed her fingers, and she rubbed her hands together, blowing hot air on them before knotting the remaining two corners. The result was a crude travois sled.

"Kathhhh ..." Mrs. Vos moaned, regaining consciousness, and she feebly assisted Katherine as she pulled her from the car.

"Don't speak, Mrs., save your energy for the baby."

Katherine gently rolled Mrs. Vos onto the blanket, and using the golf clubs as handles, pulled the pregnant woman along. She set out in the direction the chauffeur ran but soon lost the trail as his footprints vanished in the storm.

Her stockings provided little protection from the deep snow seeping into her shoes. Near exhaustion, her spirits lifted when she spotted a small house—at least she could get Mrs. Vos out of the cold.

No one responded as she banged on the door and yelled for help. Katherine weighed her options: continue through the storm or force her way in. Leaving Mrs. Vos at the front door, she sprinted to see if there was a back entrance—miraculously, that door opened. Racing through the house to the front, Katherine unlocked the door and moved Mrs. Vos inside to the kitchen. She lit the oven for warmth and washed the dried blood from Mrs. Vos' face. The gash across her forehead didn't seem too bad. Mrs. Vos opened her eyes, and their brightness reassured Katherine the woman would survive.

"Thank you, Kay," she said and drifted into unconsciousness again.

In all her life, Katherine had never been called anything other than her full Christian name. Puzzled by this wealthy lady calling her something so familiar, she attributed it to shock. Katherine must have fallen asleep herself, because the next thing she knew, she was being shaken by a man who kept asking, "Who are you?"

Officer Bradley was on patrol when he spotted the car on the frozen Mill Pond. After first checking to see if anyone was inside, he began searching for the driver. He had almost passed the little house, then noticed a light was on and went to check it out.

After rousing Katherine, the policeman said, "Help her up, and we'll get her to the car. I'll drive to Dr. Burgesen's; his house is closest."

While the doctor was examining Mrs. Vos, Katherine sat in the parlor, her hands cradling a cup of tea as she absently sipped the warm contents. Without warning, the front door flew open. A man burst in, shouting, "Where is she?" Frigid air and a swirl of snow followed him inside.

Officer Bradley updated Jonah Vos as best he could and introduced him to Katherine. The three of them sat stone-faced until Dr. Burgesen came out and said, "You can go in now."

Mr. Vos stood. "No, the girl," said the doctor, motioning to Katherine.

Unsure why she was being summoned, Katherine slowly stood and even more slowly walked to the room where Mrs. Vos lay. The white gauze wrapped around Mrs. Vos' head reminded Katherine of the fur pillbox hat.

"Sit with me, Kay," she said.

Katherine sat, and Mrs. Vos gently took her hand.

"Thank you for saving me and my baby. The doctor says we'll both be fine."

She squeezed the girl's hand. A few seconds passed before Mrs. Vos asked, "Monty, the chauffeur, was he able to get out?"

The girl looked down at her hands, unsure what to say.

Mrs. Vos took this to mean he had died in the accident. "I'm sorry for such an ordeal on your first day with us. Monty—his name was Herman Montgomery—was a good man."

Katherine shook her head, intertwining her fingers one way, then another, and whispered, "He didn't die."

Mrs. Vos wore a quizzical expression. "The doctor told me ... that only you and I were in the house."

Katherine bobbed her head slowly.

"Tell me what happened."

"He ran off when we stopped spinning." Then added, "He must have gone to get help," because she didn't want to say what she feared—that he had abandoned an injured pregnant woman.

Mr. Vos peered his head into the room. "My darling, I know you want to thank your savior, but it tortures me not to see for myself that you are all right." He crossed the room and took Mrs. Vos' hands in his. The couple stared at each other, sharing a private moment. Katherine turned to leave.

"Stay with me, Kay," Mrs. Vos said, then gazing back at her husband, she added, "Dearest, Monty left our car to get help. Please go look for him."

Mr. Vos and Officer Bradley found Monty at the Jockey Post, a bar that, despite its name, catered mostly to local fishermen. Inside, the building was dim and smelled of tobacco and stale beer. The bar was empty except for Monty, hunched over a glass of rye.

When the bartender spotted Bradley's uniform, he decided he had something important to check on in the kitchen and slipped out through the swinging doors. Monty lifted his head to call for another drink and saw Mr. Vos and the policeman in the mirror behind the bar. He sputtered his words, "I'm sorry, Mr. Vos, I tried, but it was too late. I've been sitting here trying to build up the courage to tell you."

"What are you saying, Monty?" asked Mr. Vos.

The chauffeur drained the last of what was in the glass. His eyes glazed over, and it took him a moment to focus on Jonah's face. "It was that girl. She went crazy all of a sudden. She grabbed the wheel. It was her fault. I tried to save Mrs. Vos."

Officer Bradley scanned the man by his side. The husband's eyes had narrowed, his hand curling tightly. Bradley shifted his stance, bracing for an altercation. Instead, he was surprised when he heard Mr. Vos say, "Let's get you to Dr. Burgesen's and have him look you over."

Monty's first attempt at walking proved unsuccessful, so Officer Bradley hoisted him off the floor and steered him toward the patrol car. Once they arrived at Dr. Burgesen's, the chauffeur was able to walk from the car to the door under his own power. His path, however, resembled that of a toddler chasing a firefly—lots of changing directions and swatting at the air.

The three men entered, and Monty saw Mrs. Vos in the parlor, seated by the fire, with the new girl at her side.

"What lies have you told them?" Monty spat at Katherine. His words slurred as he swayed unsteadily.

He turned back to Mr. Vos. "I gave you six good years of service, and you listen to the tales of that Irish pot-licker?"

Jonah Vos' face flushed with anger, but he forced his voice to stay even. "I am willing to forgive you a moment of cowardice, but I will never entrust my family to your care again. Officer Bradley will escort you back to Glenwood. Pack your things, then he will take you to the train station."

Mr. Vos joined Mrs. Vos and Katherine in the parlor and shut the door. They could hear Monty's complaints through the walls.

"This isn't right. He can't throw me out."

While a certain division between employer and employee would always remain, the Voses immediately paid in full Katherine's debt to the church. They even tried to bring her younger sister to America. Unfortunately, when they finally received word back from Father Timothy, they learned that Katherine's father had passed away and that Maeve had been adopted. The Voses hired a private detective to locate the girl, but all he could discover was that a "loving couple from a good family" had taken her in.

Katherine worked as a personal maid for Mrs. Vos until Caleb was born. After that, she became his nanny until he went to boarding school. When Mrs. Vos was diagnosed with cancer, Katherine quietly ensured the house continued to reflect Mrs. Vos' preferences. She organized the staff to handle the bulk of the cleaning while Mrs. Vos was at her scheduled treatments, so as not to disturb her. Since Mrs. Vos' diet had to be carefully monitored, Katherine learned how to prepare all of her meals according to her specific needs. Finally, the gardens were kept immaculate, one of Mrs. Vos' few remaining joys.

Caleb was home from school for Christmas break. One night, while the family was gathered in the parlor, Mrs. Vos repeated the story of Katherine's first day on the job. Caleb had heard it multiple times before but listened politely to his mother.

At the end of her story, she said, "You must listen to Kay as you would to me."

Caleb smiled and asked, "Why, where are you going, Mom? Paris again?"

She waved this off. "Kay is the reason you're here in this world. I wouldn't have made it without her. When I'm gone, show her the respect you have shown me."

Caleb hugged his mother. "The doctors say that after the next round of chemo, it will all be gone. You're going to be around for a long time yet."

"Promise me," she whispered.

On a bright winter day, Mrs. Vos asked to be wheeled into the sunroom. Katherine first made sure Mrs. Vos was warm enough, then began to read aloud while Mrs. Vos looked out over the frost-covered rose garden. When Mrs. Vos' eyes closed, Katherine got up to move her back to the parlor.

"No, I want to stay here. I'm envisioning the garden in bloom. Be a dear, Kay, and bring me some tea, and I'd like toast with butter and clover honey."

By the time the tea brewed, and Katherine found the clover honey tucked away in the back of the pantry, Mrs. Vos had passed away.

The funeral for Mrs. Eliza Vos was held at the Old Brookville Church with a large reception following at the Brookville Country Club. Katherine returned home early to tidy the house. She cleared the bouquets from the entry, dining and living rooms. Mr. Vos used to complain about the floral arrangements—he had always said they smelled worse than his cigars. Of course, Mrs. Vos always had the last word. Thinking of her former boss—and, well, her friend too—Katherine sobbed for a moment, then forced the tears to stop. There would be time for crying later; now, there was too much to be done. Katherine washed her face and set back to work. When Jonah and Caleb returned from the service, they found Katherine packing away the wheelchair.

Jonah had been stoic throughout the wake and funeral, keeping his emotions tightly controlled. But now, his grief and anger erupted. "What do you think you're doing? Get out! Pack your things now!" Tears were streaming down his face.

Stunned by Jonah's outburst, Katherine stood frozen for a moment, unsure of her place in the house that had become her home. The emptiness inside overwhelmed her. But she refused to falter. Katherine surprised herself at how normal her voice sounded. "As you wish, sir."

She turned and left the room. Her tears returned, but this time she couldn't control them.

A light rapping at her door came a short while later. Expecting the chauffeur to be waiting, ready to take her to the train station, Katherine was surprised to see Caleb.

He stood silent for a moment, his hands stuffed in his pockets, gaze fixed on the floor. "My father wants to see you in the sunroom." Then Caleb shuffled off, walking toward the family side of the house, his head down.

Katherine picked up her suitcase and headed downstairs. When she entered the sunroom, Mr. Vos stood at the far side in front of the picture window, his back to her. Without turning, he said, "Come here, please, Katherine."

She set down her suitcase and joined him at the window.

"I've been staring out this window for over twenty minutes now. It's probably the most time I've spent looking at that garden. And the damn thing is covered with snow." His voice started to rise and crack. He took a deep breath and began again. "I loved my wife. We didn't always share the same passions, like the garden, but I loved her more than I can say." He paused. "You once saved my wife and child. I shouldn't ask any more from you. Please stay, Kay. Stay and keep Glenwood exactly how Eliza liked it. That way she will always be here with us."

It would be the only time he would ever call her Kay.

CHAPTER 8

From the darkened woods, the Squire emerges and crosses the yard, heading for the back door. He grabs the knob and turns. There's always a moment of uncertainty—what if the homeowner installed an alarm this week? The silence is reassuring. He enters and walks to the formal dining room. An ornate sideboard stands against the wall, its top crowded with porcelain animals. The Squire opens the first drawer and shines his penlight across the contents—he frowns. The next drawer opens only half an inch. It squeaks and sticks. Forcing it will take some wiggling. He studies the porcelain figures, commits their positions to memory, then carefully moves them to the floor, keeping their arrangement intact.

The extra effort was worth it. The penlight beam lands on an item that piques his interest. He takes out a gold-colored teaspoon with a rose-patterned handle. The piece feels heavy in his hand. On the underside is a Minerva head mark and an 18KGP stamp, indicating silver with gold plate. The thin top layer is flawless—this will help.

He grabs the rest of the spoons along with a matching cake knife and bonbon server. The Squire takes out a dish towel from his bag and sets to work, rolling the spoons and serving pieces inside. Once the silverware is stashed in his backpack, he returns the animals to their stations on the sideboard.

The Squire retraces his steps to the back door, but a painting on the wall stops him. A lush tropical landscape: olive and celadon palms arching over a beach, turquoise water lapping at the shore, purple mountains hazed in the distance. The brushstrokes are bold and layered, patterns within patterns. He lingers, remembering a promise he made long ago—and never kept. Guilt squeezes his chest.

The grandfather clock chimes once. Half past the hour. He stiffens, listening. A faint hum drifts from another room. Refrigerator, he tells

himself, though his pulse quickens. The Squire slips out the way he
came, trotting toward the trees. At the edge of the yard he glances back.
Empty. Then—headlights. Turning into the drive.

CHAPTER 9

Daily briefings include a quick synopsis of current arrests, accidents, and open cases. When Whitney completes his case summary of the missing silver and the forged painting from Glenwood, Chief Eaves drums his fingers on the table, a faint scowl forming. The Squire has always irritated him—Whitney can tell by the way his patience seems to wear thinner each time the name comes up.

"So, the Squire is back in town?" Chief Eaves asks.

"Perhaps," Whitney replies. "But I'm not convinced that the Squire committed both burglaries."

Eaves wishes the burglaries would just stop—or that someone would finally catch the culprit. Explaining the lack of progress to town officials—who think investigations should wrap up neatly in under an hour, just like on TV—is something he clearly dreads. Watching him, Whitney is reminded how much politics impacts the chief of police position—and wonders if the promotion is worth it.

"Both? Was there a second burglary I don't know about?"

"There's no evidence the silver cups and the painting were taken at the same time or by the same person. I can't imagine the Squire suddenly changing from sneak thief to art forger."

Hackett chimes in, "Maybe he's taking art classes at Post College like Nancy Drew."

Whitney ignores the dig at his daughter, knowing that acknowledging Hackett's snide remarks only encourages him.

"Well, apparently a painting class rates better than twenty-four years on the job. Maybe I should replace some of my officers with art students," Chief Eaves says. He pauses for a moment to stare at Hackett before turning his attention back to Whitney. "Is there any evidence confirming these are unrelated?"

"No, sir."

"For now, work it as another Squire case. Silver was taken and a note was left—that's his modus operandi."

"Yes, sir."

The reports move on to more mundane instances concerning noise complaints and speeding incidents. As the officers file out of the roll-call room, Hackett slaps Whitney on the back. "Hey, no hard feelings about Nancy Drew?"

"None whatsoever, Denis. But back to the case, I got a call from Andrew Sutton. What's your relationship with the Voses' attorney?"

"We know people in common."

"You shouldn't be talking about the case with outsiders."

"He's not an outsider, he's the Voses' lawyer. Besides, it wasn't much of a case."

"It is now."

Hackett snorts and heads for the break room. Whitney returns to his desk, where a stack of case files waits on one side. He pulls the oldest free and opens it. The Squire thefts are atypical. Common thieves grab what's readily available—electronics, guns, designer clothes, even alcohol or prescription drugs—with the plan to get in and out quickly. The Squire, however, has a specific goal in mind, and he often bypasses more valuable items.

The first notable silver burglary occurred over twenty years ago at the Madison residence. Alice Madison was a movie actress during the Golden Age of Hollywood. She never made it to A-list status; most of her roles were that of the leading lady's best friend. Alice married a producer named Philip Snyder, who, following a string of flops, tragically jumped from the Hollywood sign. After losing her husband, Mrs. Madison moved east and purchased a home in Old Brookville. The town was remote enough to ensure her privacy, yet close enough to New York City for her occasional roles on Broadway before eventually retiring entirely from public life.

When the police arrived at Mrs. Madison's home, they found the actress more bewildered than upset. Several of her antique silver picture frames had been stolen. But in a peculiar twist, the thief took the time to remove all the photographs, leaving them behind.

These were casual, behind-the-scenes snapshots—not staged studio portraits—of Mrs. Madison with various co-stars. One was of Alice with Grace Kelly and Eva Marie Saint in playful "see no evil, hear no evil, speak no evil" poses; in another, she was hugging Joanne Woodward while

Paul Newman mugged in the background, crossing his eyes and making a goofy face. Her wedding picture was in the pile as well.

Even more puzzling than the photographs was the note the thief left behind.

> *My dear Mrs. Madison,*
> *It is with the heaviest of hearts that I relieve you of*
> *your lovely Booted frames. I would not dare, however,*
> *take from you what you treasure most.*
> *P.S. You were brilliant in "The Coachman's Daughter."*

At first, the detective in charge of the case thought the term "Booted" was a slang reference to the theft itself. Later, he learned the Boots Pure Drug Company in Birmingham, England had made the frames. The estimated value for the vintage sterling silver pieces was between $2,600 and $3,000, but Mrs. Madison's personal, unpublished photographs could easily have fetched double—possibly even triple—that amount to a collector.

Adding to the mystery, the thief left behind an Edwardian-era brooch, placed atop the note. The platinum and moonstone brooch had been a wedding gift from her husband. Mrs. Madison wore it in all her film and stage performances. After she retired, the pin found a new home, propped up against her wedding portrait. Valued at over $10,000, the question remained: What kind of thief would pass on something so tempting—leaving it behind as a paperweight?

Handwriting samples collected from Mrs. Madison's staff did not match the enigmatic note. Given her celebrity and the quirkiness of the story, the Madison burglary received national news attention. Soon, the sleepy town of Old Brookville was overrun with reporters, news vans, private detectives, and even a few psychics who claimed to know the whereabouts of the missing frames. For a brief period, the media dubbed the burglar the "North Shore Silver Bandit."

The following Christmas, a package arrived at Mrs. Madison's front door. The plain brown paper wrapping had no street address, no return address, and no postage—it was simply addressed to Mrs. A. Madison. Inside were the silver picture frames, each swaddled in tissue paper.

The next theft took place at the Rothstein estate. While the staff prepared for an important fundraising dinner, a maid discovered that several serving pieces were missing from the velvet-lined silverware drawer. In their place lay a handwritten note:

I apologize for squiring away with your Strasbourgs, Madam. It must have come to your attention that your servers, while similar, are not a true match to your Chantilly. A woman such as yourself should not have to suffer in silent humiliation at having to present an unmatched service. I felt it my duty to help you avoid any further embarrassment.

The detectives quickly learned that Strasbourg and Chantilly were two Gorham silver patterns. The thief absconded with a variety of obsolete serving utensils, appraised at $1,600—insignificant considering the other valuables in the home. It was this burglary, and the phrasing of the Rothstein note that led to the thief's lasting nickname: "The Squire."

With a pattern emerging, police reviewed older cases with similar modus operandi (M.O.). A few years before the Madison theft, a report that wasn't given much attention concerned a missing silver tea set. Three sisters blamed each other for their mother's missing tea service; a fight broke out, and one sister received a bloody nose. When interviewed by the police, the trio admitted their mother could have sold, or given away, the set without their knowledge. But after the commotion from the Madison and Rothstein thefts, any case involving silver got bundled into the growing list of Squire thefts.

Additional burglaries continued for a few months. People all over the Brookville area checked their sideboards and counted their silverware. Then, as mysteriously as the burglaries had started, they abruptly stopped.

Roughly a year and a half later, it started all over again. The same M.O.: always antique silver was taken; sometimes, but not always, a note was left behind. Victims weren't even sure when the thefts had occurred, since there was never a disturbance.

During one investigation, a cleaning woman broke down crying and confessed to growing marijuana in her apartment for "personal use," but as to the burglary itself, any leads quickly became dead ends.

Over the years, the public became enamored with the mystery of the Squire. Many of the victims took pride in their loss; the item's value was a trifle compared to their other belongings, and it gained them a certain status by having something worthy of the Squire's attention.

For the investigators, the crimes were a particularly frustrating enigma. No one knew if an item had been taken days, weeks, months, or even years before the disappearance was discovered.

Nothing in the files leads Whitney to believe the Squire could have created the forgery. The similarities between the two crimes are tenuous. Both involve unusual commodities, and the thief must have some knowledge of the home. But would the same person steal antique silver and modern art?

Whitney presses the contact button labeled "Laurel." His phone displays her high school graduation photo; it used to show a picture of three-year-old Laurel with ice cream smeared across her face. She complained.

"Hi, Sweetheart. The art history class you took—what was your professor's name? R-E-E-D? ... Got it. See you later."

He dials the main campus number and asks to be transferred. After a pause and a click, a woman's voice answers:

"Post College, Art History Department. How may I direct your call?"

"This is Lieutenant Richard Whitney of the Old Brookville Police Department. I would like to speak with Professor Terrance Reed."

The woman's voice drops in volume. "I hope Terry isn't in any kind of trouble."

"No, ma'am. I just need his expertise regarding a painting."

The voice brightens. "I'll give you his cell number. He's conducting a lecture right now, but he should be free to pick up his phone in about twenty-five minutes."

Whitney writes down the number and busies himself organizing the photos and files until he can call back and set up a meeting with Professor Reed. They schedule a meeting for the next day.

Post College is a private institution within the Old Brookville Police district. Between occasional incidents on campus, parent tours, and attending art shows or concerts with Laurel, Whitney is quite familiar with its grounds. He enters the two-story brick humanities building and proceeds to the upper level. A cheery soft yellow paint covers the industrial cinder block hallway. Colorful flyers announcing upcoming concerts or looking for rides during the fall break are thumb-tacked to a cork bulletin board near the stairwell.

Whitney shakes his head; do students really trust getting rides from strangers? He makes a mental note: Laurel has her own car, but she should talk to her girlfriends about the dangers. Halfway down the hall,

Whitney finds room number 281 and knocks.

"Come in," responds a rich voice.

As Whitney enters, Professor Reed rises and steps out from behind his cluttered desk, where multiple piles of books lean at odd angles. The professor towers over Whitney's 6-foot-1 frame. Reed wears a beige three-piece summer suit accented by a bright turquoise tie. The top of his head is clean-shaven, and a few gray hairs are sprinkled throughout his well-trimmed beard.

"I hate basketball," Reed says as they shake hands.

"Excuse me?"

"When most people meet me, they see a tall Black man, and assume I should've joined the NBA."

"To be honest, I was expecting someone in torn jeans and a tie-dye shirt, not a Wall Street banker. I guess the art department has changed since my patrol days."

Reed throws his head back and laughs. "So much for stereotypes. How can I help you, Lieutenant Whitney?" He motions for him to sit.

An overstuffed bookcase lines one wall, with books crammed in both upright and on their sides, the shelves sagging under their weight. Framed exhibition posters from various museums cover the other walls; the display spans over five centuries of art, from Caravaggio to Rembrandt, Cézanne to Kahlo, and Basquiat. The room has a pleasant earthy smell—the scent of old books intermingled with a trace of pipe tobacco. In the center of the room is a brightly patterned rug, anchored by two wingback chairs. Whitney chooses one, and Professor Reed takes the other.

"I have a case with a stolen painting that was replaced by a forgery," Whitney starts.

"Do you want me to examine the painting? I'm not an expert on authentications."

"No, that's not needed. Actually, my daughter Laurel—she was in one of your art history classes—spotted the forgery."

"Laurel Whitney is your daughter? She's a bright girl and very studious, but she's certainly not qualified in ascertaining whether a painting is real or forged."

"The original painting was by Kenneth Thorpe. She noticed his signature wasn't in the correct position—the painting was upside down. Upon closer inspection, we determined the paint is still fresh, so there's no question as to it being a fake."

Whitney shows the photographs to the professor, who studies them carefully, comparing the original and the imitation.

"Have you been in contact with the FBI's Art Crime team?" Reed asks.

"No. I didn't even know there's a special unit just for art. Besides, it's just one painting, and not from a museum."

"A lot of stolen art is from private residences. I'm disappointed the owners didn't notice, since it was upside down."

"They're out of town. We were called to the residence on another matter. It's just luck that the forgery was discovered so soon." Whitney says.

"What can I do to help further your investigation, then?"

"No offense, professor, but when it comes to modern art, some people look at the splatters and drips and say a three-year-old could do the same thing. How difficult would it be to copy an abstract painting? Could just anyone manage it?"

"Why do people think modern art is easy?" Reed leans forward, his tone sharp but not unkind. "The answer is no—not just anyone could capture another artist's style. I would even argue that copying a piece of modern art is more difficult than copying a traditional, subject-based painting, especially since the work in question is a Thorpe. The Abstract Expressionists were about physical movement, how the materials react to each other, and the raw emotion of the artist. The act of copying requires precision and restraint—the polar opposite of how the original was created. To replicate an existing painting, duplicating it exactly, while retaining the energy and spontaneity of the original—well, that would require an artist of considerable skill, not to mention sizable balls. Certainly well beyond a three-year-old's skill set."

"So, they'd have to be a decent artist?"

"Perhaps even a great artist. Did you know Michelangelo Buonarroti committed a forgery? He copied a classical Roman sculpture that was later sold as an ancient relic. Once exposed, the buyer, Cardinal Riario, demanded his money back. Of course, he also recognized the obvious talent in the young Michelangelo and invited him to Rome. The rest, as they say, is history."

"Michelangelo? The Michelangelo—painted the Sistine Chapel? That Michelangelo was a forger?"

"Only the one piece was bogus, and given the depth of his work, it hardly matters—except as an interesting footnote for art historians.

The practice of copying another artist's work to develop one's own skills has been going on for centuries. It wouldn't have been unusual for Michelangelo to copy an older sculpture. There was even a famous case of an artist forging his own work."

"How exactly does one do that?" Whitney asks.

"Giorgio de Chirico was an early Surrealist. Unfortunately for him, by the time Surrealism gained popularity, he had already reverted to a more traditional painting style. So, he returned to Surrealism and backdated the canvases."

"Is that legal?"

Reed shrugs his shoulders and tilts his head to one side. "It's been a quagmire for collectors and dealers for years. I wonder what caused him to be in such a rush.

"de Chirico?"

"No, your forger. With a well-planned scheme like that, and all the care he took to copy Thorpe's style. Why not wait a little longer until the paint cured? And then to hang it upside down. Amateur."

Whitney agrees with Reed on the surface; hanging the painting upside down was a bone-headed move, but he wouldn't go so far as to call the forger an amateur. The perp is talented, and Whitney suspects he's applied his talents elsewhere.

He thanks the professor for his time and leaves the humanities building. Whitney starts down the path toward a long, forest-green structure housing the fine arts department. Once, when the campus was a private estate, the building had served as horse stables; the college later converted it into studio space for art students. Since he's already in the area, he figures he'll drop by the studio to see Laurel. It's a pleasant walk of less than five minutes.

Whitney is barely ten yards down the path when he thinks better of his plan and goes home instead—but first, he needs to pick up a few supplies.

n preparation for her trip, Laurel spends the afternoon shopping for necessities. Isadora had emailed the crew a list of items she considered essential: a power adapter for Italian outlets, jet lag relief pills, noise-canceling headphones, at least three nice outfits, and filtered water bottles. Laurel also picks up something she views as a must-have, even though it wasn't on her mother's list: an Italian phrase book.

Laurel is a little surprised to see her father's car parked in front of the house at this time of day. Both his office and bedroom are empty. "Dad? Are you here? Dad?" she calls out.

"I'm in the basement."

Putting down the shopping bags, she peers into the cellar.

"What are you doing?"

"An experiment, come see."

She descends the stairs and finds her father standing in front of two pieces of cloth, each about the size of a bath towel. By his feet is a gallon of Sherwin-Williams' gray paint. Behind him, on the floor, are other swaths of fabric arranged in pairs, each decorated with swashes and splotches of paint.

"First, I make a painting, then I try to make another just like it," he explains.

"With house paint?" Laurel asks.

"Do you know how expensive art supplies are?"

Her first instinct is to say 'Duh,' but her father hates that. She nods instead, hoping her 'mm-hmm' sounds sincere.

"I had this can lying around. Besides what difference does it make?"

"None, I guess. So, how's it going?"

"The ones marked with a 1 are my originals, the 2s are my attempts to duplicate the first. I'm trying to create something like the Thorpe painting, but I really don't know what I'm doing."

Laurel has her doubts about that last part. A watercolor painting signed by her father—a forest scene with birch trees and a stream—has hung in their dining room since she was a little girl. It's the only painting by him she's ever seen, and whenever she asks about it, Whitney only shrugs and changes the topic.

"So, what inspired your experiment here?" Laurel asks.

"I saw Professor Reed earlier. He explained how difficult it would be for a forger to copy a painting like this. Honestly, I don't know how the forger did it. Copying splotches and drips is impossible. Picasso couldn't pull off a counterfeit like this. It's not the Squire, I'm sure of it, but I haven't figured out how to convince the chief of that."

"You'll work it out"

"What are you up to? Want to get some dinner?"

"I have to get back to the studio to finish a painting myself before the trip," Laurel says.

"How about I take you to dinner on Thursday?"

"It's a date."

Laurel disappears, and a short while later the front door bangs closed. The hum of her car fades as Whitney studies his last two paintings and decides he's made enough attempts. Rapping the brushes vigorously in frustration as he washes them, his experiment yielded mixed results: he couldn't successfully duplicate any of the paintings. Professor Reed was right—not just anyone can copy an abstract painting—and whoever did this was knowledgeable in art. Unfortunately, it also doesn't rule out the Squire as a suspect.

Whitney goes upstairs to his office and types "art + FBI" into the computer's browser. Multiple links to the FBI's art theft page populate the screen. He clicks on the official .gov link. Established in 2004, the FBI Art Crime team's mission is to recover stolen art and artifacts. The site features a searchable National Stolen Art Database. Whitney leans closer to the screen, scrolling through the extensive list of stolen items, surprised by the volume and variety of "art."

While he expected to see traditional art—paintings and sculptures— he also finds items ranging from ancient fossils to a collection of World Series rings once owned by Yogi Berra. Whitney leans back in his chair, closing his eyes. Highlights from the 1956 World Series play in his head— the Subway Series—Don Larsen's perfect game and Berra's two home runs in the final. That would have been a hell of a series to see in person.

† † †

The following morning, as soon as he arrives at the station house, Whitney calls the FBI Art Crime Department. He's transferred to Agent August Smith, who leads the Manhattan bureau. Smith describes his team's huge backlog of cases and then quotes a discouraging statistic: Less than ten percent of stolen art is recovered. Whitney realizes the FBI won't be much help except as an advisory.

However, Agent Smith takes the time to explain the fundamentals of his job and the distinction between art theft and art fraud. Most art crimes fall under the classification "Art Theft"—stealing, looting, and smuggling. Despite his full workload, the agent must feel particularly helpful, or chatty, as he then recounts two colorful cases. The first occurred in 1972 at the Montreal Museum of Fine Arts. The daring heist seemed to be scripted straight from an action movie, with the criminals lowering themselves through a skylight and making off with paintings, jewelry, and figurines valued at $2 million.

The second, and more infamous, robbery took place at the Isabella Stewart Gardner Museum in Boston. During the early hours following Saint Patrick's Day in 1990, thieves disguised as police officers subdued the guards and cut several paintings from their frames. They escaped with $200 million worth of art, including works by Rembrandt, Degas, Manet, Vermeer, and Flinck, along with a Chinese bronze and an eagle finial. The stolen art still has not been recovered, making it number two on the FBI's top ten list of art crimes. The Gardner Museum continues to display the empty frames as a tribute to the missing pieces.

"Art fraud, however," the agent clarifies, "is more con than robbery, encompassing forgery, misattribution, and provenance deceit."

Whitney takes out a pad and pen as Agent Smith describes notable examples of art fraud.

One of the most notorious forgers was a German artist named Wolfgang Beltracchi. He studied Cubist and Expressionist styles meticulously to create paintings he could then pass off as undiscovered works by famous artists of that period. To bolster the scheme, he and his wife, Helene, fabricated a story of a family member buying the art from Jews fleeing Nazi Germany. The couple went as far as to stage vintage-looking photos of Helene, posing as her grandmother, with the paintings.

Beltracchi forgeries sold for hundreds of thousands of dollars at reputable galleries, duping prestigious institutions, including the Metropolitan Museum of Art and collectors such as comedian Steve Martin.

A careless mistake exposed the con. Beltracchi had used titanium white in a painting dated seven years before the pigment was available for artistic use, leading to his arrest. He served four years in a German prison.

"Now, the mere act of duplicating another painting isn't a crime," Agent Smith says. "Copying the works of old masters has been a common learning technique for artists for centuries. If it were illegal, we'd be arresting art students on a daily basis. It's the selling of that painting, claiming it's by a specific artist while knowing it's not—that's a crime."

Whitney recalls Professor Reed's story about Michelangelo and the Roman statue, and writes "Michelangelo," circling it and drawing an arrow to "ART FRAUD"—a shorthand to help him distinguish fraud from straightforward theft.

Agent Smith describes the antics of another forger, Mark Landis— though he differed from Beltracchi by copying existing paintings. Landis' imitations were so convincing that he fooled over sixty museums into believing his works were authentic. But because he donated—rather than sold—his paintings, he was never charged with a crime.

"So, Landis never went to prison?" Whitney asks. "What happened when the owners learned their paintings were fake?"

"Like I said, it's not a crime to copy a piece of art; it's also not a crime to own or display a forgery. In Landis' case, many of the owners wanted to keep the paintings."

"Why? Aren't they worthless?"

"Some institutions use the piece as a study tool, and some just like the painting, regardless of who actually painted it."

Whitney hears a muffled voice through the receiver, followed by the agent telling someone he'd be a few more minutes.

"Your case is especially intriguing since it involves both art theft and art fraud," Smith says. "I only know of two similar cases: One in Uzbekistan, a museum director replaced original paintings with imitations, selling the real art on the black market. The other occurred at the Academy of Fine Arts in China, where their director swapped over 140 Chinese paintings with his own. He claimed the practice was so prevalent that other forgeries subsequently replaced many of his counterfeits."

Whitney furrows his brow. "That's ... a lot of forgeries."

"And it's more common than people think."

"What's the motive? Are these crimes about money?" Whitney asks.

"Not necessarily. While money is often involved, especially with art theft, it has its challenges—finding buyers can be difficult. Even unscrupulous collectors, who'll go to great lengths to amass their dream acquisition, struggle to keep their ownership of a Rembrandt or Van Gogh secret. Art fraud, on the other hand, is often driven by ego. Many forgers feel unappreciated and want to prove they're just as talented as the greats. Other forgers simply enjoy thumbing their noses at the established art world and get off on fooling appraisers and wealthy patrons."

"In the cases you've described, it seems like the perpetrator sticks with a specific genre, like Cubist paintings, for example. Are there cases where someone steals both antiques and modern art?"

"Art fraud takes extensive knowledge of the artist, style, and period. Forgers rarely venture into different areas. Are you looking to tie this to the Squire?"

"You've heard about our resident thief. I know it's a reach, but my chief is looking for a simple solution."

"I'd say it's highly doubtful you have only one perpetrator. But, like the saying goes, 'birds of a feather flock together.' Criminals tend to share information, so maybe a pair is involved. You could look at INTERPOL. While they focus on international terrorism, illegal drugs, and criminal organizations, they also maintain a comprehensive stolen art database. Your art forger has worked hard to stay under the radar, and I doubt the Squire has made it onto INTERPOL's Purple Notice list—that's where they collect criminal methods and procedures. But maybe something will turn up. You'll need to apply for authorization for access; it's just an online form," Smith says.

"So how do we catch them?"

"Whoever did this had to have access. You said the painting was from a residence? Check everyone who works for them, as well as the family themselves."

"The family is wealthy, prominent."

"Doesn't mean they weren't involved with the crime."

CHAPTER 11

Whitney pulls up in front of the family-owned Italian eatery *Il Giardino* (The Garden), known for its freshly made pasta and pizza that rivals any pie in Manhattan's Little Italy. The restaurant sits between a card shop and a menswear store in a strip mall. An extended roof overhangs the sidewalk, protecting diners and shoppers from inclement weather. Iron posts topped with horse-head finials line the walkway, a nod to the equine farm that once stood there. Each holiday season, the shops take turns decorating the posts—red garland one year, tiny Santa hats another. It used to be a Whitney family tradition to pose Laurel with the decorated posts for their Christmas cards, but that stopped by the time she reached middle school, when she declared the photos "cornball."

"*Il Giardino*, really, Dad? We always come here."

"Would you prefer Cobb's Mill?"

"No, this is okay. Maybe they can help me with some basic phrases."

They enter, greeted by the rich smell of garlic and basil. Whitney tells Sophia, the hostess and owner, about Laurel's trip to Italy. In between hugs, Sophia insists Laurel look up her sister Lucia, who has a younger cousin on the other side of the family who would be a perfect match for her. Whitney places a dinner order for both of them.

Just after their salads arrive, Whitney spots one of the Old Brookville patrolmen at the takeout counter.

"I'll be right back," he says to Laurel as she spears a tomato.

"How's it going, Ryan? Anything to report?"

"Lieutenant Whitney, sir. I'm just getting some dinner. Lieutenant Hackett said it was okay to order from here."

"Relax, pickup, right?"

Ryan nods. "I have an update, but it isn't very good news."

"Go on."

"I've been checking the local antique and thrift shops for Miss Tierney's cup. Nothing. I even checked online auction sites. Still nothing."

"What's that tell you?"

"Well, it could still be the Squire, since none of the items he stole ever resurfaced. But it could just as easily be someone else."

"Assume it's the Squire. What do we know? Based on your research, he doesn't just hock his gains at any old place. He's either hired by someone or is a collector himself. Instead of tracking down the actual items, let's figure out who would want them."

Laurel joins Whitney at the counter. "Hi, Ryan. Dinner's ready, Dad."

"Oh, I didn't mean to keep you," Ryan says.

"I'm just taking my little girl out for a bon voyage dinner; she's going to Italy for a few weeks."

Sophia hands Ryan a brown paper bag with "Il Giardino" printed on the side in large, rustic lettering. He holds the bag in one hand, supporting the bottom with the other, and says, "*Buon viaggio, bella.*"

Laurel's cheeks flush at the compliment. She quickly pivots away, hoping neither man noticed. She gives a small wave over her shoulder to Ryan as she returns to the table.

"Any breaks?" Laurel asks when Whitney sits down.

"No, not really. Just whittling down the possibilities. The kid is thorough—not lazy at all."

From her father, that's a real compliment. Whitney has always been a little reticent about new recruits; contrary to what's shown on TV and in the movies, being a police officer requires patience and fortitude, not steely stares, a big gun, and gritty one-liners. Breaks come from diligently reviewing evidence and asking the same questions over and over. In the 1970s, New York City police solved one of the most notorious serial killer cases—the Son of Sam murders by David Berkowitz— through his parking tickets.

During dinner, the pair chat about the Squire and which museums Laurel hopes to visit. After the busboy finishes clearing the table, Sophia returns with a cappuccino for Laurel and a mug of black "Coffee Americano" for Whitney. "That young *poliziotto*—is that why you don't want to meet Lucia's cousin?" she asks with a wink and a smile.

Laurel's cheeks heat up again; she sips her cappuccino, hoping to hide behind the cup, praying Sophia and her father don't notice.

Whitney waves his hand dismissively. "None of this *amore* stuff until she's finished with school. We'll take the check, please, Sophia."

"School, bah, what's she need that for? A husband, *marito!*"

Sophia places the check face down and wanders off to check on other customers.

Whitney leans in toward Laurel. "You could do worse, you know."

"What?"

"Ryan. He's a decent enough guy."

"I thought you didn't want me dating cops?"

"That's absolutely right," Whitney says, smacking his hand on the table to punctuate his point. "I just meant that type—steady job, hard-working, hair cut above his ears."

"How about I agree with you on your first idea: None of this *amore* stuff until after I graduate?"

Whitney lifts his mug, clinking it against hers in agreement. They chat a little longer and finish their drinks, as the restaurant empties. After saying goodnight to Sophia, they head home.

Early the next morning, Whitney gets up to wait with Laurel for the airport shuttle service that Isadora arranged.

"You going to be okay?"

"Yeah, Dad."

"It's just ... I want you to be careful—no talking to strangers."

"I'm going to a foreign country; everyone is going to be a stranger. Don't worry, I'll be with Mom."

"That's the part that worries me."

A town car pulls up to the curb, and the driver takes Laurel's luggage and places it in the trunk.

"I'll be fine, and I'll miss you." She kisses him on the cheek and walks to the car. Before she gets in, she calls back to him, "I left you a present. It's in the basement."

Whitney watches as the car pulls away and waits until it turns the corner. His chest tightens as he feels a sudden pang of loneliness. He admonishes himself—it's just a short trip—but he also knows that soon enough, she will be striking out on her own. The chilly grayness of the early morning deepens his melancholic mood.

When Laurel decided to live at home while attending Post College, Whitney was glad. In his heart, she'll always be the little girl he taught to ride a bike and bandaged up when she skinned her knees. But there's no denying Laurel has grown, and soon it will be time for her to move on with her own life. It's also time for Whitney to consider moving on with his life, too. He had always held up being a single father as a shield to keep other women at bay, but now it might be time to lower that shield.

He feels the familiar craving for a cigarette. His fingers tingle, and he yearns to draw in some nicotine despite having quit well over a dozen years ago. Instead, Whitney ambles back to the house to make coffee. As he scoops the grounds into the filter and starts the machine, he remembers Laurel saying she left him something.

At the bottom of the cellar stairs, Whitney spots two paintings. The first is one of his originals, with the number 1 in the corner; the other is an exact duplicate, with the number 2 followed by (L). He stares at the paintings. How'd she do that?

Since he's up, Whitney figures he might as well go to the station house and get some work done. By the time the midnight shift ends, and the morning shift starts, he has cleared off a pile of reports from his desk and has begun sorting through vacation requests.

His speakerphone crackles to life, interrupting his progress. "Hey, Lieu, there's an Andrew Sutton here for you. Want me to send him back?"

"No, have him wait."

Whitney checks the clock—it isn't even 8:45 a.m. He picks up *The New York Times* and opens to the crossword puzzle. After filling in a few answers, he decides it's time to see Sutton.

"Mr. Sutton, good morning. How can I help you today?" Whitney asks as he enters the waiting area.

The lawyer smiles, unfazed at being made to wait. "Is there somewhere we can talk?" Sutton asks.

"What's this about?"

"I'd prefer not to say until we're in a more private setting."

It's just the two of them in the reception area. The dispatcher is behind a wall of bulletproof glass. The setting is private, but Whitney humors his request.

"Follow me."

Whitney tilts his head toward the door, and the dispatcher buzzes them into the inner sanctum of the police station. He leads the attorney to his office and asks if Sutton would like any coffee. Relieved to hear him decline, Whitney closes the door and motions for Sutton to take the seat in front of his desk.

"Okay, Mr. Sutton, why are you here?"

Clothed in a custom-tailored navy suit and emerald green tie, Sutton certainly looks the part of a high-priced attorney. After their previous phone call, Whitney looked into the lawyer's background. The man has cultivated a solid reputation in town, dealing primarily with estates, contracts, and family matters for Gold Coast elites.

"I came to apologize for how I spoke with you," Sutton says, fidgeting with his watch.

The action strikes Whitney as a pantomime, an actor trying very hard to look humble.

"That isn't necessary."

"Oh, but it is. The Vos family is practically American royalty—everyone wants a piece of them. It is my role to be the gatekeeper, to protect my clients, the watchdog, if you will. Sometimes I come off abrasively while performing those duties."

"I was under the impression that Miss Tierney is the gatekeeper," Whitney says.

"Dear old soul, she's as devoted as they come. But I'd describe Miss Tierney as more of a toothless, gentle old sheepdog, while I'm more of a doberman pinscher, possessing strong protective instincts regarding my clients."

Sutton pauses. "Just not as scary as a pit bull."

The corners of his mouth raise, but the expression is not a warm, genuine smile. The toothless old sheepdog description stands in stark contrast to Miss Tierney's nickname, "The General," but Whitney keeps this thought to himself.

Between Sutton's attempt at looking humble, his effusive apology, and his self-described role of watchdog, Whitney isn't sure what to make of him—other than he's someone to keep his eye on.

"Anyway, I'm sorry if my manner offended you, and I wanted to thank you for your pursuit of this case. Your professional dedication led to the discovery of the stolen painting," Sutton says.

"It was a team effort."

"You are being modest, I'm sure. How soon will you be bringing in the Squire? And how long before the original painting can be returned?"

"We're still gathering evidence and have multiple persons of interest."

"Oh, Lieutenant Hackett led me to believe this was the Squire's doing, and his capture is imminent."

"As I said, we're still gathering evidence."

"I understand it is your policy not to discuss the details of an investigation, but I would consider it a professional courtesy, not to mention a personal favor for the Voses, to ease their concern."

"Where are Mr. and Mrs. Vos again?"

"Sonoma, California. They aren't due back for a couple more weeks. I was supposed to join them, but the disturbance at Glenwood has left Miss Tierney unnerved. I recommended to Mr. Vos that I cancel my flight and remain to reassure her. This whole ordeal has frightened her terribly."

Sutton's depiction of a timid and scared Miss Tierney is antithetical to Whitney's impression of her, so much so that he wonders if Sutton has even met the woman.

"When were you supposed to join them?"

"A week ago. Mr. Vos called, excited about acquiring a vineyard. He wanted me to fly out to draw up some papers."

"Do you remember when, specifically?"

"Why, Lieutenant, are you interrogating me?"

"This is just a casual conversation, Mr. Sutton. You came to see me. I'm just trying to get a timeline and figure out how much information regarding the Vos family the thief could have been privy to."

Sutton surveys the room, noting the thick leather-bound tomes of criminal codes on the bookcase, interspersed with photos of a girl at various ages. A blue and gold college pennant with "Post College" embroidered on it hangs from one shelf. A more recent photo of the girl, now a young woman, sits on the lieutenant's desk.

"Yes, of course, I see. Well now, I planned to leave on the seventeenth. The Squire must have broken in a day or two before, or else I would have already been on my way."

"That must have been disappointing. It's beautiful out there this time of year."

"It wasn't a vacation. And as a last-minute trip, it was more of an inconvenience. I have other business dealings here that require my attention. Caleb Vos is not my only client." Sutton leans forward and lowers his voice. "But don't tell him that."

The attorney adjusts his position and settles into a more relaxed pose crossing one leg over the other.

"I strive to make each client believe I am one hundred percent at their disposal. Now, back to the Squire—what can I tell the family? Are you close to apprehending him, or should I suggest they hire a private detective? The Squire has, after all, eluded you in the past."

Whitney sees how prominent families, such as the Voses, would want a person of Sutton's caliber working for them; the attorney is smart, tenacious, loyal, and charming when it suits his needs. At the same time, Whitney can't help but feel manipulated. Sutton has offered both carrots and sticks in pursuit of his goal: a favor for the Voses, sympathetic concern for Miss Tierney, and now replacement by a PI.

Whitney gets up from behind his desk, signaling the meeting is over.

"You can tell Mr. and Mrs. Vos that this case is a priority and that we are working diligently on it. If they have questions, they are free to call me here at the station. If there's nothing else, I need to get back to my work."

"Very good, lieutenant. I will recommend to Mr. Vos that, for now, things should be left in your capable hands. Thank you for your time."

CHAPTER 12

For many, Labor Day is the end of summer. However, as long as the temperature stays warm, the pool at the Curtis home remains open. But now the days are getting shorter, the nights colder, and it's time to close the pool house.

Margeaux Curtis instructs her housekeeper, Carmen, to strip and wash the cushion covers, clear out any lingering food from the cabinets, and pack away the remaining towels. Then, she tells her to give the entire building a good scrubbing before locking it up for the season.

"I'm having guests over the weekend, so wait until Monday to start. Don't come too early—I plan on sleeping in," Mrs. Curtis says with a dismissive wave of her hand. Then she deliberately locks eyes with her housekeeper. "And if Mr. Curtis calls, tell him I'm unavailable."

On Monday morning, Carmen also opts to sleep in and arrives at the Curtis house later than usual. She circles around the property to the pool house, a broom in one hand and her housekeeping caddy in the other. The lilac-scented, eco-friendly cleaners (as Mrs. Curtis insists) slosh pleasantly as she walks.

But as she steps inside, an array of odors, both sweet and chemical, assaults her. Carmen wrinkles her nose at the combination of stale wine and chlorine. Another scent hangs in the air, but she can't quite place it—rotten meat?

The aftermath of Mrs. Curtis' gathering is significantly less chaotic than she anticipated. This doesn't even crack the top ten list of after-party disasters. Relief washes over her—cleaning the pool house won't consume the entire day.

She scans the room, her gaze landing on a nearly naked body bent over an ottoman. Years of experience have prepared Carmen for encountering Mrs. Curtis' party guests in various stages of undress. Carmen approaches, but something feels off.

As she reaches to gently shake the woman's shoulder, her fingers tremble. No movement. The body isn't breathing. She jerks her hand back in horror.

Carmen's scream shatters the late morning stillness.

aurel called when she arrived in Rome and every day for the first week. Since then, however, Whitney hasn't heard from her. He figures she must be having a good time. Meanwhile, his days are uneventful. Usually, he enjoys the serenity of a quiet house, but this time it just feels empty.

Tired of warming canned soup for dinner, Whitney goes to The Black Walnut Inn. The restaurant has been around since the early 1900s and brags about having served Theodore Roosevelt, Grace Kelly, and Billy Joel. Despite changing ownership multiple times over the years, The Black Walnut has always thrived, thanks to cooking the best steaks in the area.

As he enters, Whitney holds the door open for two women who are on their way out. He recognizes the first—she was a couple of years behind him in high school.

"Hi ya, Susie," he says with a smile.

"Hi back at you."

He turns to the second woman, and his smile spreads into a huge grin.

"Why, Nora Remick, what brings you to town?"

"Ricky? It's been so long." She hugs him. "I don't believe it."

A group of diners excuse themselves as they move past the threesome.

"We should go," Susie says.

"Have a drink with me. Let's catch up," Whitney says.

"We just had drinks." Susie takes a step toward the parking lot.

"Coffee then, come on, ten minutes."

"I'd like coffee. Ten minutes, Suz. Ricky here dated my sister Peggy and was my first crush."

"Is that right?" Susie grumbles. "Okay, but just a few minutes."

The bar area is separate and more casual than the main dining room. Forest green walls serve as a backdrop for vintage sepia-toned photographs of the inn and the ancient black walnut tree that once grew on the property. The trio finds a bistro table near the stone fireplace and settles into overstuffed leather chairs.

When the waitress appears, Whitney orders a glass of Cabernet Sauvignon for himself and two coffees.

"Or would you prefer cappuccino?" he asks the women.

"Actually, I'd like a white wine instead. How about you, Suz?"

"Fine, I'll take a Pinot Grigio."

Ten minutes stretch into a full ninety as they reminisce and catch each other up on their lives. Whitney doesn't realize how hungry he is until he returns from walking the women to their car. He's tempted to quiet the gnawing in his stomach with a quick bowl of chili, but he refrains, knowing the steak will be worth the wait.

His patience is rewarded. As he slices into the steak, a stream of pink juice flows across the plate, colliding with the melted butter oozing from the baked potato in a battle for territory. Whitney devours the first two bites, then savors the rest of his meal while replaying his conversation with the women. He knows he made a point of asking Susie just as many questions as he asked Nora, but now he can't remember a thing she said. Nora, on the other hand, lingers vividly in his mind. She's as he remembered—fun, animated, her laughter ringing out over the bar's din. She looks good too—damn good.

At one point, their conversation grew solemn when Nora spoke about her husband's unexpected death. He had been an operations consultant, which meant they moved frequently, leaving her with a résumé full of odd jobs and no established career. After the funeral, she moved back home with her mother to figure out her next steps.

While her loss cast only a passing shadow over their lively talk, it gave Whitney pause. He eagerly wants to see Nora again and wonders how long he should wait before asking her out.

The next evening, Whitney is home channel surfing, but the lineup is dismal: a soccer match, reruns, and a police drama (he detests these). Thankfully, the phone rings, breaking the monotony. Expecting Laurel, he says, "Hi honey," cheerily into the mouthpiece.

There's a brief silence before the caller speaks. "How'd you know it was me?" followed by a laugh.

"Nora? I thought it was Laurel calling."

"Oh, I don't want to tie you up if you're waiting on a call. I just had such a good time last night, so I wanted to talk some more."

"It's fine. I'm not waiting on Laurel. I mean, I'm glad you called. How'd you find me?"

"I looked you up. You're in the same house."

"Some things never change. Last night was fun, but I don't think Susie thought so."

"She was in a bad mood because of her guy—she's dating Danny Mullen, do you remember him? He married Cookie Davis shortly after high school, they divorced, he remarried but divorced again. Anyway, now he's dating Susie."

"Third time's a charm, I hope," Whitney says.

"I don't think so. Last night wasn't the first time he's broken a date with her. That's why she was so prickly."

"Personally, I think she deserves better. She's a good kid."

"Kid? She's my age."

He lowers his voice conspiratorially. "You know Nora, you'll always be sweet sixteen to me." Even through the telephone, he knows she's blushing.

"Oh, you big tease! That's just how you used to be."

"I told you, some things never change."

Hours slip by unnoticed as they talk. His cell rings, but Whitney ignores the calls. He doesn't want the conversation to end. Finally, when they're saying goodbye, Nora asks if he wants to get together again. His first impulse is to say yes. But, instead, he balks, claiming a busy work schedule, and promises to call later in the week.

Whitney checks the recent calls on his cell. There are a couple of voicemail messages from Laurel, and a half dozen missed calls with no message from her as well. He sees there's also a message from Isadora. Whitney adds six hours to the current time and decides to call Laurel back in the morning.

At 5:30 a.m. his phone rings. Whitney mumbles a groggy "Hello."

"It's about time," Laurel says. "I've been trying to reach you."

He ignores the urgency in her voice—after all, she hasn't been in touch for over five days.

"Hi, Laurel, nice to finally hear from you. How's Italy? How's your mother?"

"That bitch!"

Whitney sits bolt upright. In her entire life, Laurel's never said a harsh word against her mother.

"What'd you say?" he asks, surprised by the venom in her voice.

"I'm sorry, Dad, I know you don't like cursing, but if the shoe fits."

"What's going on, honey?"

"I don't want to talk about it. I left mom and her traveling band of sycophants. She's on her way to Milan, but I'm staying in Florence. I refuse to be on the same plane as that woman. I'm trying to switch flights now, but I'll need a ride from the airport. Any chance you can come pick me up there?"

"Of course. Let me know which flight and I'll be there. Sweetheart, you can always talk to me. What happened?"

"No, I can't go into it now."

The pain in her voice is evident. Whitney wishes he could reach out and hug his daughter.

"Okay, call me back with your arrival time, I'll meet you and take you for ice cream, or gelato. We can talk then."

"Thanks, Dad, but ice cream won't make things better this time. I'll call back soon."

Whitney figures he should listen to his messages. The first is from Laurel; she sounds excited, "The most amazing thing happened Dad, I can't wait to talk to you about it."

The second is also from Laurel, but her tone is completely different, "I can't believe I'm related to that witch! She gives Narcissus a bad name! How could you marry her? She's the most insensitive, self-centered person on the planet. Arrgh! I can't stand her. I'm getting on the next flight out of here. The home phone is busy. Is it off the hook?"

Finally, he listens to Isadora's message: "Hello, Rick. Laurel may—or may not—call you. She doesn't want to go to Milan, which is the next stop on my itinerary. She'll lose out on an important opportunity. I think she's missing that boyfriend of hers. She spends a lot of time going to museums on her own. Whatever she does, tell her she must be in Rome next Tuesday for our flight home. *Ciao.*"

Whitney shakes his head in disbelief at Isadora's blindness to how her actions affect Laurel. Everyone else says he's lucky that Laurel and Isadora's relationship is "drama-free." Whitney isn't so sure; he thinks Laurel caters too much to her mother's whims. Even as a child, Laurel never seemed disappointed by her mother's broken promises. She always made excuses for Isadora. He understands, to some extent—Laurel often has to defend her mother against critics who think any celebrity is fair game—still, she never seems to have any trouble when it comes to getting mad at him.

He remembers their early days together when they were first getting acquainted. Isadora modeled in her teens and twenties. The dramatic contrast of her jet-black hair and ivory skin set her apart from the popular blonde surfer-girl models of the time. She had some success, most notably landing a national shampoo campaign. While she never reached supermodel status, she gained a certain celebrity cachet in the tri-state area.

Both Isadora and Whitney lost their fathers as children—one to a heart attack, the other simply disappeared. The absence of a father forced them to grow up quickly. It was a shared experience that bonded them, though each developed very different views on family. Isadora resented helping her mother raise her younger siblings and resisted any responsibilities that were thrust upon her. In contrast, Whitney vowed never to abandon his family or his obligations.

Isadora continued to model after they married but soon realized her front-of-camera career would be fleeting. She then transitioned to behind-the-camera, initially focusing on fashion photography, before moving to portraits. Perhaps it was all the hours spent posing as a model that inspired her to capture her subjects at ease. Her portraits strip away pretense, allowing viewers to see her subjects in intimate moments, as though the picture was taken by a close friend.

At first, their life together worked. Whitney supported Isadora's growing career, in part by taking late shifts so he could spend time with Laurel during the day. But over time, their delicate balancing act unraveled.

Something big must have happened in Italy for Laurel to be so upset.

As Whitney heads to the police station, he braces for whatever the day holds. Entering through the main entrance, he's relieved to make it to his office unencumbered—no disgruntled attorneys, no messages to meet with the chief, and no new burglaries.

With no pressing issues, Whitney's mind drifts to Nora—her eyes, her smile, her laugh. He catches himself grinning and quickly refocuses on work.

Mid-morning, Laurel calls with her new flight information.

CHAPTER 14

Margeaux Curtis devotes the day to a meticulous inventory of her shared assets with her soon-to-be ex-husband. She marks a star by the items she thinks Ben will fight her over and notes what she'll counter with if necessary—certain items she can part with easily. Dividing their property has become a calculated game of chess—best to be prepared with her sacrificial pawns.

The day is bright and warm. Margeaux opens the windows, a faint aroma from the mums perfumes the air. She lingers, admiring the brilliant maple tree in the backyard. The leaves are having their final colorful display before they turn brown and die. Margeaux always loved watching the tree transform through the seasons. A sadness envelopes her; this will be the last year she'll see the maple in its autumnal glory. She blots away a tear with the back of her hand.

A flicker of movement catches her eye. She whirls around, pulse quickening, but it's just a breeze teasing the drapes.

Three pages of notes later, Margeaux decides she's had enough cataloging for the day. A bottle of white wine has been her companion throughout the inventory process, its light body reflecting her mood. But now, as evening approaches, she craves something bolder. Pouring herself a glass of red, she savors the first sip, letting it linger on her tongue before swallowing. She feels an illicit thrill at liberating yet another bottle from Ben's cherished wine collection. A minor act of rebellion in an otherwise accommodating life.

A growing chill snakes through the house. Margeaux weaves through the rooms closing windows. The act of lowering sashes and locking them in place feels oddly final.

The effects of the second bottle of wine work their magic. A familiar warmth emanates from deep within her, and the perpetual knot at the back of her neck fades away. Earlier in the day, she called the Winterberry

Club for a dinner reservation. Eating alone in public doesn't bother her; it's eating alone at home that depresses Margeaux. She starts toward the stairs to shower and change.

Ben's office door creaks open. Heart racing, Margeaux lets out a surprised yelp as a man steps out. After the initial shock, relief sets in—she recognizes the familiar face. It's him, a former lover from a brief affair—a fling that blazed brightly at the start but soon faded. They navigated the aftermath with polite detachment when seeing each other at business or social functions. At times, it still seems like he is looking after her, which, depending on the situation, Margeaux finds either sweet or creepy. His unexpected presence feels ominous.

"Margeaux." His voice is low and seductive, the sound stirring long-buried memories of limbs entwined.

He starts a casual conversation, opening with a comment about the weather—as if lurking behind Ben's door is a normal occurrence. "I've been thinking about you, about us. Wondering if maybe the timing's right. I let myself in to surprise you ... but then I got scared." Margeaux crosses her arms, squinting. Humility was never part of his personality, though the explanation sounds plausible enough. "The house is empty. We could ..." His eyes flick toward the stairs. The hairs on the back of her neck prickle. Her instinct registers the danger before her brain can catch up.

He suddenly lunges and grabs her neck, fingers tightening around her throat, his thumbs pressing against her trachea, their pressure steadily increasing. She flails at her attacker with sluggish, ineffective blows, the wine having dulled her reflexes.

His grip is vice-like, and he lifts her off the ground, her toes barely grazing the floorboards. The panic in her chest turns to terror as she meets his eyes—once sexy and inviting, now cold and dead. She might as well be begging for mercy from a shark.

The room dims as darkness swallows her whole.

Looking down at the corpse slumped against the wall, he feels annoyed. The body of Margeaux Curtis lies at his feet, guilty of being in the wrong place at the wrong time. Why is she here and not with her current lover? As he calculates what to do next, fragments of memories—or are they fantasies—creep into his thoughts.

He was college-aged when it first happened, and the combination of terror and excitement overwhelmed him. He described the incident to the school therapist, though he left out the violent details. "Hyperphantasia—experiencing extremely vivid mental imagery," the therapist said. "I want you to keep a journal and start weekly sessions." But he never returned. Instead, he ritualized the episode—privately, obsessively—revisiting it as a tool to focus his mind during particularly challenging moments. Now, he settles himself on the couch, leans back, and closes his eyes, allowing the scene to unfold.

Some coworkers had invited him to dinner. Normally, he didn't socialize, but to avoid seeing the old woman, he'd agreed to meet them at a diner. He arrived first, chose the last booth, and sat facing the door. The layout was typical—booths along one wall, a counter with backless stools on the other, and the obligatory rotating pie case. The place was empty—just him and the waitress. She was plain-looking and overcompensated with too much makeup. What she lacked in prettiness, her curves more than made up for, filling out her mint-green diner uniform in a way that was hard to ignore. The zipper was undone just enough to reveal a hint of a lacy ivory-colored bra.

The waitress explained that the cook was out sick, so she was working double duty. Apologizing in advance for her limited cooking skills, she recommended he order something that would only need to be heated rather than actually cooked.

"That's okay, I'm not very particular," he said.

"What's your name, sugar?" the waitress asked.

"Tom." A lie.

They had exchanged smiles, talked, and flirted. Eventually, he had ordered meatloaf, mashed potatoes, and gravy. She then sashayed toward the kitchen.

His coworkers arrived and wasted no time making lewd comments about the waitress. His jaw clenched. This was a hard-working woman who deserved respect, not the crude remarks these slobs made. He fingered the retractable box cutter in his pocket as they guffawed. In one swift motion, he swung his arm across the table and sliced both their throats.

The next thing he knows, he's in a bathroom surrounded by green ceramic tiles, the waitress gagged and tied to a toilet, her uniform pushed up to her waist.

He heard a voice outside himself say, "I like when women wear matching underwear. Otherwise, they look cheap. You're not cheap, are you?" He traced a finger along the top of her frilly bikini bottoms. The waitress responded by shaking her head wildly.

He raised a fillet knife in front of her face. "Your cook needs to take better care of their utensils. This one was dull. You know, an unsharpened knife can cause more damage than a sharp one. You have to apply so much more force to cut with a dull knife."

His eyes shifted from her face to the blade. "Don't worry, though— I took the time to hone the edge."

Her body thrashed against the bonds; the toilet held firm.

"Don't do that. I could nick an artery."

He pushed her legs apart and dragged the blade across her inner thigh, watching the blood swirl and fade into the toilet water. His focus shifted to her neck. With minimal pressure, he made a small incision. Blood trickled down her chest; he stared, mesmerized by its path and the red flower blossoming as it reached her bra.

His excitement overtook him. Rather than making a precise cut, he slashed violently at her chest instead. Blood splattered across the green tiles in a macabre Christmas pattern. In her weakened state, she struggled to speak.

He leaned closer, her scent familiar—Canasite perfume. It reminded him of the old woman—who could have easily afforded the real Chanel No. 5 but liked to think thrift made her clever—it did not. He squeezed his eyes shut, banishing her from his thoughts. When he opened them again, the waitress's eyes were pleading. He lowered the gag.

She whispered, "What do you want?"

Suddenly, a tapping noise interrupted her, followed by a blinding light. Disoriented, he looked around and realized he was alone in the booth. The waitress was tapping the menu with her pen.

"What do you want?" she had asked again.

His head exploded with pain. Grabbing his head, he rocked back and forth, moaning, "No, no, no."

"Sugar, are you okay?" the waitress asked.

"Splitting headache just came on," he gasped.

"Oh, I hate those. I have aspirin in my bag. Wait here, I'll be right back."

But he didn't wait. As soon as she passed through the double doors, he ran out, leaving $20 on the table. Never stiff a waitress, he reminded himself.

Lying on Margeaux's couch, the last wisps of fantasy fade. The memories settle his mind, leaving an odd, satisfied smile on his lips. He opens his eyes and returns fully to the present. Now he knows exactly what to do. He glances around Ben's office, already forming a plan. Margeaux is still slumped against the wall. During the heat of their exchange, he hadn't noticed—but now, there's no mistaking it: Chanel No. 5. The real thing. No bargain imitation. Margeaux always had class.

CHAPTER 15

L ieutenant Whitney arrives at the scene just as the uniformed officer strings yellow crime-scene tape around the pool house. He nods to the patrolman as he heads toward the tent being used as the incident command post.

To reach the backyard, Whitney had to circle around the sleek, modern-style residence—the kind one might expect to see perched on a California cliff rather than in suburban Long Island. The pool house mirrors its architectural style, with floor-to-ceiling glass panels that provide a clear view of Detective Swift photographing the scene.

Sergeant Stone draws up alongside him. "We're waiting on the coroner and crime scene unit. The victim is Margeaux Curtis, wife of ..."

"Soon-to-be-ex-wife of Benjamin Curtis, named partner at a Wall Street investment firm," Lieutenant Hackett cuts in as he swaggers over. "Check this out."

He hands Whitney a Polaroid print of a woman's body. She is draped face-down over a hassock, or a "poof," as Laurel called it when she bought one for his home office—a poof doesn't belong in a man's office. Whitney bats the stray thought out of his head.

"What happened?" Whitney asks Stone.

"Homicide. Looks like strangulation. There's a braided cord around her neck. We'll know for sure once the medical examiner submits his report."

Whitney looks back at the building. Sheer white drapes hang in the center of each glass panel, all gathered at their midpoint, except for one that dangles limply.

"You said soon-to-be-ex-husband. Trouble between them? You like him for this?" Whitney asks.

"Out of town. Chicago, the maid said. Could be a boyfriend, or it could be the Squire." Hackett hands another Polaroid to Whitney and sneers. "She looks like a pig—just needs an apple in her mouth."

Whitney frowns. Plenty of cops use gallows humor to compartmentalize the ugliness they see. He understands that, but Hackett always manages to twist it into something uglier. Inside the squad room is one thing— but a careless slip in front of a family member could blow back on the whole department.

The photo is even more abhorrent than Hackett's comment. Taken from behind the victim, it shows her skirt hiked up around her waist, a silver candlestick inserted into her rectum. Sleek and modern, its coiled base gleams under the camera flash. With a gauze-wrapped hand, Hackett plucks the photo from Whitney's grasp.

"Murder is far from the Squire's typical M.O.," Whitney says.

"She could have caught him in the act, tried to stop him," Hackett offers.

"But sodomy? Seems like a very personal act for a thief."

"It takes all kinds. Plus, Curtis was a cougar—into kinky shit, too."

Whitney narrows his eyes and scowls at Hackett. "Is that from personal experience, Denis, or are you repeating locker room gossip?"

"As a matter of fact, Whit, it's something I know for a fact. About four, maybe five, years ago, I was coming back from a burglary call when I spotted a car parked by the entrance of the nature preserve. Figured it was some rich kids making out since it was a Benz and the windows were all steamed up. I opened the door, and there were three half-naked people, all wearing bird masks. I asked for ID, and one of them was Margeaux Curtis."

"So, there's a report. We may want to talk to those two other people."

Hackett glances around the yard, as if it's a rental property and he's looking for flaws. When his gaze returns to the pool house, he frowns.

"Well, this was like five years ago," Hackett says. "I didn't want to cause any undue embarrassment for anyone. Besides, they were all consenting adults. I gave a verbal warning."

"Do you remember the other two people?" Whitney asks.

Hackett twists his mouth to one side. "Not after all this time."

"Why do I suspect you'd have remembered if they were women?"

Hackett throws his arms into the air. "Are you giving me the third degree, Whit?"

"Just asking questions. What happened to your hand?"

Hackett waves his bandaged appendage. "This? Nothing, just some plumbing repairs."

The coroner arrives. Seeing an opportunity to exit the conversation, Hackett strides to greet him.

Sergeant Stone shares a knowing glance with Whitney. "You know how he is," she says.

Across the yard, Carmen, the housekeeper, sits in an Adirondack chair, an emergency blanket wrapped tight around her shoulders, her face puffy from crying. Whitney approaches, asks if he may join her, and offers his condolences.

She stares at the pool house with a vacant expression, and though she's slow to respond to questions, she eventually draws strength from helping the police. Carmen confirms Hackett's hearsay regarding the upcoming divorce and adds that since Mr. Curtis moved out, Mrs. Curtis has dated quite a few men. The most recent was the tennis pro at her country club.

Whitney writes Carmen's contact information in his notebook and tells her she's doing just fine. People often need reassurance when dealing with tragic situations. She bobs her head, wiping away fresh tears. Whitney moves off a few paces, giving her space, when his radio crackles with static: "We found a note."

Suicide? Not a chance—just based on the photos, no one would do that to themselves. "Say again?" he asks into the transmitter.

"It's the Squire. He left a note," Detective Swift reports over the radio.

Whitney makes his way back into the command center and joins Hackett and Stone. They watch as Swift carefully traverses the path of contamination—the designated route that allows him to enter and exit with as little disruption as possible to the crime scene. He heads straight for the trio.

"We found this tucked into her bra," Swift says, holding up an evidence bag containing a small note card.

"What's it say?" Whitney asks.

Swift turns the bag around. The card has been unfolded and flattened, revealing both sides. It stands out from the others—previous Squire notes were always plain, but this one has a silver border, and the tone is different.

Monstrous Beast! How like a swine she lies. – The Squire

Hackett chimes in first. "That cinches it. There's silver and a card—it's the Squire."

"Seems flimsy to me, Whitney says. "Whoever did this didn't steal the silver; they used it as a prop—or a weapon. And all the previous Squire notes were unsigned."

Hackett makes a dismissive "pfft" and shrugs his shoulders. "Anything's possible."

The exhibit custodian takes possession of the evidence and Detective Swift starts back toward the pool house. He stops just inside the threshold, places an evidence marker, and begins taking photos of his new discovery. Rather than waiting for the detective to finish, Whitney decides a better use of his time would be to meet with the tennis pro. It could take hours before the crime scene is fully processed and the body readied for transport to the morgue.

Whitney calls the club to get the tennis pro's name and schedule.

Once there, he drives past the main clubhouse, a huge brick colonial building with two-story white pillars, and continues down a meandering driveway that leads past the first tee and the 18th green. He parks in front of a massive air-supported dome that covers the tennis courts. Someone having an affair with their tennis instructor seems cliché, but it must happen often enough for it to become one.

Inside the bubble, on the first court, a pair of doubles teams are mid-match; the second court is empty, and the third is clearly being used for a lesson. Whitney walks along the back edge toward the farthest court. A woman alternates between forehands and backhands from the baseline while a man on the other side of the net feeds her tennis balls. Two young boys—about four and seven—have made a game of chasing the balls and returning them to the standing basket beside the teaching pro. Their laughter interrupts the steady thwack, thwack of the rally.

The tennis coach is tall and fit-looking, just as one would expect. Whitney jots down the pro's name and appearance in his notebook: "Aaron Jennings, 5'11", 180 lbs., sandy hair." Despite it being autumn, the pro also has a healthy-looking tan.

Once the lesson ends and the mom and boys are leaving, Whitney approaches the pro. "Aaron Jennings?"

"Call me AJ."

The pro's bright smile fades when he notices Whitney's shoes. "You really should be wearing sneakers out here."

"Lieutenant Richard Whitney, Old Brookville Police. Is there some-where we can talk?"

AJ motions to a couple of folding chairs beyond the court's perimeter. The men sit.

"What can I do for you, Lieutenant Whitney?"

"I'm looking into an incident involving one of the club members. When was the last time you saw Margeaux Curtis?"

AJ's eyes dart left and right; he shifts in his seat, intently studying the tennis racket's string pattern. To some, that might look like guilt. Whitney knows better. In the past, eye movement was used to determine a person's truthfulness, but relying solely on body language is now a debunked method of lie detection—especially when the interviewer has no baseline behavioral pattern with which to compare.

The housekeeper already told Whitney about the affair, but he's curious to see how AJ responds to his questions.

"Let's see, the summer session ends with a round-robin tournament over Labor Day Weekend. Mrs. Curtis, like a lot of our other members, only plays during the summer session. Even with the heaters, it still gets chilly here in the bubble."

"I was under the impression that your relationship was of a more personal nature."

AJ jumps to his feet, the racket clattering to the ground. His voice raises, bordering on a shout. "Hey, just what is this all about? Has something happened to Margeaux?"

Whitney doesn't respond. He waits quietly for a moment, and looks AJ in the eye, then nods his head toward the chair. AJ sits. "Why don't you tell me about you and Mrs. Curtis?" Whitney asks.

Realizing his outburst inadvertently revealed his secret, AJ's broad shoulders droop. He looks around at the nearly deserted tennis courts, sits back down and he lowers his voice. "It's against club policy to be involved with a member."

Why do people speak in hushed tones when making a confession? The foursome at the far side of the bubble is completely engrossed in their match. Even if there was a lull in the action, they couldn't possibly hear AJ at this distance.

"I don't care about any club infraction. I'm investigating Margeaux Curtis' death," Whitney says.

AJ jerks his head up. The golden tan drains from his face.

"Murder?" AJ asks.

"What makes you say that?"

"If it was a car accident, you wouldn't have come out here to question me. And there's no way Margeaux would commit suicide."

"You were having an affair, then?"

"It wasn't serious. We were just having fun."

"So, you've seen her since Labor Day. When exactly?"

"Thursday night. She came over, but didn't stay the night."

"Mrs. Curtis threw a party over the weekend. Did you go?"

"No, we weren't a couple like that, and we didn't want anyone at the club to know. We would just get together sometimes, and well, you know. I didn't want an actual relationship, and I'm tired of one-nighters. Margeaux is smart, beautiful, and sophisticated. We both wanted the same thing—sex with no complications. We weren't in love or anything, but I did like her."

"Who would have been there?"

"For sure Suzanne Francis—they were doubles partners. As for the others, I could only guess. You should talk to Mrs. Francis. Margeaux's really gone?"

Whitney nods.

AJ puts his head in his hands and starts muttering, "Oh God," over and over again.

Whitney goes to the courtside cooler and fills a paper cup with water. When he returns, AJ's eyes are glistening with tears.

"Drink this." He hands the cup to the tennis pro. "Can you think of anyone who would want to hurt Mrs. Curtis? Her husband, maybe?"

"I don't think so, but then we didn't talk about Mr. Curtis."

He gives AJ time to drink more water. "Can you tell me where you were on Sunday?"

"Um ... I went to a buddy's house to watch some football. I was there most of the day."

Whitney writes the details in his notebook and adds "brown eyes" to his initial description of AJ.

"Am I in trouble?"

"The investigation is just beginning. We'll have more questions. It'd be best if you don't leave town."

Whitney hands AJ his card. "If you think of anything else, call me."

When he returns to the station, Whitney walks in on Hackett holding court with some of the other officers. Hackett likes to surround himself with a small group of followers; they sometimes have drinks after their shift or barbecue together on weekends. Whitney operates by a different philosophy. He's friendly with everyone at the station but doesn't socialize with any of his subordinates outside of police functions. Having to answer to the chief and five different mayors is enough politics for him. He works hard to avoid any appearance of favoritism.

Hackett calls out to him, "Hey Whit, how's the tennis pro look?"

"Athletic." Whitney doesn't like discussing cases across an open squad room and goes straight to his office.

Hackett follows. "No, really, did he do it?" he asks.

"I'll need to confirm his alibi, but he has no apparent motive, and he doesn't strike me as the murdering type."

"All men are the murdering type, given the right circumstances," Hackett says.

"True enough."

"Whit, look, there's something I'd rather not have become part of the report," Hackett glances toward the squad room, then eases the office door shut before lowering his voice. "I don't know if Margeaux held on to any mementos, but there's a chance you might find some letters from me."

Whitney meets Hackett's eyes but says nothing.

"We had a fling. It ended years ago—ancient history."

"This was after the incident in her car? How'd you end it? Any problems?"

"No, nothing like that. We just went our separate ways. That's how it goes sometimes."

"What was that show of yours about on scene? Pretty damn callous for someone you were involved with."

"You know how it is out there, especially around the guys. I've got an image. Besides, that photo ... that wasn't ... Margeaux," Hackett says, dropping his gaze, the last syllables of her name barely a whisper.

"Did you have anything to do with this, Denis?"

Hackett's head snaps in Whitney's direction and he locks eyes with the other lieutenant. "Christ, Rick, you know me better than that."

"You just said, 'All men are the murdering type, given the right circumstances.' All I know is that you've dumped a hot mess at my feet. The chief will not be happy with his investigating lieutenant compromising the case."

"I didn't compromise anything. Besides, it was ages ago. I haven't seen her in two, maybe two and a half years." Hackett blusters, his face becoming peppered with red splotches.

"Want to tell me where you were on Sunday?" Whitney asks.

"Sure thing. I was visiting my mother."

Whitney's eyebrows raise, "Your mother is your alibi?"

"She's in a home, Meadowbrook Gardens. The staff knows me."

"How long were you there?"

"From 6:30 until 11:00."

Whitney stares at him, but says nothing.

"What? I'm a good son," Hackett says.

"Tell me what really happened to your hand."

Hackett paces around the office, muttering about professional courtesy and covering each other's backs. Something on the bookshelf captures his attention. He moves a photograph an inch and a half to the left. "I told you, a plumbing problem. I showered before going to visit my mother. There was a leak behind the access panel. It was a tight fit, and I scraped my hand."

"Why not call a plumber?"

Hackett spins around. "With what they charge? They probably take home more than you and me combined."

"You're off the Curtis murder."

"You can't do that. You're not the boss. That's my case."

"Not anymore, and you know the chief will back me up on this. It's a high-profile murder—you had an affair with the deceased. Right now, you're toxic. We can't have you anywhere near the investigation, let alone act as lead. You know the routine. You'll have to give a statement. I'll have Stone meet you in the conference room."

Hackett sighs, his beefy frame deflating, "Could you do it in here? I want as few people as possible to know."

Whitney is a little surprised by Hackett's sense of decorum. Or is Hackett just covering his ass? Either way, Whitney likes this side of Denis better than the blowhard version. "OK, here's a pad, start writing."

Hackett looks down and pauses, takes the pad, then peers up at Whitney with a look of sincere gratitude. "Thanks, Whit. I knew I could count on you."

"Don't thank me yet," Whitney says. "I'll have more questions after I read your statement, and the chief has to be brought in on this once we're done."

Whitney circles around his desk and sits. To pass the time, he grabs the newspaper and a pen, starting in on the Monday crossword. Clue thirty-seven across jumps out at him: One who misleads by statement or appearance. A soft sigh escapes. Whitney hopes it's not a harbinger. He fills in the letters: D-E-C-E-I-V-E-R.

aurel scans the faces of people waiting at Terminal Four. Some wait eagerly, clutching flowers and stuffed animals. Others wear the haggard expressions of people dragged into battling traffic just for a JFK pickup. She searches the crowd for her father. Amidst the throng, someone stands out. They're waving with one hand and holding up a sign with her name in the other. She weaves through the crowd to reach him.

It's Ryan. He looks different in jeans and a casual Henley pullover shirt. For the first time, she sees beyond the police uniform—his lanky frame, storm-cloud gray eyes, and a mop of unruly hair. Her hand lifts of its own accord, ready to brush the stray lock from his forehead. But her sour mood takes over, and instead she turns the gesture into an awkward stretch.

"Where's my father?" Laurel asks.

"Something's come up. He planned to schedule a shuttle service, but I told him I have the day off—at least until 8:00, when I start my volunteer shift at the Oyster Bay EMS."

"Did something happen? Is he alright?"

Ryan takes the bags from her hands. "He's fine, just ... busy. Follow me."

They walk to the short-term parking lot in silence. Ryan chalks up Laurel's reserve to jet lag. He stows her bags in the trunk, and as they pull out of the parking garage, he tries to break the tension.

"Long flight?" Ryan asks.

"Yeah."

"How was the weather?"

"Okay." Laurel stares out the passenger-side window, her tone as monotonous as the steady stream of traffic inching its way toward the exit.

"Did you get to the Uffizi?"

"Yeah."

"How was the haggis?"

She glances at him sharply. "What?"

"Just checking if you're paying attention. You seem kinda bummed for someone who's just back from Italy."

"Something spoiled the trip."

Ryan waits to see if she'll reveal more, but Laurel shifts her body and turns from him. He gives her space until they're on the Northern State Parkway, heading east, before he tries again.

"Spoiled your entire trip? It couldn't be that bad."

"It was."

"I'm a good listener," he says, leaning toward her with a gentle smile, hoping she'll see his earnestness.

"I don't want to talk about it," Laurel snaps. She crosses her arms, sinking further down into the seat and placing her feet on the dashboard.

Ryan touches her knee lightly. "That's not safe."

Even through her jeans, she feels the warmth of his hand. Her tone softens. "Oh, okay." Laurel promptly returns her feet to the floor.

The rest of the trip is silent.

Ryan parks on the street in front of her house. As he's about to remove her bags from the trunk, he says, "You're obviously upset. I'd be happy to take you out for coffee, or cappuccino, if you'd prefer."

"I don't want to talk, and certainly not to you."

Ryan steps back, stunned. "I was just trying to be a friend."

"Thanks, but no thanks." Laurel's voice cracks—she hates the sound—whiny, like a child's. She doesn't want him to see her like this, but she can't stop herself. "And where's my father? What's so important he couldn't pick me up? Why'd he send you? A car service would've been better—no annoying questions."

She regrets the words as soon as they leave her lips. Her hands fly up to cover her mouth. Ryan wordlessly carries her suitcases up the pathway. Laurel grabs her backpack and follows.

Placing her hand on his elbow, she looks up into his eyes. "Look, it was just a really bad trip."

Ryan places her bags by the front door. "So you said. Your father's at a murder scene."

He looks over his shoulder at the car and then down at his feet before meeting her gaze. After a pause, he says softly, "He didn't send me. I volunteered because I wanted to see you."

Laurel opens her mouth to say something, but it just hangs there.

Ryan walks back to his car.

She jogs down the pathway after him. "Ryan, I'm sorry. I appreciate the ride."

He opens the door and looks at her over the roof of the car. "Why do you do that?"

"Do what?"

"Call me Ryan?"

"But that's your name. Everyone at the station …"

"Yes, at the station. That's how cops talk." He pauses. "My name is Ezra Ryan, if you ever bothered to ask."

He gets in the car, keeping his eyes trained straight ahead, and drives away. Laurel stands at the curb, her cheeks burning with embarrassment, as a tear streaks down her face.

The darkened skies open up, and fat raindrops pelt everything in sight. For a moment she stands stunned, unsure what to do. Laurel swears she hears someone shout, "Get out of the rain!"

But when she looks around, no one is there. She's alone. With a sharp breath, she picks up her bags and dashes into the house.

CHAPTER 17

Hackett finishes writing and begrudgingly pushes the pad in Whitney's direction. He twirls the pen between his fingers a few times, then presses the button rapidly in succession: click-click, click-click, click-click. Whitney senses that Hackett already regrets his decision to come forward about his relationship with Mrs. Curtis.

"You did the right thing, Denis. Go home. I'll bring the chief up to speed."

With him gone, Whitney can finally tackle the tasks he'd avoided while Hackett was in his office. Whitney calls Suzanne Francis, Margeaux's tennis partner and possibly the last person to see her alive. Unfortunately, Mrs. Francis does not pick up, so he leaves a vague message asking her to call the station house.

By the time he gets home, Laurel is already in bed. Relief temporarily washes over him, but guilt quickly follows. He hasn't had the time to delve into whatever happened with her mother. His procrastination pays off again in the morning. Apparently, Laurel left early for school. On the refrigerator, a note reads: "Went to the studio, then going to see Sydney."

At least she's with her best friend, he thinks, instead of going back to that arrogant ex-boyfriend.

He forces himself to compartmentalize. Whatever happened in Italy will have to wait—the Curtis murder takes priority. Whitney showers, shaves, and heads out the door.

As soon as Whitney walks into the station house, Stone informs him that the chief is waiting. He puts his coat away and goes to see his boss.

"Good, Whit. Come in and close the door." Chief Eaves waits for the door to shut before continuing. "So, Denis slept with the Curtis woman after all?"

Whitney isn't surprised that Hackett made an end run around him and contacted Eaves first.

"He claims they had an affair several years ago," Whitney says.

"Now what, fire his ass?"

The chief's approach to problem-solving has always been swift and heavy-handed.

"We have no just cause. He could sue."

"What do you suggest?"

"Detective Vernon is going to the tri-state anti-terrorism symposium in Rochester. Send Hackett along with him. He'll still be on the job, but far enough away not to compromise the investigation."

"With Twinkle-toes? I suppose that could work. How long is the symposium?" Six years ago, detective Vernon made the unfortunate mistake of mentioning he and his fiancée were taking dancing lessons for their wedding. He's been "Twinkle-toes" ever since.

"A week. Hopefully, that's enough time to find evidence to charge him or eliminate him as a suspect."

"Do you think he did it?" Eaves asks.

"No, I don't."

"Okay, ship him off with Vernon. You're lead now."

"What about Swift?"

"Pete is a good cop, but I can't have one of Hackett's inner circle in charge. It's you, or I call in Nassau. And you know, the last thing I want to do is explain to the town leaders why the Second Precinct had to be called in."

Whitney nods his head. Requests to Nassau when Brookville doesn't have specialists on staff, like CSU or the bomb squad, is fine. But for regular police work, there's no calling in outside help.

"I know you're not part of Hackett's crowd, so you won't cross any lines. Hackett has friends here who may be tempted to help him. But doing that will only hurt the department. I need an honest investigation. Do you understand?"

"Yes, sir."

"And keep the liaison with Mrs. Curtis just between us for now."

"Chief, Denis is a braggart. Maybe Swift or some others already know about the affair."

Eaves scrunches his face, irritated by this idea. He picks up his phone and angrily jabs at the buttons, placing the call on speaker. After four rings, Hackett's gravelly voice comes through.

"What."

"Hackett, it's me. Who knew about you and Mrs. Curtis?"

"No one."

"Really? I would think she's quite the notch in your belt, too good to just keep to yourself."

"No, she was different. I didn't talk about Margeaux."

"Good. We're sending you to the tri-state anti-terrorism symposium with Vernon. Pack quick, you leave tomorrow," Eaves says.

"Wait, what? I can't go. I have cases."

"Swift can handle them."

Whitney detects a hint of annoyance in the chief's voice.

"What if I won't go?" Hackett asks.

"Then you'll be suspended." This time, Eaves' voice displays more than just a hint of annoyance.

"It's that SOB Whitney's idea, isn't it? You know he's angling for your job."

The chief's face reddens, but he keeps his voice steady. "As a matter of fact, it was Whit's idea to send you to Rochester." He pauses. "I wanted to fire you."

Eaves bangs the handset down, disconnecting the call. He narrows his eyes, staring at the phone for a moment before directing his attention back at Whitney.

"Hackett told me earlier, he was visiting his mother during the time of the murder."

"That's what he put down in his statement," Whitney confirms.

"Go check it out and send in Swift. Dismissed."

The chief spins his chair toward the window, signaling that he doesn't want any further questions.

Back at his desk, Whitney presses the intercom for the dispatcher. "Have whoever is west of Wolver Hollow Road call me."

Within a few minutes, Whitney hears from Officer McIntosh. Whitney directs the patrolman to swing by Meadowbrook Gardens and confirm that Hackett was there on Sunday night. While he waits, Whitney spreads the various Squire notes across his desk—all with the exception of the one left with Mrs. Curtis, were on plain white card stock, handwritten in a distinctive blend of cursive and print.

The media pushed the note card angle extensively, so their existence is now common knowledge. But the crucial details, such as paper type and writing method, have remained undisclosed, to weed out copycats.

Whitney thinks back to one husband's bogus claim of the Squire stealing his wife's jewelry. The obvious scam was exposed not only by his choice of stolen items—diamond jewelry estimated at $30,000—but also by the typewritten message on stationery paper he left behind. The sloppy scheme landed him a five-year sentence for insurance fraud.

The note left with Mrs. Curtis stands in contrast to the others, with its silver border and elegant cursive script. Whitney studies the handwriting, noting that the vertical strokes are wider than the cross strokes, indicating a fountain pen rather than the ubiquitous ballpoint—yet another difference.

All of the notes have an interesting, old-fashioned phraseology. The Squire's tone has always been quirky, and sometimes even apologetic. However, the latest note feels sinister. Intrigued, Whitney types "Monstrous Beast! How like a swine she lies" into his computer. Various links pop up, all pointing to Shakespeare's *The Taming of the Shrew*. In the play, the line describes a drunken man; yet in the note, the murderer has correctly revised the pronoun to "she."

Is Shakespeare, or that specific play, a clue, or deliberate misdirection? Whitney types in the wording from the other Squire notes but finds no matches to Shakespeare—one more element supporting his theory that these are two different culprits. Unfortunately, it's not enough to convince those in charge.

Officer McIntosh calls back a short while later, reporting that the sign-out sheet at Meadowbrook Gardens shows Hackett arriving at 6:30 p.m. and leaving at 11:15 p.m.

"Is there surveillance footage?"

"I didn't ask. Should I go back, Lieutenant?"

"No, that's not necessary. Thanks, McIntosh."

Whitney is frustrated by the officer's lack of initiative. But to be fair, he hadn't given him details about why he was checking on Hackett. To avoid adding grist to the rumor mill, Whitney drives out to the nursing home himself.

Meadowbrook Gardens is a two-story building shaped like a sharp-cornered "U," as if made from children's building blocks. The central section houses the main entrance, dining facilities, and a large common room. The two wings contain private rooms for the residents. Outside, neatly trimmed shrubs and flower beds create an inviting exterior. Inside, the modern lobby welcomes guests with soothing neutral tones.

Behind a semi-circular desk, the receptionist has her face hidden behind a paperback.

"Excuse me, Miss, I'd like to check on the visitors for one of your residents, Mrs. Ruth Hackett." Even though he's in uniform, Whitney reaches for his ID. The receptionist doesn't bother looking up from her reading. She taps the visitor log with a long tomato-red fingernail.

The phone rings, forcing her to put down the book. "Meadowbrook Gardens, how may I help you?" she coos into the mouthpiece, then quickly presses buttons to transfer the call. She looks surprised to find Whitney still standing there.

"Visiting hours end at 9:30?" Whitney asks.

"That's what the sign says."

"Then why does the log show several people checking out after 11:00 on Sunday night?"

She shrugs. "I only work the day shift."

Whitney notices a camera mounted on the wall. "I'd like to see your surveillance tape from Sunday."

"You'll need to see Floyd. He's on lunch right now and won't be back for an hour."

"May I see Mrs. Hackett?" Whitney asks.

"Sign in, room 247." The woman points to the left and goes back to her reading.

Whitney walks down the long hallway decorated with black-and-white portraits of classic movie stars, including Humphrey Bogart, Lauren Bacall, Cary Grant, Marilyn Monroe, and Rock Hudson. The door to room 247 is ajar. He raps gently on the door frame. "Hello?"

"And just who are you?" asks a voice from behind him.

Whitney turns around. Facing him is a petite, dark-skinned woman with silver hair. She's dressed in a floral-patterned shirt buttoned all the way to the collar. Her posture is defiant, hands on her hips, elbows pointing out.

"My name's Richard Whitney. I wanted to ask Mrs. Hackett a few questions."

"Ruth is sleeping. She sleeps a lot. Doesn't get too many visitors, and certainly not the police. What do you want to ask her about?"

"I didn't catch your name, Miss...?"

A faint smile touches her lips at the polite and youthful address. "Call me Cassie. Everyone does. My room's just across from Ruth's."

"Is there someplace we can sit and talk, Cassie? Maybe over a cup of coffee?"

Her smile widens, revealing small but even teeth. "Do you like pie, Richard Whitney?" she asks, offering her arm. He takes it, and they walk together to the dining hall.

Cassie sits at a table in the very center of the room. Whitney fetches a slice of strawberry rhubarb pie and a cup of coffee, light with two sugars. He then returns to the counter for a slice of lemon meringue pie and a coffee for himself because Cassie insisted, saying it would be unseemly for her to eat alone.

"Do you remember Sunday?" Whitney asks when he sits down.

"Of course, I remember Sunday. How old do you think I am?"

"I think you're young enough to enjoy the gossip about you entertaining a younger man who obviously isn't your son."

Cassie grins, a twinkle in her eye. "Well now, not much happens here. I need to amuse myself somehow."

Whitney leans in closer, taking her small hand in his. "Let's not disappoint them then," he says with a wink. "What can you tell me about Ruth's son?"

Cassie pulls away, crosses her arms and her voice cuts above the room's chatter, "That phony baloney!" Realizing her outburst has attracted the attention of everyone, Cassie stifles a soft laugh.

Over coffee and pie, Cassie reveals the truth behind Hackett's long visits. A group of men, Hackett among them, set up weekly Sunday night poker games under the pretense of visiting family. The men look good in the eyes of their wives by visiting their relatives, while secretly playing cards and enjoying whatever sport is in season.

"I'd curse their names and spit on the floor, but that wouldn't be ladylike," Cassie says, clearly disappointed by the priorities of these men. "At least Ruth's son arrives early and has dinner with her first."

Meadowbrook Gardens overlooked the men using the lounge as a "man cave," until they lit up cigars, violating the smoke-free policy. Shortly after the complaint, the common room was completely remodeled: fresh paint, new carpeting, big screen TVs, and new recliners, all provided by an anonymous donor.

Whitney walks Cassie back to her room, but before she provides him with the names of the poker players, she makes him promise to visit her again. He checks in on Ruth Hackett, who's still sleeping soundly, so

Whitney returns to the lobby.

Floyd is back on duty. He leads Whitney to a small electronics room where they review Sunday's footage. The video shows Hackett entering alone at 5:56 p.m. and leaving with the other men at 11:17 p.m. Though they aren't pals by any stretch, Whitney feels a surprising sense of relief seeing Hackett's alibi confirmed.

On the way back to his car, Whitney's phone pings. It's a text from Nora—a reminder about dinner that evening. He smiles. She's been asking to meet Laurel and planned something special.

Amid the murder investigation, there hasn't been much time for personal matters. He still hasn't found the right moment to ask Laurel about Italy—or what really happened with her mother. And he hasn't told her about Nora yet either.

It's been years since Whitney introduced Laurel to someone he was dating. The last time was when she was in middle school, during a brief involvement with a woman who had a daughter Laurel's age. The girls hit it off—better, in fact, than he and the mother did. The woman was smart and kind, but he just didn't feel a real connection. When the relationship ended, Laurel took it hard. She was looking forward to having a sister and cried for days.

Since then, Whitney's avoided introducing girlfriends—especially for something casual. But Nora is different. She matters. The time has come. He figures he'll leave work a little early to tell Laurel his news. An hour should be enough.

CHAPTER 18

The train idles at the Oyster Bay station as eastbound commuters head for their cars. In four minutes, at 7:38 p.m., the train will depart, this time heading west on its way to Penn Station. In the Squire's view, commuters fall into two groups, those who enjoy chatting and those who do not. He purposely sits alone in the second car. Even in a well-lit train, he needs to disappear.

It's rare for a conductor to walk through before the third stop at Glen Street, but just in case, his ticket for Jamaica Station in Queens, New York, is tucked in the small pocket at the top of the seat in front of him. Jamaica isn't his true destination—he'll hop off even before reaching Glen Street, at the Locust Valley station. But a ticket for such a brief trip is unusual and would stand out. He needs to be unremarkable—just another faceless reverse commuter heading back to the city.

The Squire is aboard the train for less than fifteen minutes, most of his time this evening will be spent on foot. He hikes away from the station, leaving the little town's hub behind him. During the day, people walk, jog, and even push strollers along this road, but at night it's different. What seems common in the daylight now looks unusual, even suspicious. His success on these excursions depends upon his invisibility.

As quickly as possible, he slips into a wooded area. Through the distance comes a wavering cry—whaaaaaa! Whaaaaaa! Whaa! Whaaaaaa!—a train announcing its arrival and the unloading of more commuters heading home. A pang of guilt tugs at him; that's where he should be—home, not out at his other job, not borrowing.

It was unseasonably warm earlier in the day. But now that the sun has set, a cool wind carries with it a light fog—a potential benefit, as limited visibility will help conceal his movements. On the other hand, he'll need to pay careful attention to his route, as it's easy to lose one's bearings in the mist. The chill and fog close in on him, an unwelcome reminder of the trap he's fallen into.

The trek takes almost an hour. Tonight's destination is a stately home, one the Squire is familiar with and has been inside many times. He hesitates, listening carefully for signs of life. A few crickets are conducting a final concert before the first cold snap, but the house itself is silent. His outstretched arm reaches up, fingers tapping along the top of the door molding until they touch something metallic. Snatching the key, he opens the door.

It's rare for him to visit a site with an alarm system, but he makes this exception. Using his knuckle, he presses a succession of buttons on the panel, 7-3-2-2-3-7. Using the house number forward and backward is an obvious code, and known to anyone who's ever worked there.

On his way to the dining room, he passes a pair of accordion doors. Without thinking, he eases the panels open exposing a floor-to-ceiling storage unit. The shelves hold a few books and board games, but mostly videocassettes—a museum of dated technology, kept out of sentiment rather than use. Shaking his head, the Squire chides himself, don't get sidetracked.

Just then he spies a container on the floor. He kneels and draws it close to him. It's made from wood and is about the size of a shoebox, with a small brass trunk clasp but no padlock securing it. The Squire flips the hasp up with his thumb and opens the lid.

Inside are velvet pouches. He picks up one, upends it, and a narrow silver box falls into his hand. Inspecting the piece, the Squire rolls it over, engraved into the top is a delicate wreath design. The metal feels cool against his palm, and he slides it back into the pouch. He opens a different bag, another silver box—this one unadorned and heavier. He estimates a dozen bags containing silver boxes.

He has to make a decision: Pack the whole thing, or take just the pouches. An empty box would be a sure sign of a burglary, whereas if the box itself is missing, there's a strong chance the family will just think it's misplaced.

Shifting the items in his backpack, he makes room and hoists it onto his shoulders. When he closes the closet, a small squeak escapes, deafening in the silence. He freezes. The pounding of his heart echoes in his ears as he scans the shadows. Reassured he's alone, the Squire takes a sharp breath, then darts out, shutting the back door firmly behind him.

The backpack feels heavier than usual, and he's winded by the time he makes it back to town and boards the next eastbound train. At this hour, the train car is nearly empty. He finds a seat away from the other riders and places his pack beside him. As the train whistles and chugs forward, memories drift into his consciousness. The Squire closes his eyes, lost in thought, while the rhythmic clatter of the train lulls him back to another time.

As a boy, he loved riding the train with his father, especially when it pulled onto the turntable at the Oyster Bay station and slowly spun 180 degrees to make the return trip to Queens. This process had become an event in itself. Children, adults, and even school field trips came to watch the mechanical marvel. The engineer sometimes let local kids hop on the running board for the turning operation. Those were great days—long before he became the Squire.

His father, Ernest Seaman Jr. (Ernie), would say to him, "My father was a train fireman, I'm a fireman, and someday, son, so will you; it's in our blood." Ernie lit up whenever he talked about the railroad and its history. "Remember, son, we don't just bring people to and from work, we move the president," he would boast, despite the fact that Theodore Roosevelt had died in 1919, long before Ernie even became a fireman. Ernie's enthusiasm was sincere and infectious. After all, his father, Ernest Seaman Sr., had been a fireman on the Oyster Bay line when it did carry the president.

Theodore Roosevelt often traveled by train to Oyster Bay on his way to Sagamore Hill, which was referred to as the Summer White House. At 42, he was the youngest man to have become president; John F. Kennedy was the youngest man elected president. President Roosevelt was outgoing and spoke easily with the train crew. Upon learning of Ernest Seaman's new son, he asked to have the baby brought down to the station so he could "meet the lad." From that point on, whenever the president took the train home to Oyster Bay, Ernest Sr. would make sure his wife met them at the station with young Ernie in her arms.

There had never been any doubt that Ernie would become a fireman. And as soon as he was old enough to join his father, he started learning the required skills. There was also never any doubt that when he married and had a son, the boy would be named Ernest Seaman III. But from the moment the baby made his first cry, Ernie called his son Teddy.

The age of steam engines was coming to a close; in its place was the promise of a modern diesel era. At the time, the change was so exciting that neither father nor son realized it also meant the death of a third generation of railroad firemen for the Seaman family.

Ernie and Teddy rode the very last steam train out of Oyster Bay. His mother, Eleanor, was not pleased with her son missing a day of school just to ride some silly old train, but his father insisted it was a historic event. They rode engine number 35 as it made its final run down the line before retirement.

The excitement over the new diesel trains faded quickly as many people lost their jobs. Ernie was fortunate—his mechanical skills were adaptable and in demand at the Jakobson shipyard, known to the townies simply as Jake's. He joined shortly after the launch of the Navy's X1-midget submarine. The Navy commissioned only that single vessel, later dismissing the project as a novelty. So Ernie's talents were put to use on Jakobson's other projects: tugs, yachts, and fishing boats.

To help the family, Teddy took an after-school job at Fleischer's Butcher Shop. His chief duty was sweeping the sawdust that was still sprinkled across the floor—a holdover from when it had been used to soak up blood or grease. On Saturdays, he rode along with the delivery man, helping carry packages. He was paid weekly, and along with his meager earnings, he was sent home with beef shanks or oxtails. His mother had a talent for turning those modest cuts of meat into meals that his father claimed were "fit to serve the Rockefellers."

Teddy never considered his family to be poor—there always seemed to be plenty to eat, and frequently he brought leftovers to the widow next door.

Once he could drive, Teddy began making deliveries on his own for Fleischer's. He was gregarious and always willing to help in some extra way. Most deliverymen just rang the service bell and left their bundles by the kitchen door. Teddy always carried the meats inside, along with anything the produce man or dairyman had left as well. At the last delivery stop of the day, he would offer to peel potatoes, chop vegetables, or even carry heavy loads of laundry. Through these acts, he endeared himself to the estate staff, which increased his tips.

While on a delivery to the Kingsley estate in Upper Brookville, he met the most stunningly beautiful girl in the world. Rose Collins had chestnut hair, alabaster skin, and large emerald-green eyes. She was the new maid. The Kingsley estate soon became the permanent last stop on his route just so he could spend more time with the new girl.

After graduation, his father got him a job at Jake's. Teddy purposely took the early shift so he could still make deliveries for Fleischer's—and, more importantly, still see Rose. He proposed shortly after her eighteenth birthday, and a small wedding followed a few months later. Mr. Kingsley offered the young couple an apartment in the former carriage house on the condition that Rose would continue her housekeeping duties and Teddy would be available for any handyman projects. The mechanical knowledge he gained from the shipyard became an asset, and the young groom was soon called upon by neighboring homes to help with small emergencies. It was an especially happy time for the newlyweds.

The train jostles the Squire from his reverie. Recently, he read an article about the restoration of number 35. He smiles faintly, thinking about seeing the old engine again.

West Shore Road passes by the window, followed by boats bobbing on the moonlit bay. The Squire is almost home. In his younger days, he would have jumped off the train before reaching the station, but now he can't risk spraining an ankle—or worse. Besides, the walk to his house on Duck Pond Lane isn't far, just barely over a quarter of a mile.

Some nights, he takes the long way home, walking through Roosevelt Park. Like the sound of a train whistle, the gentle lapping of the waves against the shore soothes him.

Tonight, however, he's eager to get home and opts for the most direct route. The pack feels heavy—whether from its contents or his guilt, he's unsure.

The Squire moves through the town center and its mom-and-pop shops. This is a blue-collar town, a working person's town, in dramatic contrast to the upscale Brookville estates. He walks past rundown, modest two-family homes clad in faded vinyl siding. A splotchy brown dog with a gray-muzzled face trots back and forth inside its chain-link fence.

"Sit," he commands. The dog obeys and waits expectantly.

"Good boy." He tosses the dog a treat. He always carries treats when he goes on these excursions, just in case.

The neighborhood transitions from attached two-family houses to small single-family homes. Clapboard and neatly trimmed hedges replace vinyl siding and metal fences. His spirits lift once he catches sight of his own home. No longer conscious of the weight on his back, he hastens his pace. But first, he makes a quick detour to the detached one-car garage to unload his bundle, before entering the house.

"Hello," he calls as he steps through the front door. "Something smells wonderful."

"You're just lucky it ain't burnt, coming home so late."

"Chandice, what would we do without you? How's my darling?"

"Come here before you go up."

Worried, he follows her into the kitchen. "Why, is she okay? Did anything happen?"

Chandice, a tall nursing student from St. Maarten, usually speaks in a lilting voice—though it can turn sharp when the mood arises. Currently, her tone is somewhere in between.

"I want to make sure you don't smell like booze or another woman. I won't let you upset her."

Spreading his arms wide, he slowly spins around while Chandice sniffs at the air. He never lied to his wife until he started "borrowing." She believes wholeheartedly that emergency jobs—ones only he can handle—just pop up. Chandice obviously has her doubts. Ironically, if both women knew the truth, he's sure the aide would understand, but his wife would be crushed.

"Everything I do is to make her happy. I don't like being away for long; you must know that by now."

Her expression softens. "I suppose I do. It's just... she gets so sad when you're out, and I don't know what to tell her."

"I'm sorry, but duty called. How is she?"

"She's a fighter—you can tell by her expression she's in pain, but she won't admit it. There's stew in the pot. She didn't eat much. What do the doctors say?"

"Same as always, they want to run more tests. Don't you have to go to class?" he asks.

"No class tonight. Study session. I have exams next week and was hoping to have Tuesday and Wednesday off."

"Okay, I'll make it work." He helps Chandice put her coat on. "See you tomorrow?"

"See you tomorrow."

He walks up the stairs to their bedroom. His wife is asleep. The only pieces of furniture in the room are a bed, dresser, and nightstand— a matching set that was his wedding present instead of a honeymoon. A carved pineapple sits atop each bedpost, and the dresser and nightstand also have pineapple designs. On their wedding day, he promised someday to take her to Hawaii; until then, they would at least sleep among pineapples.

During the day, the room is bright, with lots of sunlight streaming through the windows. African violets grow in glass terrariums on top of the dresser. A delicate violet-patterned wallpaper complements the live plants. There is no TV. He offered to buy one special for her to have upstairs after she got sick, but his wife refused.

As a young man, he worked hard to make their dreams come true. Unfortunately, Hawaii always remained just out of reach. Tragedy struck when they lost their son during childbirth. The couple was heartbroken. The pain and loss compounded after they learned that trying for another child would kill Rose. Their dream of a large family was shattered.

He watches her sleep from the doorway, her breathing steady and sure.

Her eyes flutter open. "Teddy," Rose whispers.

"I'm here, my love."

aurel and Sydney Archer have been best friends since third grade. Sydney is the youngest in her family, with five older brothers. The two girls became fast friends—Laurel being an only child and Sydney the only girl. Their friendship quickly grew into a sisterly bond. Through their teen years, interests diverged, and crushes came and went, but they remained each other's constant.

After high school, Laurel planned to go away to college with her boyfriend. But after they broke up, she decided to stay home and attend Post College. Sydney ventured north to Boston, and during her spring semester, she met David Jones, her eventual husband.

The young women meet at a café near the Post campus. After placing their orders for salads and iced teas, they dive into catching up.

"So, tell me about your trip! Was it great? Did you meet anyone?" Sydney asks, her voice dropping to a whisper on the last question.

"Sort of, but not like that," Laurel smiles and bumps her foot lightly against Sydney's under the table. "Not everyone meets their dream guy on the first day of college."

"You just pick the wrong type of guy, Laurel."

"Speaking of which ... I have some news. A bit of a bombshell, actually."

Laurel springs to her feet, startling her friend, and waves in a wide, sweeping arc. Her hand then shifts into a quick, beckoning flick. Sydney turns to see a young, uniformed officer striding toward them. Laurel can hardly wait to speak. "Ryan, I'm glad—oh, sorry, Ezra, I mean. I'm sorry about the other day." She lowers her gaze, a soft pink tinges her cheeks.

Sydney's eyes widen as she watches the interaction. She clears her throat. "Ahem."

With a quick gesture between them, Laurel makes the introductions. "Sydney, this is Ezra Ryan. He works with my dad and also volunteers for EMS in Oyster Bay. Ezra, this is my friend Sydney." Ryan smiles, leans down, and shakes Sydney's hand.

"Hey Ezra, how's the Squire case?" Laurel asks.

He winks at Sydney, allowing her to watch as his smile morphs into a serious expression. He stands tall and faces Laurel.

"It's Officer Ryan to you. And I'm sure your father wouldn't appreciate me discussing the details of a case with outsiders."

"Okay, I deserve that. I said I'm sorry. What can I do to make it up to you?"

Ryan's smile returns as he rubs his chin thoughtfully. "Hmmm … interesting proposition. I'll have to think about that. Given enough time, I'm sure I'll think of something you can do."

Laurel's cheeks redden.

"Right now, though, I have to go. I'm on duty and Sergeant Stone hates getting cold coffee. Nice meeting you, Sydney. I'll get back to you, Laurel."

Ryan exits the café. Laurel sits back down, but her eyes follow him until he's out of view. When she spins back to face her friend, Sydney is fanning herself with one hand and coos, "Officer Ryan can slap the cuffs on me, anytime."

"Syd!"

"He's cute, you should definitely go for it."

"Are you crazy? He works with my dad. Besides, I made him mad the other day."

"Oh, I think he's gotten over it, and with the way he looks at you, I'm sure Officer Hottie there would be happy to get you in a compromising position or two."

The waiter sets down their lunches and asks, "Anything else?"

"Another iced tea, please," Laurel says.

Sydney adds, "Make that two."

"So, is Detective Dreamboat your bombshell?"

Laurel exhales, her shoulders sagging. "Not exactly." She takes a deep breath. "My mom slept with Birk."

Sydney's jaw goes slack. "Wait, what? Isadora told you—to your face—that she slept with him?"

"She didn't tell me directly—she was talking to a designer she was photographing in Italy."

"And she said she slept with your ex-boyfriend?"

"No, she described him. Well, his tattoo, actually. It was Birk."

"I'm sure he isn't the only person with a tattoo. What is it, a snake? Or is it tacky to get a tattoo of yourself?"

Laurel appreciates her friend's attempt at levity, but her voice betrays the pain she feels. "It's part of a poem. In Latin."

Sydney pauses, looking more serious. "But you two broke up. Are you still into him?"

Laurel rolls her eyes. "No, oh god, no."

"Good, because he was a major ass."

Both girls smile.

"It's just, she's my mom, Syd. She should've known better."

"Did you ever introduce them?"

Laurel shrugs her shoulders, popping a cherry tomato into her mouth. She cocks her head to one side before replying. "No, not that I can remember. My mom was on assignment in Tokyo most of the time we were dating."

"Maybe he pursued her. She is famous and drop-dead gorgeous."

"That isn't helping."

"What I mean is maybe she didn't know who he was."

"So, you're on her side?" A harsh edge returns to Laurel's voice.

Sydney stabs her lemon wedge with the straw a few times, then meets her friend's gaze. "Sweetie, I am always on your side. I think right now you're mad at the wrong person. If they did ..." Sydney pauses, choosing her words before continuing, "... get together, don't you think it's more likely he went after her than she went after him?"

Laurel slowly nods. She's used to people using her as a way to get close to her mother.

"Besides, Birk is a parasite—he takes and takes until there's nothing left. I was afraid he'd play starving artist, conning you into supporting him until you finally had enough."

"Why didn't you say anything?"

"Laur, you were so over the moon, if I said anything then, we wouldn't be talking now."

"Is that why my father hates him?"

"He's going to hate anyone you bring home, except maybe Ezra. He's a real cop, right? Not a stripper cop—a real cop?"

"You are bad, Syd. I've got enough on my plate with school. I don't need to add Ryan, I mean Ezra."

"What is it between you two?"

"It's a long story."

"I've got plenty of time. Spill it."

CHAPTER 20

Whitney heads home early to talk with Laurel before their dinner with Nora. That morning, he estimated an hour would be plenty of time to ease her into the idea—but he should have left work earlier. When Whitney arrives home, there's a note from Laurel on the refrigerator.

> *Nora called. Who the hell is Nora, and how does she know*
> *so much about me when I've never even heard of her?*
> *Make my apologies, I won't be joining you for dinner.*

Crumpling the paper in his hand, Whitney contemplates canceling dinner entirely, but he's been looking forward to seeing Nora all day. Hearing her laugh is exactly what he needs. He takes a quick shower and shaves before leaving.

On the drive to Nora's house, he tries to think of what to say about Laurel, but his thoughts keep returning to Margeaux Curtis' murder. Hackett being involved with the victim is bad. It doesn't matter how long ago the affair was—in the court of public opinion, Hackett is going to be viewed as a primary suspect. On top of that, the chief keeps pressuring him to prove the murderer and the Squire are one and the same. The only evidence supporting that theory, however, is the note left with the body. It doesn't seem to matter to the chief that it's inconsistent with other Squire cards.

Nora opens the door as he's heading up the walkway. The sight of her sweeps away any lingering thoughts about the case. She's wearing a dark green sweater dress that complements the color of her eyes and shows off her curves. Back in high school, he'd always thought of her as a sweet kid. Sometimes, she tagged along when he took Peggy out on dates. He smiles at her, thinking her figure is still cute as ever—something he never acted on back then, since he was dating her sister—but that didn't mean he never noticed. She takes his coat and leads Whitney toward the dining room.

"I'm sorry about Laurel," he starts.

"Oh, that's fine. I'm glad she came early. It gave us a chance to get to know each other one-on-one."

He steps into the dining room. Laurel is seated at the table. She briefly meets her father's gaze, then shifts her attention to her feet.

Nora gushes, "Aren't the flowers Laurel brought beautiful? I love all the colors."

Centered on the table is a modest bouquet. To Whitney, they look like psychedelic daisies. Instead of white petals, each flower bursts with vivid color: pink, red, yellow, and orange. Some are a bluish-purple—Laurel probably has a special name for it, like heliotrope.

Something about the flowers tickles his brain, but he can't think of why. He mentally swats the thoughts away and instead focuses the enticing aroma coming from the kitchen.

"Smells great," he says.

Nora places a bottle of wine in front of him. "Would you open this, please? I have to check on the food."

He uncorks the bottle and pours wine into two glasses. In a low voice, he says to Laurel, "I'm mad at you. You've been acting childish."

"I know."

"But this"—he tips his head toward the flowers—"might get you out of the doghouse."

Nora emerges with a platter of sliced strip steak, surrounded by grilled vegetables. "Who's hungry?"

The dinner conversation starts awkwardly, the first topic addressing Laurel's trip to Italy, with each question receiving a one- or two-word answer. Whitney tries to telegraph his disapproval of her curt answers with a stern look.

When the conversation switches to the forgery case, it's Nora's effervescence that finally breaks down Laurel's brusque attitude.

"I'm still amazed at how you discovered the painting at Glenwood was a fake. How did you figure that out?" Nora asks.

"Well, I didn't do much. I just saw that it was upside down." Laurel responds.

"But that observation was key," exclaims Nora. "They should make you an honorary detective. That's a thing, isn't it Ricky?"

"No, that's not a real thing." Whitney mutters.

"Well, it should be. I think you deserve a medal, or at least a parade," Nora says. "Cheers to you. A smart woman is an invaluable resource." Nora raises her wine glass and leans forward.

Laurel picks up her water glass and lightly taps it against Nora's glass. "Thanks, and I like that; to smart women."

Laurel's first smile of what will be many that night appears

"Come on now, Ricky, get in on this. Your daughter is amazing and deserves to be celebrated."

Whitney glances back and forth between the two women. An amused grin slowly spreads across his face. Any trepidation he had regarding the two of them getting along vanishes.

There's still the issue with Isadora to deal with, but for the moment, relief and pride courses through him. Laurel stays through the meal and an appropriate amount of after-dinner small talk before making her excuses to leave, citing studio work she needs to catch up on now that she's back from her trip. Whitney stays considerably longer.

CHAPTER 21

The next morning, Whitney sits at his desk reviewing various reports. He's distracted by thoughts of the previous night's dinner, and the bouquet Laurel gave Nora. He didn't think introductions would be a big deal, but something has been off with Laurel. After returning home from her trip with Isadora, Laurel has had a renewed focus on her schoolwork, which is good, but she has also been distant.

Whitney rubs his temples, trying to push a swirl of colorful daisies from his mind. After his unsuccessful attempts at clearing the thought away, Whitney closes his eyes, intent on following the distraction wherever it leads. This time, instead of the colored daisies, he sees sunflowers. His eyes pop open as he remembers a photo attachment on one of Laurel's emails. Whitney scrolls through his messages until he finds the one he's looking for. Laurel was traveling by train from Rome to Florence and took a picture of the passing landscape captioned 'A sea of yellow flowers.'

This is a waste of time. Whitney clicks the X on the photo attachment. But his mind locks onto that last thought: a sea of yellow.

He rummages through the Margeaux Curtis investigation report until landing on his note regarding a substance found underneath two of the victim's fingernails; a yellow substance.

Whitney knows if he calls the lab, he'll end up bouncing from extension to extension; an in-person visit will get faster results. On the drive to the forensic services building in Westbury, he calls Detective Bert Walsh. The two worked together before Walsh transferred to Nassau County Police. The detective is waiting at the entrance when Whitney arrives.

"Hey, Whit, long time. What brings you here?"

"Thanks for seeing me, Bert. I'm working on the Margeaux Curtis murder. Waiting on the lab report, but I have a few questions and was hoping to talk to someone."

"That's a strange case. You think the Squire is back?" Walsh asks.

"Hard to say."

Walsh leads him through a rabbit warren of corridors painted a dull industrial gray. Finally, they enter a windowless room.

"Who's got Old Brookville?" Bert calls out.

The technician closest to the door glances up from his microscope, jerks his head toward the back. "Lee does."

"There you go, Whit. I have to get back upstairs. Good to see you." Walsh takes a few steps, then turns back. "Hey, Marion and I should have you over. It'd be good to catch up. And bring Laurel along, unless she's gotten married or something."

Or something; the seemingly innocuous comment shoots through him. Whitney boxes the feeling away to be dealt with later.

"Thanks, I'd like that," he answers.

Whitney strides toward the back of the lab. The only person there is a woman.

"Are you Lee?" he asks.

The woman looks up, lips pressed into a tight line. "Vivian Lee. Spelled L-E-E," she says crisply. "And yes, my mother's favorite movie was *Gone With The Wind*."

"Lieutenant Whitney, Old Brookville," he says, holding out his hand.

She ignores the gesture. "I haven't finished the report yet."

Vivian Lee's appearance fits the stereotypical "nerdy lab tech": white coat, oversized glasses, hair in a tight bun, her voice as clinical as her surroundings. She bears little resemblance to her glamorous namesake.

"I can see you're busy, but I was in the area and had a few questions. I'm hoping you can help me."

Lee looks up at him, blinking from behind her large-frame glasses, but says nothing. He continues, "I was reviewing my notes and wondered if it's possible that the murder took place elsewhere."

"Interesting that you would ask about that. I found some evidence to support the scene being staged."

She holds up a plastic baggie containing a pair of women's high-heeled shoes, made of purple suede with bright red undersides.

"Look at the toe." Then she turns the bag around. "Now the heel."

"There are scrapes on the heel," Whitney says.

"Yes, but not on the toe, right?"

The technician's voice strikes a higher pitch, and her speech quickens as she explains her discovery.

"The crime scene photo shows the floor to be stone—slate, I'm guessing. From the position of the body, if the implied act occurred, there would be scrapes on the toes of her shoes. But the toes have no marks. The shoes—they're Christian Louboutin, by the way—probably $600, maybe even $700. If I paid that much for shoes, I wouldn't risk scuffing them."

Whitney recognizes the signature Louboutin red soles from Isadora's modeling days, but he allows the lab tech to show off her knowledge.

She hands him the evidence bag. "Look closely at the heel. The scrape marks go in one direction along the vertical seam, not back and forth."

"As if she were dragged," Whitney says.

"Exactly, as if she were dragged."

"So, it's possible this wasn't a lover's tryst gone wrong?"

"Based on the evidence, I can't confirm or refute that hypothesis. But it does suggest the body was moved postmortem. You'll want to compare my notes to the ME's. I'm sure he'll be able to expand upon my findings."

"What about the substance under her nails? Have you analyzed that yet?" Whitney asks.

It's paint and it's old, specifically a color compound called chrome yellow. Today its use is highly regulated because the pigment contains lead and other heavy metals. I'll have a more detailed analysis once the lab reports are complete.

"Thank you for taking the time to talk with me, Miss Lee. Your insights have been very helpful."

The technician's attitude transforms as a smile lights up her face. "Oh, you're welcome, Lieutenant. And call me Vivian."

Whitney drives to the Curtis Estate. It's still an active crime scene, though at the moment, the only person there is the security officer. Whitney signs the logbook noting his intention to remain outside the building. The predominantly glass structure allows an ample view of the interior. It's all white. White walls, white upholstered chairs with white pillows—no decorations, no candlesticks, and, most importantly, no yellow.

"Detective Swift said he thinks we can release the scene in another day," the security officer says.

"Has anyone gone up to the main house?"

"No, sir."

"Got the search warrant?" Whitney asks.

The security officer hands over the warrant papers. Whitney scans the pages. The section describing the premises goes into specific detail, ensuring the affidavit covers the pool house. Unfortunately, the language focuses solely on the outbuilding, omitting the main house.

"Crap."

He looks to see which officer made such a rookie mistake. Despite the mark looking more like the scratchings of someone trying to get their pen to write, Whitney immediately recognizes the "signature"—Hackett.

"Shit."

As soon as he's out of earshot of the security officer, Whitney calls Eaves. "Chief, I've been to the lab. We have an issue with the Curtis murder that's gonna require calling in Nassau's forensic unit. I'll tell you when I get there. Meanwhile, don't let Swift close the scene."

Once they're able to discuss Whitney's new hypothesis face-to-face, Chief Eaves' response goes a step beyond Whitney's previous thoughts.

"Effing shit. Amend the warrant. I'll put Swift on hold. But find something before we call in Nassau," Eaves says.

Whitney drives to the courthouse with Officer Ryan for another procedure for the recruit to become familiar with: obtaining a judge's signature on an amended warrant.

They return to the Curtis residence. At the front door, Whitney holds out his hand. Ryan pulls a single key with an ID tag from his pocket. Whitney tries the door lock, but it won't turn. "You sure you grabbed the right one?"

Ryan nods somewhat nervously. "I also called the alarm company and Mr. Curtis."

"Let's see if there's another door."

As they circle to the rear of the house, Ryan asks, "How's Laurel?'"

"She's fine."

"When I met her at the airport, she seemed ... I don't know, distracted? Certainly not happy, like people usually are when returning from vacation."

"You haven't spent any time with her mother. ... I'm just kidding. She was probably tired from the flight."

Whitney, of course, noticed something was off with his daughter, but he's not about to discuss it with a subordinate. He and Ryan gain access through the back door and enter the kitchen. Whitney strides purposefully to the opposite end of the house. He wants to first investigate the room abutting the patio because of its proximity to where the body was found.

Like the pool house, this room is also entirely white—white walls, white furniture, and a huge white grand piano in the center. Wall-to-wall white carpeting covers the floor, punctuated by three zebra-skin rugs. Vacuum lines run in parallel patterns; reminding Whitney of a freshly mowed football field. Heavy white drapes frame each window. As he stands in the doorway, Whitney is puzzled by the contradiction of a woman who boldly wears purple shoes but also decorates her home in such a safe, bland style.

On the opposite end of the room, a sleek modern candlestick sits on the mantle—it appears to match the one found with the body. Ryan is about to enter the room when Whitney stretches out his arm, preventing him. "Shoot some pictures from here. I'll call Nassau and find out when they can come."

Whitney points at the candlestick. "Zoom in on that."

"Do you think Mrs. Curtis and her ..." Ryan pauses, "... friend were in the living room, she accidentally dies, he freaks out and moves her to the pool house?"

Whitney appreciates the young officer's attempt at tact. He can only imagine what Hackett's description of events would have been.

"Okay, let's say it was sexual asphyxiation gone wrong, and her partner panics," Whitney says. "Wouldn't he just run? Why move the body?"

"The Squire then. She catches him stealing, they fight, he kills her and stages the scene."

"Again—why move the body and does it look like a fight occurred here?"

"He cleaned up?" Ryan says knowing it sounds implausible.

"Let's see what CSU finds before we do any more speculating. We're also waiting on the medical examiner's report for the definitive cause of death."

Whitney enters the CSU number into his phone, and he walks back toward the entrance. On his left is a small room—Mr. Curtis' office, perhaps. The room is painted a rich burgundy, standing in colorful contrast to the white living room and exudes a masculine aura.

Once connected to the Nassau CSU investigator, Whitney explains the expanded warrant while he casually scans the office. To one side is a leather couch, a green and gold plaid blanket is draped over one arm. Opposite him, a pristine desk stands devoid of the usual home office clutter—no papers or computer, not even a phone. Behind it hangs a large landscape painting.

He finishes the call and pivots to leave when he spots another painting, also a landscape—wheat fields. Something about the painting feels significant. Is it famous? Maybe a Monet?

A year ago, Laurel convinced him to attend a seminar with her on how looking at art can enhance observational skills. He was reluctant to go, but later agreed after learning that similar programs are presented to the FBI. To Whitney's pleasant surprise, the seminar was both interesting and practical. The lecturer explained that the key was to describe each painting without editorializing or jumping to conclusions.

Whitney squares himself to the painting and closes his eyes; when he opens them again, he forces himself to just say what he sees. Amber haystacks lined in rows, with mustard-colored shadows stretching across a golden field. At the top, a sliver of blue sky fades to butterscotch at the horizon. After a moment, it clicks: the whole thing is basically yellow.

Maybe Margeaux Curtis wasn't the target. Could this painting be another forgery? If Mrs. Curtis caught him in the act, would the forger kill her? And if so, how could he be sure he wouldn't get caught? Moving a body takes strength and time. Whitney moves toward the painting, noting its wide, ornately carved frame. The surface doesn't appear to have any scratches, at least none that he can see with his naked eye. He draws a deep breath to check but doesn't detect any odor.

"I'm all set," Ryan calls from the hallway.

"Come here. See this painting?" Whitney gestures with his thumb. "Can you get a close-up? Really close?"

"Sure, how close do you want it? I have a macro lens in the bag."

A voice calls out, "Hello? Is someone here?"

Whitney and Ryan move toward the sound. Two men are standing near the front entrance. The first Whitney recognizes: It's Andrew Sutton. The other, he surmises, is Benjamin Curtis.

"Oh, it's you," Sutton says. "My client learned there would be a search of his home."

Whitney introduces himself to Mr. Curtis then says, "We all need to leave. Recent evidence has emerged that could affect the investigation. The residence is now a crime scene."

Sutton glares at the two officers before walking outside.

"You already know what happened. The Squire killed Mrs. Curtis. My client was out of town."

"There's reason to believe the murder took place inside the house and Mrs. Curtis' body was moved later. The Crime Scene Unit is on its way— here's our search warrant."

"This is ridiculous. The murder took place in the pool house. Subjecting my client to your preposterous theory is cruel."

Sutton's chin juts out. His angular jawline and aggressive manner remind Whitney of their earlier conversation when the attorney described himself as a doberman pinscher.

"There was a yellow substance on the body. Nothing matching that substance has yet to be found at the pool house."

"That could be anything. Maybe she was crushing saffron earlier in the day. What difference does it make?" Sutton paces back and forth, his feet tapping a staccato rhythm on the slate patio.

"Initial analysis suggests it's paint," Whitney says. "Mr. Curtis, can you think of anything she may have handled in the house? A painting, perhaps? We noticed a small yellow painting in an office. Can you tell me about it?"

"Could be paint, could be something else," Sutton says. "This is absurd. You're reaching, Lieutenant. Stop wasting my client's time. Let's go, Benjamin."

"No. It's fine, Andrew," Mr. Curtis replies, finally joining the conversation. He wears a haunted expression typical of someone in the early stages of grief. "I want to help."

"Is it a Monet?" Ryan asks, cutting through the tension.

Everyone turns to him. Whitney catches Ryan's eye and nods slightly, finally approving of one of his interjections.

"Etienne Renarde," Mr. Curtis answers. "*La Saison des Récoltes* or *Harvest Season*, is the title. Renarde was a contemporary of Monet. Same quaint haystacks, but at a fraction of the cost. I bought it as a first-anniversary gift for Margeaux. Turns out she isn't—sorry, I mean wasn't—a fan of Impressionists, so it got relegated to my office."

"The forensics team will need to take the painting to make comparisons," Whitney says.

Sutton positions himself between Whitney and the front door. "It's a valuable piece of art. No, you may not take it."

Whitney addresses Mr. Curtis directly. "The technicians are specially trained and will carefully prepare your painting for transport to the lab."

Mr. Curtis nods slowly, visibly shaken. Being at the crime scene must have cemented the tragedy. "I'm ready to go. You have my number if you need anything else."

"One more thing. It may be awkward, but I need to ask—Mrs. Curtis had several affairs …, could one of those men come after her?"

Sutton huffs. "That crosses the line. Come with me, Benjamin."

"We both have jobs to do, Mr. Sutton," Whitney says. "Yours is to protect your client; mine is to apprehend a murderer. It may be an uncomfortable question, but the answer could be pertinent."

The attorney sighs and gives a slight nod.

"It's possible, I suppose," Mr. Curtis says calmly. "Also, she didn't limit her affairs to just men."

"That didn't bother you?" Whitney asks.

"We had an open marriage with very few rules."

"Then why divorce?"

Mr. Curtis shrugs. "Maybe being free to do whatever you want is its own kind of cage."

"Do you need anything from the house? I can escort you," Sutton says.

"I can't allow you in. The residence is part of the investigation."

"Really, Lieutenant? You know my client had nothing to do with the murder. Surely, he's free to go about his own home?"

Benjamin Curtis waves his hand in the air, dismissing the lawyer's protest. "I moved out months ago and split my time between my fiancée's condo and an apartment in the city. There's nothing in there I need." He descends the few steps to the driveway.

Sutton hurries after his client. The officers watch as the two get in a dark sedan and drive away.

"Is it me, or did Mr. Curtis age ten years during the time he was here?" Ryan asks.

Whitney sighs. "The reality of it all is sinking in."

When the CSU team arrives, Whitney speaks with the supervisor regarding the body being moved, the matching candlestick, and his theory that the yellow substance found under the victim's fingernails could be from the painting located in the office.

The supervisor wants his team to first locate supporting evidence that the pool house wasn't the primary scene before taking possession of the Renarde painting. He assigns one agent to start at the cabana and trace the path back to the house. Whitney watches as the officer crouches at various fieldstone pavers, taking photographs and setting evidence markers. Eventually, the findings are placed into plastic evidence bags. A trail of purple fibers seems to satisfy the supervisor, who then orders his team inside.

CHAPTER 22

A soft knock at his door breaks his concentration. Whitney looks up to see Laurel leaning her head through the doorway, waving a sheet of white paper as a sign of truce. "Is it safe?" she asks.

"That depends."

"I've made dinner."

The rumbling in his stomach is insistent, and the familiar aroma from the kitchen—one he's been trying to ignore—is too good to resist. He follows her to the table.

"Smells good," he says as he eyes the pot pies—one of his favorite meals.

Laurel slices into the pastry crust, dividing it into wedges, and moves the pieces to the side of her plate—a habit she started as a child, saving the crust, or "cookies" as she calls them, until the end of the meal. Whitney attacks his pie with gusto, mashing the crust with the chicken and vegetables.

"Is this your way of an apology?" Whitney asks.

"I'm sorry, and thought this might make up for being moody."

"You mean petulant and selfish?"

"Those too. I was mad at Mom."

"You could have talked to me. I'm usually mad at your mother. I would have understood."

"This was something I couldn't talk about with my father."

She lowers her gaze to the plate and pushes a carrot around. Whitney says nothing; issues with Isadora can be delicate.

"And Nora surprised me."

"I'm entitled to a love life."

"I know. I mean, of course you do, but you should have told me. And are you?"

"Am I what?"

"In love?"

"I'm your father, not one of your girlfriends. For now, let's just leave it at—I like seeing Nora."

"You deserve to be happy, Dad. There should be more to your life than just work, golf and crossword puzzles."

Laurel brings a forkful of pot pie toward her mouth and blows on a steaming chunk of chicken. She pauses, resting her elbow on the table. "And I guess there comes a point in every young woman's life when she has to push her father out of the nest and into the world." Laurel grins before popping the chicken into her mouth.

"I'm the one who needs to leave the nest?"

"What, you don't think I'm going anywhere? I still have, hmmm," she pantomimes calculating in her head and counting fingers, "four, maybe five semesters to go."

Whitney frowns.

"Just kidding, I'll be wearing a cap and gown in May."

"You better."

"How's the case?" Laurel asks, trying to change the subject.

"Complicated. How about you tell me about your trip?"

"That's complicated too."

"Come on now, Laurel."

"Okay, it started fine, but the thrill of working on set wore off pretty quickly. She treated me like an intern. All I did was fetch espressos and *sfogliatellas* for the crew."

"What's that?" he asks.

"Sfo-lyat-te-las," she says, pronouncing the word slowly, "are a pastry with ricotta and candied fruits. It's not like I was expecting special treatment, but I thought I'd be more than just a gofer. Then when we were in Florence, there was a scheduling glitch leaving us with a few free days. Mom was busy sorting out the schedule, so I spent my time at the Uffizi Gallery."

"And you met someone," Whitney says.

Laurel hesitates. "No, well technically yes, but not like that. I was working on a sketch of a painting by Botticelli. An older gentleman came into the salon and watched me for a while. The second day he came back to see how my drawing was progressing. Turns out he's Senior Fabbri, the museum's director, and he asked if I wanted to see how they repair damaged paintings. It was cool. They have x-rays, infrared imaging, and special tools to apply tiny dabs of paint to the damaged areas. Senior

Fabbri then asked if I would be interested in their conservation training program. Dad, I think I found what I want to do, for real, for me."

Despite her enthusiasm, Whitney is not entirely sure he can support yet another change in her academic career, especially one that means studying overseas. But it's her last words, "for me," that stand out. Until now, all her other majors were chosen to follow a boyfriend. Each time she offered excellent, practical reasons to enter into those studies, yet she never expressed a personal desire—until now.

"In Italy? What about Post? How will this work, and what kind of career can you have with this?"

"I'll graduate in May, then spend the summer interning in Florence. If that goes well and I'm accepted into their conservation program, I'll train there for two years."

"Two years? Aren't there any local schools?"

"It's the Uffizi, Dad, and I was personally invited by the director. There'll be breaks when I can come home, and you could visit me. As for a career, I'll have a lot more opportunities in conservation than I would as a fine artist. I could get a job with a gallery, auction house, or even a museum. I'd be doing something worthwhile, but still creative. I've been wanting to talk to you about this, but so much other stuff has been happening."

Laurel's passion shines through, reminding Whitney of the last time she was this enthused over a career—she was eleven and completely enamored with Eileen Stone, the department's new officer. All throughout middle school, Laurel dreamed about becoming a police officer herself. This is one of those moments that tears at a parent. Whitney is happy for Laurel, for this opportunity, but is also concerned about her being overseas for such a long time. Aside from vacations with her mother and occasional time spent with Sydney's family, he and Laurel haven't really been apart.

They continue talking for over an hour, and Whitney finds himself caught up in her excitement, captivated by her dreams. At one point, he mistakenly uses the word "restoration" instead of "conservation," prompting Laurel to explain the differences between the two fields.

"They're different, dad. Restoration is about making the art look good, focusing on aesthetics. But conservation—conservation is about preserving the original as much as possible. It's about cleaning, repairing, and sometimes even removing past restoration attempts. Most people don't understand the effects modern materials have on centuries-old art. To become a conservationist, like I want to, you need an advanced degree and hundreds of hours of training as an apprentice."

She pulls up a pair of pictures on her phone. The side-by-side comparison shows the original *Ecce Homo* fresco along with a novice's botched attempt at restoration.

"This is what can happen if people don't know what they're doing," Laurel says.

What once was a painting of Jesus Christ wearing a crown of thorns now looks like a furry pancake-faced creature.

Whitney remembers Lee's comment about the yellow substance being old paint and asks, "Do you know anything about chrome yellow? Is that an old paint?"

"Well not old in terms of art history," Laurel says. "It was popular with the Impressionists: Van Gogh, Cezanne, Monet, so mid-1800s. They liked its vibrancy, but unfortunately the paint darkens over time. Why do you ask?"

Whitney doesn't want to admit it was found on the murder victim. "A lab tech mentioned it; the name stuck in my head." He turns his focus back to the meal.

The idea of his daughter working at a museum is becoming more appealing—it would be full-time work with health insurance and a reliable paycheck. Better that than starving in some seedy studio loft.

When their conversation resumes, it's about the Squire. Laurel, like most people, enjoys hearing about his latest escapade. However, unlike Chief Eaves, she refuses to believe he's capable of murder. She, along with a majority of the public including his victims, indulge themselves with a romantic fantasy that the Squire is a modern Robin Hood because the injured parties are those who can afford the loss.

CHAPTER 23

Officer Ryan's day off coincides with an antiques show in Fairfield, Connecticut. He drives the hour and a half to the old textiles manufacturing building that houses the event. Vendor stalls are dispersed throughout the multi-level structure, and luckily for him, the event organizes merchants according to their wares: textiles in one area, furniture in another, and, most importantly to Ryan, all the silver and jewelry dealers are together in one section.

A steady stream of antique hunters explores the show floor. The din of overlapping conversations reverberates off the walls and the tin ceiling. A mustiness permeates the room—dusty old things with a hint of decay clash with the bright overhead fluorescent lights.

The show has a transient, circus-like feel, traveling up and down the eastern seaboard from March through December. Some dealers attend every exhibition, while others focus only on those within a few hours' drive of their shops. Even in the age of credit cards and transaction apps, cash remains king, making it easy for anyone—including the Squire— to sell their pieces anonymously.

Ryan methodically works his way up one aisle and back down the next. The booths with only silverware aren't as busy as the ones with jewelry, so the merchants seem happy to chat—a benefit for Ryan. One dealer, specializing in early American silver, claims to have bought—and since sold—a pair of grape shears from Ryan's file. Another dealer thinks the ornate fish knife looks familiar but can't be sure based on just the photograph.

This show encourages the local community to bring in their family heirlooms for appraisals. Sellers and buyers are both on the lookout for a rare find worth big money. Typically, though, most of what turns up is unremarkable.

Ryan learns that most of the items the Squire has stolen are mediocre in the antique silver world. The items would fetch a decent price but aren't so unusual as to attract unnecessary attention. The exception is the tastevins—all the dealers are interested in those. However, no one purchased any recently or even heard a buzz about them coming on the market. Ryan hands out his card to each of the vendors, even though he has little hope anyone will call.

Squeezing past a crowd of people gathered at a mid-century modern furniture booth, Ryan makes his way over to the paintings section. All the artwork on display is in the style of American primitive. There is nothing akin to the Abstract Expressionist Thorpe painting. He asks if any of the buyers have had dealings with someone selling paintings and antique silver and is repeatedly told there is no crossover between the two markets.

Before leaving, he circles back to the silver section, hoping the vendors might have remembered something new. They have not. At one booth, a display of small decorative boxes catches his eye: Some are plain silver, others have colorful enamel work. He's drawn to one with an engraved design: a number entwined in a wreath. Ryan picks up the box. It feels cool in his hand as he rubs his thumb over the etched lid.

The merchant explains that the boxes were for carrying calling cards, an important part of social etiquette during the Victorian Era. People would leave their calling card—similar to a business card—when they visited a friend or stopped by to express condolences. Homeowners would prominently display the cards of influential people as a way of showing off their social circle—a nineteenth-century version of likes and follows.

He can't recall who he purchased this box from, only that he recently bought several from one collector. Eager to make a sale, he claims the box in Ryan's hand once belonged to an Olympic athlete, pointing to the etched design, "See? 1896, the year of the first modern Olympics. And look at the wreath—it's not a Christmas wreath, it's laurel branches. Those were used to crown champions."

Ryan is skeptical of the tale and walks a few yards away, but then turns back, buying the box on impulse.

On the drive home, Ryan is deep in thought. While he didn't recover any stolen items at the antique show, he still hopes Lieutenant Whitney will appreciate what he learned on the trip. He's so engrossed he nearly misses the ramp for the Throgs Neck Bridge. Midway across the East River, traffic becomes stop-and-go, with a stalled car blocking the center lane. Ryan drums his fingers on the steering wheel, frustration building. He turns on the radio and spins the dial, searching for a traffic report. The announcer says there's moderate eastbound traffic, so he still has a chance to catch the lieutenant before he leaves. The dashboard clock reads 3:47.

When Ryan pulls up to the police station, the lieutenant's unmarked car is in its usual spot. He grabs the files, leaving the silver box in its brown paper bag nestled on the floor, and sprints into the station.

"Lieutenant Whitney, do you have some time?"

Whitney glances at Ryan's jeans and sneakers. "Is it casual Friday already?"

"It's my day off, sir, but I had an idea regarding the Squire case. I'd like to go over it with you."

"Fine, have a seat."

Ryan then recaps his Fairfield trip for the next forty-five minutes.

"I gotta say, good initiative. Does this antiques show come to Long Island?" Whitney asks.

"No, last year, it was at the armory in Manhattan. This show is a big East Coast event. I thought I'd look into any that are held only on the Island."

"What about paintings? Did they have paintings?"

"Some, just early American folk art, nothing modern. Does the chief still think the Squire committed all the burglaries?"

"I doubt he truly believes that theory. It's more wishful thinking on his part. Right now it's easier having one criminal to discuss with the mayors rather than a thief, a forger, and a murderer. When are you back on duty?"

"Tomorrow, 8:00 a.m."

"Okay, thanks for this. Go home and get some rest."

CHAPTER 24

The voicemail light blinks, taunting him—could be something important—or not. Movement on the Curtis murder case has stalled. Whitney eases himself into his chair with a sigh before pressing play. The first message is from Isadora. Whitney places his elbow on the desk, resting his forehead on his palm. "How many times do I have to tell her not to call me on the station line? She has my cell," he mutters.

Laurel hasn't spoken to her since she returned home. He's surprised by the tone of her voice; it sounds like legitimate concern. At home, Laurel's mood has brightened, so Whitney assumed she and her mother resolved whatever happened in Italy. The last thing he wants is to be the go-between, and yet he resigns himself to talk to Laurel that night.

The second message is from Suzanne Francis. Whitney sits up straight and grabs a pen. Her voice cracks and falters as she explains she was on a cruise and only just learned of Margeaux's death. She leaves the number for the hotel where she is staying.

Whitney flips through his notebook looking for the page with Suzanne Francis' info and the questions he prepared. Just as he starts entering the area code, Lois pokes her head through the doorway. "The chief is looking for you."

He stares at the handset a moment before placing it back in its cradle and walks to the Eaves' office. "You want to see me, sir?"

"Come in, sit. How's the progress on the Squire?"

"I was just about to call the tennis partner, Suzanne Francais. She may be the last person to have seen the victim alive, and she's only just become reachable.," Whitney says, then pauses for a moment. "Sir, I don't believe the Squire murdered Margeaux Curtis."

"I know, you've said that before. But do you have any evidence supporting that theory?"

"There are too many discrepancies between the note found on the body and the ones left at the burglaries. Plus, the Squire has never so much as broken a window, let alone hurt anyone. In his notes he apologized for taking trivial items, does that sound like someone who would commit murder? And the way the corpse was posed ...," Whitney wrinkles his nose and shakes his head slightly, then lets out a long breath before finishing, "I don't think he did it."

"That's supposition, unless you can show me hard evidence, something concrete. I don't want to hear this from you again. It's just as possible the Squire escalated his behavior," Eaves says, smacking both hands onto his desk. He leans forward. "I have five town leaders breathing down my neck, wanting answers. I can't have you floating this theory that there's more than one criminal out there creating a panic."

The chief leans back with a small sigh. "Meanwhile, Caleb Vos is back in town, and his pain-in-the-ass attorney demanded an in-person meeting to update Mr. Vos on the status of his case." Whitney opens his mouth to speak, but Eaves holds up his hand. "I have to send someone, and you're it. I told that lawyer, what's his name?"

"Sutton."

"I told Sutton you'd be at Glenwood first thing. When you're finished there, you can call the tennis partner back."

"Yes, sir." Whitney nods, jaw tight. A lead in a murder investigation, and he's being sent to play politics. He stands, squaring himself to the chief before heading out.

On the way to his car, he first detours to the bathroom. Whitney cranks the cold faucet clockwise as far as it will go and thrusts his upturned wrists into the icy stream.

"What the hell?" his inner voice snaps. He keeps his arms under the water until the cold begins to burn—sharp, stinging—a shock to the system. He shuts off the faucet with his right hand and presses his left wrist to the side of his head. The makeshift cold compress soothes the pressure pulsing at his temple. He draws a deep breath and lets it out slowly, then grabs a couple of paper towels to pat himself dry.

The drive to Glenwood is pleasant, which helps to ease his frustration. It's a crisp, cloudless fall day. The trees lining the Voses' driveway have turned a vibrant crimson since his last visit. Not a single leaf litters the ground—as if their landscaper comes by daily. His own yard, meanwhile, is buried under a thick red, orange, and yellow carpet. Whitney knows how he'll be spending the weekend—it won't be as fun as playing eighteen holes, but at least it won't involve twisting conflicting evidence into a tidy theory just to satisfy the powers that be.

Katherine Tierney greets him at the door even before he presses the doorbell.

"Good morning, Miss Tierney. A pleasure to see you again."

"Nice to see you too, Lieutenant Whitney. Mr. Vos is in the library. This way, please."

Whitney follows and quickly finds himself face-to-face with Mr. Vos, who extends a hand to shake. "I'm Caleb Vos. Thank you for coming. This is my wife, Jordan, and I believe you've already met Andrew Sutton, our attorney."

Mr. Vos is wearing tan corduroys, a green polo shirt, and loafers. His wife has on a bright coral cashmere sweater and white jeans frayed at the bottom. Despite Mr. and Mrs. Vos being a notable power couple with prominent standing in Gold Coast society, they look like regular folks one might see at the grocery store—or, more likely, at the local organic farmers' market. Andrew Sutton, however, appears overly formal in his custom-tailored gray wool suit and navy-blue silk tie. Whitney shakes hands with Mrs. Vos and Sutton.

"Would you like some coffee, Lieutenant?" Miss Tierney asks.

"No, thank you, Miss Tierney."

"Very well, then. I'll leave you to your meeting."

Whitney turns back to face Mr. Vos. "Actually, we've met before—at a police benefit golf outing at the Brookville Club. We were in the same foursome."

"That's right! I thought you looked familiar. Please, call me Caleb. If I remember right, you were on a hot streak on the back nine—three birdies, wasn't it?"

"You have an excellent memory."

"This is charming," interrupts Sutton, "but can we move on to the reason the lieutenant is here? Have you caught the Squire killer yet?"

"The investigation is ongoing," Whitney replies.

"What's the hold-up?"

"Andrew, I'm sure the police are doing their best," Mrs. Vos says.

"I want to make sure it's a priority. What if something had happened to poor old Miss Tierney when he broke into Glenwood?" Sutton says, his tone growing sharper. "I think you should hire a full-time security detail."

Caleb Vos chuckles. "A bit like locking the barn door after the horse has escaped, don't you think? Whomever this person is, he's just lucky Katherine didn't catch him moving the flower vase or tracking dirt across the patio."

"You may still see her as the commanding house manager she once was, but time is catching up with her. She's become frail and fearful," Sutton says.

Jordan Vos huffs and shakes her head. "You obviously haven't crossed swords with Katherine. We hire security for special events, but on a regular basis, it just feels intrusive. What do you think, Lieutenant Whitney?"

"As long as you and Mr. Vos haven't been the target of any threats, I'd say it's a personal preference." A fleeting thought crosses Whitney's mind: What would the chief have said about this? But since he's not here to weigh in, Whitney adjusts his stance and straightens his shoulders. The chief be damned.

"Getting back to your earlier question, Mr. Sutton, there isn't much I'm at liberty to discuss, except that we are continuing to investigate," Whitney says.

"Is there anything we can do?" Vos asks. "Offer a reward?"

"More often than not, a reward—and the media attention that goes with it—hinders rather than helps an investigation."

"I see. Besides, it's just a painting and a couple of cups."

"Tastevins," Sutton says.

"My point is, they're just things. They don't matter compared to losing one's life," Vos says.

"Poor Margeaux," Mrs. Vos adds.

Whitney shifts his attention to her. "Were you and Mrs. Curtis friends?"

"I wouldn't call us friends, but I didn't dislike Margeaux either, as many other wives did. We just didn't run in the same circles."

"Did you have any friends in common? Use any of the same services?" Whitney asks.

"Do you think the person who ..." Mrs. Vos pauses for a moment as she chooses her words. "... who hurt Margeaux, is the same person who stole our painting?"

Sutton cuts in before Whitney can answer. "Of course it is. It's the Squire. He stole the silver tastevins and the Thorpe, and he killed Margeaux Curtis."

"We're looking into every possibility," Whitney says.

"It's obviously the same criminal," the attorney says, lifting his hands into the air. "There was silver and he took a painting."

Mr. and Mrs. Vos exchange surprised looks.

Caleb Vos asks, "Did they have a painting stolen as well?"

"That's yet to be determined. The crime lab is evaluating several key pieces of evidence," replies Whitney. He then reiterates his previous question concerning friends and services.

"I think the only person we share in common is Andrew, along with the staff at the Brookville Country Club," Mrs. Vos says.

Mr. Vos corrects her. "Ben and Margeaux belonged to Winterberry."

"Oh, that's right."

"You belong to both clubs?" Whitney asks.

"And several others. It helps for business connections," Vos says.

"I understand it was your daughter who discovered the fake Thorpe. Is she also on the police force?" Mrs. Vos asks.

Whitney smiles—he can't help it. "She's a student at Post College, studying fine art. She spotted a discrepancy on some material I brought home to review."

As soon as the words leave his lips, Whitney knows he shouldn't have given away any personal information—fatherly pride got the better of him. He surveys the trio facing him: a well-regarded philanthropic couple and a suit. Not much of a threat level here.

Mrs. Vos' face lights up with interest. "That's incredible. Lucky for us, the university provides a quality education. Maybe we should increase our donation this year, Caleb."

"I believe your commitment to the school has been more than generous," Sutton says.

"Andy, relax. You worry more about our finances than my CFO."

Whitney notices the lawyer cringing ever so slightly at the familiar use of his name.

"Maybe it was someone from the college, a painter who needs drug money," Sutton suggests.

"I think that's unlikely, Mr. Sutton. How would a student know what paintings are here at Glenwood?"

"Andrew, don't you have a cousin who studied art?" Caleb Vos asks. "I remember he came to some parties at Cornell."

"You knew each other in college?" Whitney asks.

"As undergraduates, different years, but the same fraternity," Vos says. "I liked your cousin. He was a painting student at Buffalo. Whatever happened to him?"

"He died," Sutton replies somberly.

"I'm sorry, Andrew. I didn't know. It's been years since I even thought of those times. Henry Lockhart, that was his name—he was a little shy, but a good guy. The fraternity brothers took to calling him Rembrandt."

"It was a long time ago. Drug overdose. I don't like to talk about it. Can we focus instead on the task at hand and stop the Squire?"

All eyes fall on Whitney.

"I know being patient can be frustrating," he says. "Let us do our job. We'll notify you immediately when your property is recovered."

"Thank you for coming, Lieutenant. We'll wait to hear from you on any updates," Vos says as he shakes Whitney's hand again.

Miss Tierney promptly appears at the doorway. "I'll see you out."

The meeting went more smoothly than he expected, though its necessity seemed to stem more from the attorney's insistence than Caleb Vos' interest.

Once Whitney returns to the station, he jots a few notes but doubts they'll lead anywhere. He then calls Suzanne Francis. After a round of introductions and condolences, he asks about the Saturday party.

"Well, it was a small gathering—just Margeaux, me, and a very fine bottle of Leflaive Meursault," Suzanne says, mangling the French name with a little laugh. "Actually, make that two."

Whitney checks the time. Still morning. He wonders if she's already had a drink—or taken something to settle her nerves. Gone is the teary hesitancy from her earlier message. "Was Mrs. Curtis worried about anything?" he asks. "Did she express concern for her well-being?"

"No, not at all. She seemed to be in a really good place emotionally. The divorce would have been finalized in a few weeks. Margeaux had come to terms with it. She was at peace."

"I was under the impression she initiated the divorce." Whitney hesitates, then adds, "I don't mean to be indelicate, but there's been talk about affairs."

A pause. Then Suzanne's tone sharpens. "Of course—paint the murder victim as a whore."

"That's not what I said," Whitney replies, mindful to sound professional. "I need to get a clear picture of her life, the people in it, and whether any of them may have had a reason to hurt her."

"You know all the club gossips are wrong." She pauses briefly.

"Margeaux wasn't a tramp. She was hurt. You know what that bastard did to her? After two decades of marriage, Ben wanted to spice things up, Margeaux went along just to make him happy. But it was never enough. He started having affairs—quietly at first, but when Margeaux walked in on him with another woman in their bed, that was the last straw. She started having affairs of her own. They were short-lived. I think she was hoping to make Ben jealous."

"Do you know who these men were?"

"A few were men at the club—Ben had already cuckolded one of them. Oh, and one was one of you guys—a cop."

"An Old Brookville police officer?" Whitney asks. He feels a slight tightness in his throat.

"I don't know where he was from. Margeaux just said she didn't have to worry about speeding tickets anymore because she had a 'get-out-of-jail-free card.'"

Whitney corroborated Hackett's alibi, but if word of his affair with the deceased became public, it would complicate the investigation. Was it possible Mrs. Curtis dated another cop, or even a few? Some women find the job sexy.

"What about the wives? Was anyone so mad they'd exact revenge?"

Suzanne snorts. "That's rich. The women at the club don't do their own grocery shopping. No way they'd risk breaking a nail attempting a murder. They're more the poison-pen type. Rumor and innuendo are the tools of their trade."

Whitney thanks her and confirms the best way to reach her if any additional questions arise, before ending the call.

The conflicting accounts of Margeaux's life, as told by her friend and ex-husband, swirl through Whitney's mind. Is one of them lying—or both? And to what end? People lie for a variety of reasons: self-protection, self-promotion, or to protect others. Then there are those who lie simply for the pleasure of it. In a murder investigation, all of these possibilities have to be considered.

His thoughts are interrupted by the ringing of his desk phone. Initially he ignores the noise, deciding whoever it is can leave a voice message, but after five rings he relents and presses the speaker button. "This is Lieutenant Whitney."

"Finally. I have more important things to do than track you down," Vivian Lee says.

She continues by grumbling about the top priority the Curtis case is receiving, upending her other assignments. Apparently, the lab technician doesn't view murder as any more of a priority than any other crimes. Whitney is grateful that the focus of her aggravation is some nebulous higher-up and not him. He listens patiently while she vents. After a final exhale, Vivian's tone softens.

"The reason I called is because I finished testing the Etienne Renarde painting. Radiocarbon dating of the canvas fibers proves it's from the late 1800s, but the paint is new, composed of modern chemical compounds."

"So, a forgery," Whitney says.

"Looks to be. To run the test, I had to remove the painting from its frame. On the inside edge, I discovered a small spot of blood. Preliminary lab tests show the sample is recent and from a Caucasian male. Though a complete DNA test to match against people in the system will take a while."

Identifying the suspect as a white male offers little help to Whitney: statistically, women are more likely to be murdered by men, and most violent crimes occur within the victim's own ethnicity.

Lee continues, "Now, regarding the note card found with the body. I researched the watermark; it's by Smythson, a high-end British stationer. The ink is German, Starwalker Gray, manufactured by Montblanc, only available as bottled ink."

"Good work on the painting. That could help establish motive."

"I get it's important, and that it's for you," Lee says. "But I have other cases to work on. It's not right to pull me off those."

"I understand, and appreciate your dedication to all your cases, big and small."

"At least someone does. Bye, Lieutenant."

Whitney reviews the notes from their conversation. Now that a second forgery has been confirmed, it adds a new layer to the case. He feels a small sense of satisfaction at having his fountain pen hypothesis validated by the bottled ink, but that feeling is fleeting. There's still nothing linking the crimes to, or separating them from, the Squire thefts.

He purposely held off on asking Lee to explain radiocarbon testing, hoping to stay on the tech's good side. Irking her with questions she would view as a waste of time might make her less agreeable to help in the future. After the call, he checks online: radiocarbon testing measures carbon-14 decay to date organic materials, accurate within forty years—

enough to tell whether a canvas is modern or from the 1800s.

Whitney remembers Agent Smith briefing him about the German forger who mistakenly used Titanium White paint, which led to his capture. Was that case well known? Could the forger he's searching for be familiar with it, and if so, wouldn't he want to avoid the same mistake?

The paintings in his case are privately owned, and not likely to be subject to an authenticity check soon. Maybe that's why the forger considered the paint a low-risk concern. But then why bother with an old canvas?

Whitney can't wrap his head around it—some details meticulously handled, others ignored.

Agent Smith also said forgers typically work within one genre. The person who copied the Renarde paintings must be the same person as who made the Thorpe, even though the artistic styles are completely different—one Impressionism, the other Abstract Expressionism. The first forgery was a modern art piece. Why not stick with that genre? The materials would have less impact on determining authenticity.

The insurance papers supplied by Benjamin Curtis show that *La Saison des Récoltes* by Etienne Renarde, was purchased at auction over two decades ago. Photographs accompany the insurance papers and show the painting encased in an elaborate hand-carved frame. Mr. Curtis didn't mention the frame being different. The forger must have been in the house for a while in order to swap out the painting. And the blood found on the frame is probably from scraping his hand or forearm while releasing the original.

Questions swirl in his head, more than he can answer. Whitney decides to head home. At least he'll resolve the Laurel/Isadora situation— he hopes.

CHAPTER 25

While driving home, a conversation Whitney had with Laurel earlier in the week flashes through his mind. She explained that her conservation training would require extensive research into various artistic movements. If the forger studied art restoration, it could explain their ease in copying different styles.

He turns into the driveway and parks behind Laurel's car. Whitney grabs his briefcase—there are always papers to review, legal updates, technological advances and new procedures. "Not tonight," he says under his breath as the solid "thwomp" of the shutting door punctuates his words. Tonight's agenda is sorting out what happened between Laurel and Isadora.

Entering the house, he finds Laurel is sitting in front of the TV watching a cooking show, snacking on a bowl of dry cereal.

"That's some meal," he says.

"I wasn't expecting you. I can fix something quick for dinner. How's that?" Laurel asks.

"Sure, thanks."

Whitney walks to his office and puts his briefcase next to the desk. He looks around the room remembering its transformation. Isadora used the spare room as a walk-in closet, stuffing it with half a dozen garment racks of her clothes. After she left, it became a home office, allowing Whitney to spend more time at home with his daughter. The desk itself is nothing fancy—he purchased it at a neighbor's yard sale. However, he did splurge on a quality ergonomic chair.

He even created a special spot for Laurel by building floor-to-ceiling bookcases that flank the double-hung window, with a bench seat in between. This nook became Laurel's favorite reading spot. While he worked, she'd cuddle up with her stuffed tiger and read: first, J.K. Rowling stories about wizards, and later, Middle Earth adventures by J.R.R. Tolkien.

Laurel spends less time in his office now—only on rare occasions does he find her there, reading one of her college textbooks. The tiger, however, has taken up permanent residence at the window seat.

Whitney sighs as he realizes those moments will be coming to an end soon. He heads upstairs to change and shakes off the melancholic shroud.

Laurel's voice calling from downstairs brings him back to the present. "Breakfast for dinner," she says, setting down plates piled with fluffy scrambled eggs.

After a few bites, he asks, "This is good. What's in it?"

"Ham, cheddar, tomatoes, and a little green onion."

"I've been thinking about the talk we had on art preservation and was wondering if any local colleges offer similar programs."

Laurel scrunches her face a little as she mentally begins to pull together her case for studying in Florence. Her father deliberately ignores her furrowed brow.

Whitney goes on, "We discovered a second forgery, and it got me thinking; Could someone who studied conservation have made it, since part of that training requires learning different artistic styles? Can you find out which schools offer a program like that, or if any Post students went into that field?"

"Sure," Laurel says. The tension in her face vanishes; the request has nothing to do with her post-graduate plans. Besides, she likes the idea of helping her father with a case.

Whitney fortifies himself with a few more bites of eggs before delving into the issue with Isadora. He takes a deep breath, releases it slowly and then says, "Your mother called me today."

Laurel looks down at her plate and pushes some food around.

"Are you ready to talk about what happened on your trip?"

"I don't know if I can tell you what happened exactly. It's ..." Laurel hesitates and pokes her eggs. "... humiliating," she says, the last word barely a whisper.

Laurel looks up at the ceiling before meeting her father's eyes. "I don't know if I can forgive her. What she did was wrong, selfish—even for her. I'm afraid if I bring it up, she'll just say I'm making a big deal out of nothing. You know how she brushes away any criticism."

He's well aware of Isadora's penchant for not accepting responsibility for her actions. It was a source of countless arguments he had with his ex-wife. "You need to talk to her. Despite her faults—her many, many faults—your mother loves you. When she learns why you're upset, she'll want to make amends."

Laurel sits silently.

"Her many, many faults. Her many, many, many faults."

Laurel starts to smile.

"Many, many, many ... I mean a lot of faults."

"Okay, I get it," she says. "I'll call her."

"Many, many, many faults."

"You're the one who married her," Laurel says, giggling.

"My one and only fault."

In the morning, Whitney is almost out the door when Laurel wanders from the kitchen with her breakfast in hand—a bowl of yogurt with dry cereal sprinkled on top.

"Call your mother," he says.

"I will."

"Today."

"Okay."

"Many, many, many."

"Shouldn't you be on your way to work?"

"Right, by the way, I'm having dinner with Nora, so it may be late before I see you."

"That's cool, say hi for me."

Laurel watches her father drive away as she spoons some yogurt into her mouth and considers how to approach the subject of Birk with her mom. She pinches her lips together and breaths a heavy sigh. Don't prolong the pain, she thinks to herself, do it fast—like ripping off a band-aid. Standing straight and steeling her shoulders, Laurel walks purposely into her room, takes her phone from the charging station, and taps the contact button labeled "Mom."

CHAPTER 26

The short commute from his home to the station house provides Whitney the time to tuck away parental concerns and shift into police mode. When he arrives, a message waits on his desk.

Officer Young, from the Sands Point Police Department, called regarding a forged painting, wants you to call him back.

Whitney heads to the break room for a cup of coffee before settling in at his desk and returning the phone call.

"Young here."

"This is Lieutenant Richard Whitney from Old Brookville. You wanted to talk to me?"

"Yes, hi, Lieutenant. Thanks for getting back to me. I was working at the Sands Point Conservancy yesterday when a fight broke out. They were filming one of those TV shows, you know, the kind where people bring in junk they found in their attic, hoping its worth millions. Anyway, this guy, Mark Baldwin, caused a scene because the appraiser said his painting is a fake. Baldwin starts swearing it's a setup, that they switched paintings backstage, and he pummels the appraiser. Now, that would make for some exciting reality TV," Young says.

"And how exactly can I help the Sands Point Police?"

"Oh right, Baldwin—the guy with the painting—has a statement of authenticity and the original receipt. The whole thing made me think of your case with the switched paintings. I read about it on the stolen articles page of the NCIC."

Whitney remembers posting information about the Thorpe painting to the National Crime Information Center database. With the crime being so unique, he thought it was worth putting the details out there, just in case another agency has a similar case. Whitney writes down all the details and thanks Officer Young. As soon as he hangs up, he calls Mark Baldwin to arrange an appointment for later that day.

Whitney dedicates the rest of the morning to reading the medical examiner's report. He closes the office door, hoping to be able to read without interruption.

The ME's report immediately reveals contradictions. Manner of death: homicide. Cause: asphyxiation from manual strangulation. Her hyoid bone was broken, with finger marks on her neck. If the braided drapery cord found with the victim was the actual murder weapon, there would be a patterned ligature mark.

The report further describes hypostasis in the gluteus maximus, hamstrings, and gastrocnemius muscles, indicating the body was in a high Fowler's position at the time of death.

Whitney lets out a wearied sigh. These reports would be easier and faster to process if written in plain English. He translates in his head: Blood pooling was found in the buttocks and in the back of the thigh and calf muscles, meaning Mrs. Curtis was seated, not bent over a hassock when she died. As Vivian Lee predicted, the ME's report validates her earlier findings, suggesting the body was moved.

The ME cites the time of death as 10:15 p.m. (plus/minus four hours). The calculations used in assessing time of death are influenced by multiple factors, hence the large time swing. Many doctors give a rough time range, while others like to sound more authoritative by declaring an exact hour and minute but still qualify the time with a plus/minus factor. The ME who wrote this report falls into the latter category.

The time range is troubling to Whitney; Hackett's alibi doesn't cover the entire span. The two of them have worked together for a long time, and Hackett is a lot of things, but it's hard to imagine a cold-blooded murderer is among them.

Secondary details regarding the victim are on subsequent pages. The yellow paint found underneath the fingernails is presumed to be pre-murder. While the insertion of the candlestick was post-mortem, since the lacerations lacked any signs of inflammation.

Whitney imagines the scene: Mrs. Curtis discovers the forger in her husband's office. They struggle, and she grabs the original painting, scraping the surface during the scuffle. The perpetrator attacks from the front, strangling her, and the body slumps to the floor. The murderer leaves her that way while he substitutes the fake painting for the real one and decides what to do with the body.

The defilement of the body has Whitney stumped. Why would someone stage the body in such a debasing position? A stranger wouldn't do that—or would they, simply to throw off the investigation? No, it had to be somebody who knew her and her habits. A stranger would have bolted—they wouldn't spend time altering the scene and risk getting caught.

Whoever did this must have some knowledge of police procedures. They probably knew their note wouldn't match previous Squire messages—but the presence of a note card would force the police to consider the Squire. This criminal is skilled in more ways than just with a paintbrush. The ability to pivot under pressure, casting suspicion onto the Squire—that was smart.

Whitney's cell phone buzzes right before it's time for him to leave for his meeting with Mark Baldwin. It's Laurel, so he accepts the call. She says that she spoke with her advisor regarding art conservation, and he thinks the internship at the Uffizi will be a wonderful opportunity for her.

Of course, the advisor feels that way, Whitney thinks—it's not their daughter who will be gone for two years.

Laurel tells him that her advisor mentioned no other students have pursued conservation; to his knowledge, she would be the first. He also lists a few East Coast colleges that offer similar programs: New York University, the University of Delaware, Buffalo State, and Savannah College of Art and Design. Whitney writes down the school names, circling NYU because it's the closest to Old Brookville. He ends the call with a quick "Thanks, sweetheart," and dashes to his car.

Whitney arrives for the meeting, and from the moment he's buzzed in at the entrance gate, he suspects the painting wasn't taken while in Mark Baldwin's possession—in the short distance from the driveway to the front door, he passed two security cameras.

Baldwin greets him in a white shirt with "MB" stitched on the pocket, the fit sharp enough to suggest it was made to order. His khakis are pressed, his shoes polished loafers with tassels—an outfit that projects a classic Ivy League look. Baldwin shows no signs of having "pummeled someone," and Whitney suspects Officer Young embellished the conflict.

"We'll join my wife in the living room," Baldwin says.

A petite brunette woman sits on the couch. She's also wearing khaki pants, a crisp white blouse, and loafers.

"My wife, Beth." Whitney leans over to shake her hand.

"So, why is Old Brookville Police investigating my stolen painting?" Baldwin asks.

"We have an open case with some similarities."

"Was another Vincent Mellor stolen?" Beth Baldwin asks.

"No, not a Mellor, but another painting was replaced by an exact duplicate. What can you tell me about your painting?"

"My grandfather bought *Cold Spring Harbor* directly from Mellor himself in 1936. It was handed down to my father, and then to me."

"How long has it been in your possession?" Whitney asks.

"Twelve years, last May."

"Where did you keep it?"

"Right over there," Mr. Baldwin points to an adjacent wall.

"What made you decide to bring it to the Sands Point Conservancy to be appraised?"

"I thought it would be fun, being on TV and all. My father had certain items appraised about thirty years ago, after my mother passed away. At that time, the painting was valued at $223,000. I didn't tell the show— I thought it would make for better TV if I acted like I had no idea."

Baldwin opens a slim leather portfolio and hands several papers to Whitney.

"Here's the old appraisal, along with the analyst's statement that the painting is fraudulent."

"To be clear, sometime in the past three decades, your Vincent Mellor was substituted with a copy," Whitney says.

Mr. and Mrs. Baldwin nod in unison.

"Your home appears quite secure based on the gate and exterior cameras. Did you have any special protection for the painting itself?"

"Yes, there's a trip alarm if the painting is removed from the wall," responds Baldwin.

"One time Hanna—she's our housekeeper—set it off while cleaning the room. I thought she was going to have a heart attack. But there's no way Hanna had anything to do with this," Mrs. Baldwin says.

"I tend to believe you, but I'd like to talk with her just the same. Where does Hanna live?"

"In Brooklyn, with her sister."

"This is an ongoing investigation, so I'm unable to give out any details, but do you have friends or relatives in the Brookville area?"

The Baldwins again move in sync, shaking their heads.

"How about your father's home? Where was that? Did he have the same kind of security you have here?"

"He lived north of the city, in Westchester. He used to say, 'Nosy neighbors are better than any security system money can buy.'"

"Were there any people he saw regularly?" Whitney asks.

"For the five or so years before he died, there were his nurses. He had quite a few—Dad could be a handful. There was also the lawyer who updated his will, and some workmen who made renovations: safety bars in the bathroom, railings for the outdoor steps, that type of thing."

"Do you remember the companies you dealt with?"

"I kept the business cards," Mrs. Baldwin says. She excuses herself to get the contact info.

Mr. Baldwin leans in and whispers "She's a stickler for paperwork and keeps everything."

"Could prove handy," Whitney says. "Was anything missing when you packed up your father's things?"

"It was a while ago, but nothing that I recall," Baldwin says.

Mrs. Baldwin returns with a list of names and numbers. Whitney hands Baldwin his business card in case they remember anything else, and he thanks them for their time.

During the drive back to the station, Whitney mulls over the implications of yet another switched painting—three forgeries. When did Long Island become a hotbed for counterfeit art? He's reluctant to admit it, but the stealthiness of these crimes reminds him of the Squire.

Once back at his desk, Whitney goes over the list Mrs. Baldwin provided. At the top, she wrote "Helping Hands Home Care," followed by "R. Zimmerman, attorney at law," and finally "Keats' Construction."

He calls Zimmerman first, assuming the lawyer will be the easiest to reach. Unfortunately, he's wrong. The lawyer died shortly after Mark Baldwin's father. His son has taken over the practice but is in the middle of relocating. For now, digging through old files is out of the question.

Whitney calls the contractor next. He doesn't hold out much hope of getting any useful information and is surprised when the owner immediately remembers Mr. Baldwin.

"Old man Baldwin, I remember him well," Keats says. "He was quite a character. We handled a number of projects at his home over the years."

"I'm impressed you remember him from so long ago," Whitney says.

"Poor old guy had Alzheimer's. Initially, I sent my crew, but Mr.

Baldwin got upset, saying they were there to steal from him. The son, Mark, had to deal with his father's ranting a lot. They lost other contractors because of his father's dementia and offered to pay more if I would stay on and personally finish the job," Keats says.

He pauses before continuing. "My mother had the same thing—kindest woman you ever would have met, never said a harsh word. Then the disease took hold, and my sweet, gentle mother started cursing like a dock worker. So I understood when Mr. Baldwin had an off day."

"You were the only one who worked there?"

"Mostly, but there was also Hank. Good kid—worked summers for me when he was home from school. Hank was the best, so neat—his drop cloth was virtually spotless. Quiet, too. The homeowners often forgot he was even there."

"What's Hank's last name and phone number?"

"Lockhart. Hank Lockhart. Sadly, he died—car crash. All this happened a long time ago. Why are you asking about Mr. Baldwin?"

"There's an issue with something Mr. Baldwin owned that may relate to another case. I'm just trying to get as much background information as I can. Thanks for your time."

Whitney calls Helping Hands Home Care next. After being transferred to the manager, he receives a list of the few nurses who worked with Mr. Baldwin and are still with the company, along with their contact information. The care workers confirm Keats's description of Mr. Baldwin's paranoia and suspicion of strangers. Several aides sound far less compassionate than the contractor, prompting Whitney to wonder if they're in the right profession.

Whitney places two more calls: one to Ben Curtis and the other to Miss Tierney. Neither of them recognizes any of the workers' names. It's another dead end. If there's a connection between the three painting heists, Whitney has yet to find it.

He's just about to shut his office door and leave for the day when a patrolman hands him a small black box wrapped with a silver ribbon tied into a bow.

"What's this?"

"Sergeant Stone asked me to bring it back to you. It just came in by messenger," Officer Byrne says.

Whitney puts down his briefcase, leans against the door jamb and pulls off the ribbon. Assuming it's a present from Nora, he isn't prepared for what he sees. Inside is a note card along with a silver baby spoon nestled on a bed of cotton batting. His chest tightens as he reads the message:

> *You may not have riches, but your little Post artist is*
> *still something of value I can take. –The Squire*

The card has the same silver border and formal script handwriting as the note found with Mrs. Curtis' body. Whitney immediately calls Laurel's cell phone, only to get her voicemail. A pounding starts in his head.

"Byrne!"

The uniformed officer quickly reappears.

"Who brought this? Did you see him?"

"I think it was a bicycle messenger. I was coming in while he was going out. That's when Stone told me to bring the package to you. I don't even know for sure if he dropped it off—I just assumed. Is something wrong?"

Whitney doesn't answer. He's already sprinting down the hall.

CHAPTER 27

Whitney bursts into the dispatch booth, startling Sergeant Stone. She spins around in her chair to face the lieutenant. Whitney has a reputation for being cool under pressure, so the sergeant is surprised to see him flustered.

"Are you okay, Lieu?" Stone asks.

"Who brought in that box?"

"Some bicycle guy. It was just a few minutes ago. I can pull it up."

Stone punches a few buttons on the console. One of the video monitors switches on and begins scrolling through footage of the reception area. They watch as an athletic-looking man enters the building. He's wearing black bicycle shorts, a yellow and black striped shirt, and a yellow helmet. He looks like a giant bumblebee.

"Package for Lieutenant Whitney," is all he says before turning and going back outside to his bike.

"Which way did he go?"

Stone taps a different button, pulling up the exterior footage. They watch the cyclist make a left onto Northern Boulevard, heading east.

Whitney bolts from the station and leaps from the top of the entrance steps, landing hard on the pavement. He cuts across the lot and slides into his car, then peels onto the street.

Briefly pausing at the intersection, he then blows through the red light. Each car he passes spikes his adrenaline. A quick glance at the dash: over 90 miles per hour.

Doubt creeps into his brain—what if the bike is a ruse, and the guy has a partner with a van? What if I've missed him? The small uncertainty burgeons into a deeper panic. Whitney's heart beats wildly in his chest. Gripping the steering wheel tighter, he scans the road ahead, searching for the cyclist.

As he crests a small ridge, Whitney spots the yellow and black striped shirt. He slows the cruiser as he approaches; the siren makes a few whoop-whoops, followed by Whitney announcing for the cyclist to pull over and get off the bike.

He gets out of the car, his hands trembling. The urge to slam the cyclist to the ground is overwhelming. Do your job — follow the rules, you don't know anything yet, he tells himself, then orders the cyclist to remove his helmet, get on his knees, and place his hands on his head.

Another car pulls off to the side of the road. The gravel crunches beneath its tires. Officer Byrne enters Whitney's peripheral vision.

"Name?" Whitney asks.

"I'm Tim Van Der Meer. I was just out for a ride." The cyclist shifts his position slightly.

"Address?"

"Here in Old Brookville." He shifts again.

"Where's Laurel?"

"Who?"

"Laurel!"

"I don't know any ..."

The man suddenly makes a lunging roll to the side. Byrne is instantly standing over him, gun drawn. "Don't move a muscle."

The cyclist now looks less like a bee and more like an upended turtle, on his back, hands and legs raised into the air.

"Please!" The man's voice is shaky. "The gravel, my knees. I'm Tim Van Der Meer, I live on Sugar Maple Road. Call my wife. My ICE card is in the helmet."

Whitney nods to Byrne, who picks up the helmet and hands a small card to the lieutenant. Printed across the top in capital letters is "IN CASE OF EMERGENCY," followed by a telephone number. Whitney calls and speaks with Mrs. Van Der Meer. After reassuring her that Tim is fine, he tells her to meet them at the police station and to bring identification for her husband.

Whitney approaches the cyclist and offers an extended hand to help him up.

"Mr. Van Der Meer, I'm Lieutenant Richard Whitney. I need to talk to you about the box you left for me. It will be more comfortable at the station. You'll ride with me. Officer Byrne will pack up your bicycle. Also, I want to have someone clean up your leg."

Van Der Meer looks down at himself and notices the indentations on his knees, along with a trickle of blood dribbling down his shin.

"I'm okay," he mumbles, feeling more shaken by the sight of a pistol pointed at him than by any cuts from kneeling on the ground.

They drive to the station in silence. Whitney's mind races, worrying about Laurel. The cyclist's mind also races, but he's thinking about the gun.

At the station, Whitney directs Sergeant Stone to tend to Mr. Van Der Meer's abrasions. Then as he's about to try Laurel's phone again, he remembers the location-finding app, a condition he insisted upon for her first phone. Thankfully, she never bothered uninstalling it.

The app places her in the northeast section of the Post campus— the fine arts building—but the location isn't live. The last ping was 53 minutes ago. After leaving brief instructions regarding Mr. Van Der Meer's statement, Whitney leaves again, this time heading west on Northern Boulevard.

It's dusk when he pulls into the parking lot for the arts building. Laurel's blue VW Beetle is there, temporarily assuaging his fears. Whitney enters the building and strides toward the painting studios. Two girls are washing their brushes at a sink. He asks if either of them has seen Laurel Whitney.

The first girl looks Whitney up and down, frowning at the uniform. "I don't have to tell you nothing."

The second girl is wearing a Michelangelo parody T-shirt, *The Creation of Adam*, but instead of reaching his hand toward God, Adam is offering his middle finger.

"Please, she's my daughter. Something's wrong," Whitney says, purposely choosing the tone of a concerned father over an authoritarian police officer.

The girl hesitates for a moment, sizing him up before answering. Despite the attitude conveyed by her wardrobe, the girl's expression softens. "She was here earlier, but I haven't seen her in a while."

"Her car's out front. Is there somewhere else in the building she could be?"

"There's a lounge on the second floor with a vending machine," the girl says, pointing toward the door. "Up those stairs to the right."

Whitney takes the stairs two at a time and heads straight for the lounge.

Behind him, the first girl smacks the second in the arm. "What'd you do that for snitch?"

"That's her dad. Can't you tell he's worried?"

The vending machine is there, but Laurel isn't. At the far end of the room, a student drums on the table with his palms, earphones clamped to his head. The music is loud enough that Whitney can hear the beat from several paces away. He waves his hand in front of the student's face, capturing his attention. "Have you seen Laurel Whitney?" he asks.

"She left with some dude."

But when he presses for more information, all Whitney gets is a shrug and "Dude definitely wasn't a student."

He races back down the stairs, checking each studio again, and calls Laurel's cell and their home. No answer. There is one missed call—Nora. But he doesn't call her back.

Outside, night has crept over the campus. Whitney jogs to the parking lot and a sour taste spreads through his mouth. Laurel parked under a streetlight, as he taught her, but instead of her car being bathed in a circle of light, it's swallowed by shadow.

A shiver runs down his spine. The art building's isolation, tucked away from the main campus, now feels dangerous. Whitney grabs a flashlight from his car.

Drawing near, he realizes Laurel's car is leaning at an odd angle. He walks around to the passenger side; there's a crunching beneath his feet. He flicks on the beam, scanning it across the ground—broken glass twinkles back at him. The streetlamp didn't burn out, the bulb was shattered. Whitney points the light at the car and sees both of Laurel's passenger-side tires are flat.

A single flat tire is one thing, two is deliberate, that combined with the note he received, and Laurel leaving "with some dude" has Whitney struggling to keep his rising panic in check. He calls the station, requesting that a squad car and detective team come to the campus. Whitney doesn't want to appear like an overprotective parent, but getting a kidnapping threat changes everything.

He remembers the day she was born—cradling that tiny, swaddled bundle. Tears filled his eyes as he gently pressed his lips against her forehead. Waves of emotion coursed through his body so intensely he rocked back on his feet. The nurse placed a steadying hand on his back laughing, "Whoa there, dad. How are you going to take care of this little one if you fall over?" He vowed then, as all new fathers do, no one would ever hurt his baby girl.

In his dual roles as a father and a police officer, Whitney tried to balance shielding his daughter from the ugliness of the world, while also preparing her for the dangers that do exist. He warned her about obvious cons and not to be too trusting. Serial killer Ted Bundy fooled women by faking car trouble and a broken leg. Laurel would never leave with a stranger just because she had a flat—she'd know better than that. Whitney shakes his head vigorously—don't go there. Stay focused. He pushes down the growing queasiness in his stomach.

During one of his calls to the station, Whitney learns that the bumblebee man is who he claims to be. While on his usual bike ride, a man drove up to him offering a $100 bill if he would deliver the box to the police station. The man claimed it was for his girlfriend, "Lieutenant Whitney." They had a fight, and he was afraid to deliver it himself, thinking the other cops would give him a hard time.

Unfortunately, Mr. Van Der Meer can provide only a vague description of the man: white, dark hair, no visible tattoos or scars, and no idea as to his height or weight since the man never got out of his car. Van Der Meer provides even fewer details about the vehicle: dark, blue or black, and a car (as opposed to a van or SUV). He can't even recall if it had two or four doors. The one unique thing Van Der Meer remembers is that the man wore leather driving gloves.

Whitney's phone buzzes again; a glance shows Nora. He can't ignore it; otherwise she'll keep calling. He texts: situation — can't talk.

Three patrol cars and one unmarked detective vehicle arrive on campus. The parking area pulsates with red and blue flashes.

Detective Swift spots a small valve cap lying on the ground and crouches by Laurel's car. His find confirms Whitney's suspicion that this was an intentional act. Now evidence, Swift places the cap inside a small plastic bag. Underneath the light pole with the shattered bulb lie a couple of cigarette butts, which are placed in a different evidence bag.

Swift reports there's no sign of a struggle. This news does not ease Whitney's mind; his pacing picks up speed, as does the vehemence with which he jabs at his phone.

He's so engrossed in his thoughts about what to do next that he's shocked to hear Laurel's voice.

"Dad, why are you here? And what are they doing with my car?"

Whitney grabs his daughter, pulling Laurel into a tight embrace. His voice is strained. "I thought something happened to you. Where have you been?"

"The Townsend Gallery, for a show of student work, including a painting of mine. I asked Ezra if he wanted to go."

Whitney loosens his grip on Laurel but does not let go. "Ryan, you're the dude?"

"Hello, Lieutenant." He awkwardly reaches out his hand to shake. Whitney ignores the gesture.

"You didn't answer your phone." Whitney says to Laurel.

"Gallery policy requires all phones silenced. This is a little over the top, even for you. What's going on?"

Whitney finally releases her.

"You got a flat."

Glancing around at all the police activity, Laurel says, "Well, this is some kind of service."

Whitney turns toward Laurel's date. "Officer Ryan, walk with me."

Once they're several yards away from Laurel, he shows Ryan the card. "This was delivered to me at the station."

"It's just like the note found with Mrs. Curtis. How's he even know about Laurel?" Ryan asks, a slight quiver to his voice.

"That's what worries me. Take Laurel home and wait with her until I get there. No wait, change that. Take her to the station. I want the house checked out first."

"Yes, sir. Should I tell her what's happening?"

"Might as well. She'll drive you crazy with questions until you do."

Ryan takes a couple of steps back toward Laurel. Whitney calls to him before he reaches her. "Oh, and Ryan, right now your job is to keep her safe. Later, we'll talk about you dating my daughter."

As he nears Laurel, Ryan raises his hand to signal her to wait with her questions. "I'll tell you everything I know once we're at the station house, including why I'm taking you there."

Whitney watches Swift instruct the other detective to finish processing the scene. Then the two of them drive to East Norwich and inspect the lieutenant's home. It's close to midnight when Whitney returns to the police station. Ryan is at a desk in the squad room, reading.

"Where's Laurel?"

"She had me drive her to her friend Sydney's house so she could get some sleep. I spoke with the husband, David, and told him to call 911 immediately if anything seems out of the ordinary, no matter how minor.

Did you find anything suspicious at your house?"

"No, but I feel better with her staying somewhere else tonight. I'm going to write this up. You go home."

Whitney knows it's best to describe everything while it's still fresh in his mind. Unfortunately, his thoughts keep bouncing between trying to remember as many details as possible and worrying about Laurel. Obsessing over "what if" questions is pointless and a waste of energy, but Whitney can't help himself. What if she was alone? What if he goes after her again? How did he know where to find Laurel? He tilts his head to one side and furrows his brows. That last question isn't so pointless. How did he know to find her at Post College?

CHAPTER 28

Chief Eaves stands in front of the desk, observing his lieutenant for a moment while deciding what to say. Finally, he opens with, "You look like crap, Whit."

Startled, Whitney jerks his head up from his desk, meeting the chief's gaze.

"Honestly, though, I'd be more worried if you looked like your usual dapper self after everything that happened. Been here all night?"

Whitney stifles a yawn and glances at the window, watching dust particles dance in the morning sun. "Apparently."

The chief pulls up a chair and sits.

"How's Laurel?" he asks.

"She's fine. To be on the safe side, she's staying elsewhere. I think it was a scare tactic, and this guy's either very lucky or calculating as hell."

Eaves leans forward. "Or feels threatened. You may be right—this is unusual for the Squire. Whoever's behind this has a dangerous agenda. But until we know more, the official line is one suspect. I don't need mayors micromanaging us."

He glances at his watch. "Stone's starting the briefing soon. You should be there, then go home."

If the killer feels threatened, he must be onto something, but Whitney doesn't feel any closer to figuring out who he—or she—is. The murder, the forgeries, the thefts—the crimes are each so distinctive. Nothing connects.

Whitney nods absently and lumbers away, first to the lounge for a black coffee, then to the briefing room. Exhaustion clings to him, weighing him down. He doesn't even realize Stone has finished until a couple of patrol officers come over, offering reassurance. "We'll get the bastard," one of them says.

Sergeant Stone approaches Whitney and waits for the others to move on. Standing beside him rather than facing him directly, she asks in a low voice, "You okay, Lieu?"

"I'm all right, thanks, Eileen." Whitney faces her and musters a faint smile, but his eyes stay dull. "What did you find at the scene? Cigarettes? I'm a little distracted. Was there a DNA match?"

"No, too early for that. Just that they're French cigarettes. At first, we thought they were hand-rolled since they have no filters, but it turns out they're a brand called Gauloises."

Whitney's smile falters. The glaze lifts from his eyes, replaced by something sharper.

"Does that mean something to you?"

"Laurel's ex-boyfriend smoked those stupid French things. I'm gonna have a chat with that boy."

A buzz of activity interrupts their conversation. Hackett has shown up at the station before his scheduled return and is now holding court with his usual crew. He had asked for two weeks personal time following the anti-terrorism symposium—which normally requires advance notice—but under the circumstances, the chief approved the request.

If Hackett has any lingering concerns about his connection to the murder victim, they're well concealed by his boisterous display.

He spots Whitney at the far end of the room and calls out, "Hey, Whit! Turns out you sending me to Rochester was the best thing you could have done for me. You're looking at the new chief of Harper's Cove—nice town, even better fishing."

He breaks free from the circle of patrolmen and strides toward Whitney. "I'd rather be a big fish in a small pond than second fiddle for the rest of my career," Hackett says. "You know Eaves is going to recommend someone from outside Old Brookville to replace him."

Whitney has bigger concerns than the politics of promotion. "Denis, congratulations," he says, managing a smile as he extends his hand.

Hackett grips it firmly and leans in. "I heard about Laurel. Let me know how I can help," he says, his tone unexpectedly sincere. He releases his grip and returning his attention to the other officers, Hackett announces, "I'm here until the end of the month. Plenty of time to catch that Squire prick."

Whitney turns to leave, but Stone places her hand on his forearm, stopping him.

"You know you can't go after him. I'll look into it. Give me the ex's name and where to find him. Go home, get some rest. And don't worry, I'll bring back-up," she says, and jerks her head in Hackett's direction.

Sergeant Stone and Lieutenant Hackett drive to the campus security office at Post College. Stone explains the situation to the supervisor, who looks up Birk's schedule and assigns an officer to retrieve him from class.

Birk enters the office, swaggers to a chair, and sits down. His eyes dance quickly over the woman police officer, assessing the physical attributes he can see. His gaze shifts to the manila folder on the table. "So, what's this all about, sweetheart? Do you need a date to the policeman's ball?" he says. Birk lowers his chin, lifts his eyes, and blows a kiss at her.

A growl emanates from behind him. Birk looks over his shoulder, and sees there's another cop, this one male, standing with his back against the wall, arms crossed.

"This, Mr. Dunn, is about destruction of property," Sergeant Stone says. She opens the folder, taking out several photographs, and lays them out in a row on the table.

Birk scans the photos. One is a picture of a car with flat tires, the others are close-ups: a valve cap, cigarettes crushed on asphalt, and a car fender with a dusted palm print.

Stone lifts a medium-size black case from the floor and places it on the table with deliberate slowness. She unlatches the clasps with a sharp snap, her eyes never leaving Birk's. "We're going to need prints." She removes an ink pad and paper cards, placing them next to the manila folder.

"Is this a joke?" Birk scoffs, looking from one officer to the other.

"This is not a joke." Stone stares at him, counting to ten in her head before continuing. "You can make this easy by telling us what happened, or you can make us go through the process of fingerprinting and swabbing you for DNA. But I gotta tell you, the prosecutor doesn't like when we waste valuable resources and usually tacks on additional charges just for spite."

"Charges? What charges?"

"Vandalism, destruction of property, malicious intent."

"Littering," grumbles Hackett as he steps closer.

"This is stupid. It's a flat tire, no harm, no foul."

"So, you admit this was your doing?"

"Yeah, so what? There's no damage. Can I go?"

"There's the broken street bulb," the campus security officer says, surprising everyone with his comment. "Those are special-ordered, and we have to book a bucket truck to install."

Stone picks up the manila folder, flips through the papers until she finds what she's looking for. "We also have the matter of this note, delivered to Lieutenant Whitney on the day you tampered with his daughter's car."

She pushes a photocopy of the note toward Birk. "Threatening in the second degree. Typically, a year in jail, plus a fine."

Hackett leans down, so he's face-to-face with the student. "More if it's against a police officer or his family."

Birk pushes his chair away from the table and jumps to his feet.

"Whoa, whoa, whoa. Yeah, I let the air out of Laurel's tires and threw a rock at the streetlight so her car would be in the dark, but that's it! Only someone with a death wish would send a note like that to Mr. Whitney."

Stone softens her voice. "Sit down. Do you need anything, a glass of water, maybe? Let's go over all the facts and see if we can clear this up."

At home, Whitney can't relax. He has memorized the note's wording and repeats it in his head, willing the eighteen words to impart a clue.

He considers the upside to Laurel's ex being the culprit: He's not much of an actual threat, and he'd be out of her life for good. "Sculpture Boy" did not make a favorable impression on Whitney when they met. The kid lacks the initiative to get a job, so he certainly can't pull off a crime as ambitious as murder.

Whitney slaps his desk with his palm. Don't excuse him just because he's lazy. Think like a cop!

The note threatening Laurel, and the note found with the body, appear identical. There must be a connection. Birk is an artist—he could have made the forgeries. Maybe he has partnered with someone—someone who is dangerous. Whitney must have dozed off at some point, because he's awakened by the ping of a text: "Birk let out the air but claims he didn't send the note. Talk tomorrow." The message is from Eileen Stone's cell phone.

Whitney then texts Laurel: "Love you." She responds right away:

"Love U2." He gets ready for bed and falls into a restless sleep.

First thing the next morning, Whitney meets with Stone and Hackett to hear about the interview with Birk. Stone summarizes Birk's statement while Hackett leans against the wall with his arms crossed. "He admits to causing the flats and breaking the light. Says he saw Laurel with a new guy and got jealous. Does Laurel have a new beau?"

"Eileen, please."

"Right, sorry, Lieu. Post College will deal with the fine for damaging campus property. They're also putting him on probation. He's not allowed to have any contact with Laurel, but that only applies when she's on campus."

Hackett mutters, "Letting the kid off easy. Probably don't want to refund any tuition."

Part of Whitney agrees with Hackett—the dad side of him would like to see the ex-boyfriend expelled. But Whitney focuses on his police role and asks, "Is there anything that can tie him to the forgeries or murder?"

"He claims he was away with his new girlfriend the weekend of the Curtis murder. We spoke to her. She's pissed about his stunt with Laurel. He'll be in the doghouse for a while, but she confirmed their weekend away," Stone says.

"Calls himself an artist," Hackett scoffs. "I've seen better-looking dog turds than the crap that guy makes. No way he could copy those paintings."

"Could he have a partner?" Whitney asks.

"I doubt it," Stone says. "He was way too eager to save himself and would have told us if he does. Despite his rebel-without-a-cause persona, I don't think he's been in trouble before."

"Thank you, Eileen. Thanks, both of you."

"Yeah, yeah. No good deed goes unpunished, I'm betting," Hackett mumbles.

Over the next few hours, Whitney devotes himself to catching up on work that got pushed down on the priorities list due to recent events. Whitney is still troubled, even after learning that the incident with Laurel's car has no connection to the threat he received. Somehow the person who killed Margeaux Curtis also knows about his daughter.

Suddenly, an out-of-breath dispatch officer bursts into his office. Whitney braces himself.

"A guy just called in saying he caught the Squire."

CHAPTER 29

Bobby enters the shop and dings the service bell in rapid succession. He's young, sporting an acne-spotted complexion, long hair, and a patchy first mustache. Most importantly, he doesn't look like he belongs in the antique shop.

"Yo, here to do some business." Bobby calls out, craning his neck to see into the back of the shop.

He upends a tube sock, dumping a cell phone and some jewelry onto the glass countertop with a loud clattering. One bracelet spins in circles faster and faster, mesmerizing Bobby. He senses a presence—or rather, smells a presence: garlic.

"Dude, get a mint."

A low voice grumbles, "This ain't a pawnshop. Beat it."

Bobby turns. The shop owner looms over him. "C'mon, man, you got bling right here." He taps the glass case. Inside is a display of vintage jewelry, along with some small porcelain figurines.

"Let me get my loupe."

The owner makes his way behind the counter and busies himself rummaging through a drawer. Bobby glances around the shop. It appears to have high-end stuff, so he's hoping the payout will include a couple of Benjamins. The man makes a throat-clearing sound, drawing Bobby's focus back to the counter.

Bobby's jaw slackens, and his eyes widen. There's a gun, almost engulfed by the big man's baseball-mitt-size hand. It would be comical, except the muzzle is pointed at Bobby's chest. Reflexively, he raises his hands.

The gun makes a jerky move, which Bobby interprets to mean he should move to the right. He's desperate to look around for an escape, but can't pull his eyes away from the weapon, and startles himself when his back bangs into a wall. Bobby's leg feels warm, followed by a faint splattering sound.

Keeping the gun trained on Bobby, the shop owner uses his other hand to grab the phone and call the police. In a gravelly voice, he says, "I caught the Squire. Send a squad car right away."

Bobby gathers his courage, attempting to sound cool; instead, his voice squeaks, "Dude, you got it all wrong."

"Shut up!" The voice rumbles, spraying Bobby with garlic-scented spittle.

The boy slowly slides into a crouched position as tears stream down his face. Bobby wraps his arms around his knees and sobs. "I just wanted cash to buy some weed, man."

Between gasps for air, the police dispatcher relays the details of the call. The owner of Dovetail Antiques & Consignments claims the Squire is there trying to sell some silver. After getting the address, Whitney has Officer Ryan join him and directs Detective Swift to meet them there.

Cedar Lane weaves in and out of the towns of Locust Valley and Matinecock. The south side of the road, which includes the Dovetail shop, lies within the Old Brookville Police district—a zoning benefit Whitney is sure the chief will appreciate—if they catch the Squire.

Whitney, Ryan, and Swift enter the store. Small vignettes of furniture paired with decorative items populate the showroom. At the counter sits a beefy man, his face buried in a boating magazine; he looks out of place surrounded by all the genteel ornamental objects.

"Are you the owner?" Whitney asks.

"That would be my wife," the man answers without looking up.

"I'm Lieutenant Whitney. Are you the person who called?"

The man puts down the magazine. "Oh yeah, that's me. Sorry, I thought there would've been sirens."

"You said this is your wife's store. Is she around?" Whitney asks.

"No, I'm just filling in. She's visiting her sister in Jersey."

"And your name?"

"Tilbrook. Larry Tilbrook."

"And you claim the Squire was here?"

A grin spreads across the man's face. "Is here. The Squire is here. I get a reward, right? I've got my eyes on a nice 32-footer." He taps the magazine with a finger the girth of a sausage.

"I think the reward expired," Ryan says from behind Detective Swift. "At least that's what I read."

"Isn't there always a reward?" Tilbrook asks.

"First, tell us what happened," Detective Swift says as he scans the store's interior.

"This guy comes in trying to sell some jewelry—nothing fancy—but I realize it's all silver, and he must be the Squire. So, I took out my piece, marched him to the back, and tied him up."

Swift glances around the artfully arranged shop—no broken glass, not a chair out of place. He huffs. "You have him here? Tied up?"

"Yeah, in the back. Follow me."

"Slow down," Whitney says. "Where's your gun?"

Tilbrook opens a drawer and reaches for the weapon.

"Stop! Officer Ryan will get that. Do you have a pistol permit?"

"I don't need a permit. I got the Second Amendment."

"Actually, in New York State, handguns require a permit. You could face a felony charge," Whitney says.

"But I caught the Squire. I'm a hero."

"We'll see about that. Let's meet your Squire," Detective Swift says.

Tilbrook snakes his way through a narrow passage toward the back of the building, and the three officers follow. The storage area is a disaster—far different from the well-crafted display in the front. Lamps balance precariously on top of chairs, which teeter on tables. The officers follow, navigating through the chaos, careful not to topple a pile. They stop in front of a utility closet; muffled sounds emanate from within. Tilbrook opens the door, looking very pleased with himself, his chest puffing out as though he's expecting Whitney to pin a medal on him.

Inside the small room sits what appears to be a teenager, bound to a folding chair. His eyes are bloodshot, his jeans soaked through. A pungent mix of urine and marijuana hangs in the air around him.

"You've got to be kidding me," Swift says, turning his head away from the stench.

"I'm going to take the rag out of your mouth," Whitney says to the boy.

Bobby spits on the floor. It's not clear if this action is to expel lint, or if it's commentary on being tied up. "Thank God you're here. That dude's crazy. Pulled a gun on me for no reason."

Whitney cuts the duct tape that's wrapped around the captive. "What's your name?"

"B-Dawg."

"Let's try that again. Name?"

"Bobby."

Whitney turns around in the cramped space. "Detective, get Mr. Tilbrook's statement. Check to see if he has a permit and confirm it's up to date. Otherwise, confiscate the weapon. Bobby will come with me to the station."

"What?! How is that fair? What about my reward?" Tilbrook whines.

Swift makes an exasperated huff. "Does that kid look like he's been stealing antique silver for over a decade?"

Tilbrook pauses for a few seconds, his eyes dart between Swift and Whitney. "He could be," he mumbles.

Tilbrook initially refuses to produce his gun permit, insisting that the Constitution alone gives him the right to carry a firearm. But the possibility of jail time proves persuasive, and he eventually hands it over. Still, avoiding arrest doesn't seem to make up for losing the reward— and the new boat that would have come with it.

At the station house, Bobby makes himself comfortable by straddling the back of a chair—a posture he believes re-establishes his coolness. It doesn't work. Whitney knows better; the boy still reeks of fear and urine.

"Tell me what happened, Bobby."

"I told you, dude's freaking crazy. I came in to do some business, you know, sell some stuff, and he pulls a piece on me."

"What were you selling?"

"Just some old stuff—a cell phone, gold coins, jewelry. Like that."

"Your stuff?"

"Yeah, mine. Well, the jewelry was my grandma's. She left it to me. What are you gonna do about that guy? Pulling a gun is crazy shit."

"The detective is talking with him."

"Talking with him? Lock him up is what you should do."

Whitney takes out a manila envelope and shakes its contents onto the table.

"This is what you were selling?" Using his pen to separate the items, Whitney lays the chains in straight lines. "We have four chain necklaces, one cell phone with a gold glitter case and cracked screen. Really, Bobby? Sparkles? They don't seem your style. Eight Sacagawea coins ..."

"Gold coins."

"No, Bobby. They're just dollar coins, not made of gold."

The boy's reacquired bravado deflates.

"Six bracelets and four rings. None of these items really belong to you, do they?"

"I told you, man. It was my grandma's."

"The thing is, the jewelry you have here isn't the jewelry an older woman would wear. The charm on this necklace is a pony, and this other one is a volleyball. I'm thinking this jewelry belongs to your sister. How old are you, Bobby?"

The boy hangs his head. "Sixteen. You gonna call my parents?"

"I think that's best, don't you?"

"They're gonna be pissed."

After the boy is released into the custody of his mother, Whitney writes up his report on Bobby, the criminal mastermind—probably the worst he'll get is being grounded by his parents. He's lucky that the shop owner's husband didn't shoot first and ask questions later. The husband is even luckier he didn't shoot an unarmed kid.

CHAPTER 30

Whitney enters his home, a turquoise backpack decorated with anime pins lying on the floor. He frowns and steps into the living room. Laurel is typing on her laptop. The television plays a cooking show in the background.

"What are you doing here?" he asks.

"Good to see you too, Dad."

"No really, why aren't you at Sydney's?"

"They're newlyweds. I can only crash on their couch for so long. I was feeling like a third wheel. Besides, isn't it over? The internet is on fire with posts saying the Squire's been caught."

Whitney sits down and pulls his daughter close, "It wasn't him—just some stoner kid. Besides, I don't think the Squire sent that note to me."

He doesn't want to tell her yet that her ex was the one who caused the flat tires. The real threat is whoever sent the note to the station house. If she were to think it was all "Sculpture Boy's" doing, she would let her guard down.

"I'm meeting Nora for dinner," he says. "Want to come along?"

"And be the third wheel again? No, thank you. I really need to work. I'm fine here."

Whitney leaves the room to shower and change. He returns shortly, having done neither. "Go pack your things. Your mother's traveling, you can stay at her apartment."

"What?! Why? I'm fine here."

Whitney narrows his eyes and purses his lips.

"This isn't up for debate."

"How am I supposed to get around? I don't have my car yet."

"Isadora's sending her assistant to pick you up. He'll take you to school when needed."

"You called Mom?"

He nods. "We'd both feel better with you away from this, for now. Plus, Isadora's building has a guard and security system."

Laurel knows better than to argue with her parents on the rare occasions when they agree with each other.

Within an hour, Isadora's assistant arrives at the house. Whitney brings a small suitcase and Laurel's backpack to the car. Pressing $400 into the driver's hand, he says, "It should only be a few days. If it's longer, I'll make it up to you."

The man shrugs and pockets the money like it's a gum wrapper he doesn't want to be caught throwing on the ground.

Laurel shakes her head as she walks to the car. "This isn't necessary."

"I want you safe. Call me when you get there," Whitney says, hugging her close.

Breathing a small sigh of relief, he watches as the car drives away. Now he needs to call and cancel dinner with Nora. He wants her safe, too, and hopes she won't be too mad.

Ever since receiving the threatening note, Whitney hasn't slept well. His days and nights are haunted by the thought that someone might try to get to Laurel again. He tries to convince himself it was just a hoax meant to rattle him—after all, she's fine. But knowing the killer knows about her, and where to find her, continues to gnaw at him. His nervous energy pushes him to act, but the only option available right now is to review the case files again.

Detectives at the station have two theories: either the Squire has escalated into a violent offender, or he has a partner. Whitney suspects the chief's desire to tie all the crimes into one neat package has had undue influence. The Squire's involvement in the murder and forgeries never felt right to him, but he can't afford to rely on instinct anymore.

He starts with the oldest case, this time determined to keep his mind open to every possibility. He's at it most of the night. The pile of files is still significant, but it's starting to thin.

One photograph of a long-handled serving spoon with broad, serrated teeth captures his attention. His imagination twists it into a grisly slicing blade straight out of Edgar Allan Poe's *The Pit and the Pendulum*.

Whitney flips the photo over. The description on the back is clinical and succinct: silver tomato server. Yet the thought of red juices dripping through its pierced design reinforces his gory vision of the spoon's versatility.

He rubs a hand over his face, trying to drive the macabre images away.

Suddenly, Whitney jerks his head up from his desk. He taps the home button on his phone. The screen changes from black to a picture of Laurel, smiling in her high school cap and gown. It's 2:18 a.m. How long has he been asleep? He doesn't feel rested at all.

Whitney gets up, brushes his teeth and washes his face, but the cool water does nothing to wash away the thoughts troubling him. He settles in bed, though his dreams bring little relief. In one, he's searching for something—something important. He reaches for it, but as he leans in, he loses his balance, and he falls into darkness. The insistent beeping of his alarm pulls him out.

He wakes and heads to the station house, hoping that by keeping busy he can distance himself from his dreams. Whitney spends the day fielding questions from various media outlets about the Squire still being at large. Tilbrook's uncorrected online boast that he'd caught the Squire was picked up by a self-proclaimed "cyber journalist"—Whitney thinks yellow journalist is more accurate. The sensationalized story got so many hits that legitimate outlets were forced to investigate, leading to a colossal waste of his time.

After finally finishing the last call with the media, Whitney closes his office door. He needs time to think without interruption.

Picking up where he left off the night before, he reviews the open cases. When he reaches the most recent event—the threat against Laurel—he researches the silver spoon that came with the note. It's just a common, mass-produced item.

The person behind it must have known the police would notice the inconsistency. After all, the Squire's penchant for antiques is well known. Don't jump to conclusions, he warns himself. The Squire could have made the "slip" purposely to divert suspicion—or maybe he just grabbed the nearest thing.

But focusing on the Squire as the only perpetrator doesn't sit right. The discrepancies push Whitney back toward the theory he's been circling: there's more than one criminal operating in Old Brookville. Anyone could imitate the Squire's signature move—leaving a note at the scene—that detail has been public knowledge for years.

Whitney often organizes his thoughts by writing them down. He pulls out a yellow legal pad and divides the sheet into four columns. He labels them: "Squire," "Forger," "Murderer," and "L-Threat." Under each heading, he jots down facts and impressions, hoping patterns will emerge. Overlaps and parallels start to form. He draws lines connecting ideas, and soon the page is covered by a tangle of scribbles. But one pair of words keeps surfacing in his mind, a common connection linking all the crimes. At the bottom of the page, in large block letters, Whitney writes—INSIDE INFORMATION—and draws arrows to it from each column, circling the phrase repeatedly.

CHAPTER 31

The studio smells of oil paint and turpentine. He loves that scent. At the easel, he dabs his brush against the canvas—precise, controlled. He's not just copying the image—he's capturing the soul of the original. The painter steps back, taking in the piece. This is his first attempt at replicating the work of such a well-known artist. More people will see this painting in a day than have seen any of his previous ones. His eyes widen as he inhales sharply, adrenaline rushing through his body. He savors the moment.

Then he turns to his next task. Cleaning brushes may be anticlimactic after creating a masterpiece, but proper care ensures quality work. He dips his brush into a glass jar half full of turpentine and watches the olive-green swirls dissolve into the solvent.

A memory stirs—once painful and unwelcome, now embraced as vindication. His youth was miserable, living with a cruel and unloving family. The old woman and her little prince split their time between taunting and ignoring him. Every summer the pair would travel, and while it was a relief to have them gone, it was also lonely. His only company was the servants.

The man of the house—her husband—spent most of his time at work, and when home, hid behind the locked door of his office. His rare appearances occurred only after he found enough courage from a scotch bottle. Each year he retreated further until, eventually, he shot himself.

Ironically, it was a secret gift from this sad drunk man that would become his lifeline: painting supplies and a battered secondhand easel.

The summer after his death, the old woman and brat took their usual trip abroad. But this time, there were no servants, no drunk husband hiding in his study—only him, abandoned in the house. The first few nights he barely slept. He paced the halls and lived off frozen dinners. Looking back, he should have called the police. Though at the time, he was terrified that he—not the adult who deserted him—would be blamed. He considered running away. But a desperate combination of fear and hope held him back.

Then an idea struck: What if he could please her? Would things get better? He devoted the rest of that summer to copying a small painting by Joseph Dawson, a Hudson River School artist, whose original hung above the living room mantle. It took weeks to replicate Dawson's dramatic use of light and shadow, eventually creating a convincing copy.

As a joke, he swapped his version for the original. After the old woman and prince returned, he marked off the days as he waited for her to notice. She didn't. A week passed. Then two. Months passed by and still nothing.

His hope of winning her over with his talent faded. At six months, he thought about selling the original and escaping, but what auction house would accept a painting from a teen?

Over the years, he honed his skills, becoming a master forger—not just fooling that pretentious cow, but others as well. However, this success only partly makes up for what he endured. It seems no matter how far he's come, her abuse still haunts him.

"I showed you!" he shouts, startled by the echo in the studio and the sting in his palms. When she lingers in his thoughts too long, anger takes over. He looks down at his hands, balled into tight fists, fingernails digging into his palms. He releases his grip, revealing crescent-shaped marks in his skin.

The painter removes the brush from the solvent, washes it with soap and water and blots it dry. Then, carefully, he reshapes the bristles with his fingers and lays it flat on a cloth. He's copied many paintings since that first one. A burning compulsion drives him. Each time, he feels closer to escaping his past, but he can never truly get away.

His gaze returns to the canvas. The airy palette soothes him. He rolls his shoulders, releasing a final knot of tension. This painting is special. His most spectacular accomplishment. Maybe after this one, he'll stop. Or maybe not.

CHAPTER 32

A rash of burglary calls hits the station, all from the same cul-de-sac. Quail Ridge is one of the few developments in Upper Brookville. Identical-looking homes line the private street—the only noticeable difference between them is their slightly varied color palettes.

Whitney and Ryan drive out together to investigate and pull up to number seven, a tan house with white trim. A woman in workout gear jumps rope in the driveway, speeding up until she missteps.

"Mrs. Doxey? I'm Lieutenant Whitney. You called about a break-in?"

"Yes," she says between gasping breaths. "Excuse me, I'm training for a marathon. Plus, releasing endorphins calms me, you know? I think it was the Squire. Let me show you what I found."

Mrs. Doxey leads them to a formal dining room and points to a white lacquer sideboard. "There used to be a silver platter on that easel. At first, I thought it must have slipped and fallen, but as I got closer, I saw the drawer was partially open and spotted the note. That's when I called."

"Did you touch the note?" Whitney asks.

"No, just the handle on the drawer."

Ryan unpacks the camera case and the evidence collection box.

Whitney waves a hand toward the sideboard. "Get some shots of this."

While Ryan is busy taking photos from different angles, Whitney pulls on a pair of disposable latex gloves. He opens the drawer, removes the note and reads aloud:

I apologize most sincerely for abruptly squiring Hester Bateman to her new home. A true beauty she is. My heart would break to separate the lovely from her children. So rest assured, they are all together.

"Hester Bateman?" he asks.

"An English silversmith—actually, a female silversmith—from the

1700s," Mrs. Doxey replies.

"And her children?"

"The silverware, I'm guessing. That's what was in the drawer."

"Are you sure it was taken last night?"

"Maybe not last night, but certainly in the past few days. My housekeeper was here last week, and she would have mentioned the missing platter."

After finishing with Mrs. Doxey, Whitney and Ryan move on to a pebble-gray building with darker trim, the home of Mr. and Mrs. Lyons.

"Tell me what happened," Whitney says, addressing the couple.

"My niece is getting married next week," Mr. Lyons explains. "I wanted to give her a set of place card holders as a wedding present. They've been in my family for generations. Each piece is a silver fox with ruby eyes."

"Re-gifting," Mrs. Lyons mumbles.

"It's not re-gifting—it's a family heirloom," Mr. Lyons insists.

Mrs. Lyons lets out an exasperated sigh and dramatically rolls her eyes.

"When did you discover they were missing?"

"I kept them in the china cabinet, but this morning there was a note in their place."

Mr. Lyons hands him the note. Whitney wishes the husband had shown the same foresight as his neighbor and left the evidence untouched. The note reads:

> *This handsome set of foxes and vixens is*
> *a generous offering, and most appreciated.*

"See?" Mr. Lyons says. "Even the thief thinks they make a fine gift."

Mrs. Lyons narrows her eyes. "It wouldn't kill you to open your wallet occasionally."

Recognizing the couple has nothing more to add—other than debate their ideas of generosity—Whitney thanks them for their time. He and Ryan head to the site of the third burglary, a colonial-blue house with cream trim.

Here the Squire altered his pattern by stealing antique gold jewelry. The homeowner, Mrs. Payne, recently lost her mother and is in the midst of carrying out her duties as executor. The living room is crammed with boxes of her mother's belongings. She has been separating and cataloging her mother's valuables every day, so she immediately noticed that five of her mother's gold brooches were missing. In their place was a note:

These bits and bobs are not my usual taste, nor the current
fashion. Surely they will not be missed. Put your heart
at peace. Her legacy will serve a higher calling.

"How did he know I was struggling?" Mrs. Payne asks, her eyes glistening with fresh tears. "My mother loved those gaudy pins. I was never going to wear them but felt guilty at the thought of selling."

Whitney is accustomed to seeing the Squire's victims show the curious mix of pleasure and pride in their losses. But Mrs. Payne is the first to admit relief.

After offering what comfort they could, Whitney and Ryan take their leave.

"Something's changed," Ryan says, breaking the silence during the drive back to the station.

"What makes you say that?"

"Three homes on the same street, all broken into on the same night. It's so ... so brazen. His other jobs went undiscovered for months—sometimes even years. Maybe it's not really the Squire."

"It's him. We'll compare the notes to be sure, but I'm certain the handwriting will match the Squire's, not the Friar's."

"The Friar?" Ryan asks.

"That's what Laurel calls whoever delivered the kidnapping threat to the station. She came up with 'Friar'—a mashup of fraud and squire. You're right, though. These burglaries are different."

The three break-ins feel like an escalation. But they still follow the Squire's usual M.O.—inconspicuous, nonviolent—but something about the final note lingers: 'serve a higher calling.' What did he mean by that?

CHAPTER 33

Whitney can't shake the feeling he missed something. The past few days have been a blur of distractions: the threat against Laurel, the capture of the would-be Squire. He sighs, crosses the office, and shuts the door. Time to review his notes, yet again. He knows the case files so well by now he could recite half of them from memory.

He skims through his notebook, barely registering the words. Then his eyes land on something scribbled in the margin: "Henry Lockhart, A. Sutton's cousin, 'Rembrandt,' Buffalo, overdose." Why did he write that? He pauses, then remembers—it was from the meeting with Caleb Vos. Probably just habit. It wasn't directly related to the case.

Yet, even as he turns the page, his mind lingers on the name. Henry Lockhart. Why does it sound so familiar? Is it connected somehow? Or is it the name of a chef on one of Laurel's cooking shows?

Whitney flips through the rest of his notebook. There it is. Hank Lockhart. A student who worked for the contractor at the Baldwin house. The contractor said the boy had died in a car accident.

Which is it: overdose or car crash? A simple computer search locates the old accident report: a single-vehicle crash on the Bronx River Parkway in Westchester County, New York. The deceased had a blood alcohol content of .08—legally impaired—but no narcotics.

A drug death often embarrasses the family, and they cover it up by vaguely claiming the death was an accident. Odd that Sutton would do the opposite.

The report reads like most DWI accidents: Alcohol paired with a lead foot equals loss of control. Lockhart's car flipped over and slid down an embankment into a tree. The driver wasn't wearing their seatbelt—mercifully, death was instantaneous.

An officer was dispatched to the address on the license to notify Mrs. Patricia Sutton, the victim's aunt and next of kin of the crash.

Whitney keys the name Patricia Sutton into the computer. An article pops up reporting her death—house fire—she fell asleep with a lit cigarette. Her son, Andrew, was away at the time and it was only when he contacted a neighbor—worried because his mother wasn't answering the phone—that he learned about both accidents.

Sutton's family tragedy—losing his mother and cousin within a day of each other—could explain why he insists Lockhart died of an overdose. Few people press for details when drugs are involved; his lie discourages further questions.

No obituaries exist for Henry and Patricia. Whitney calls the only funeral home in the town, hoping they handled the burial services. The woman on the phone remembers the unusual arrangements. The son opted for cremation and declined a burial, even though the family plot still has space. And there was an issue with him continually putting off retrieving the ashes. Eventually, the funeral home shipped the remains.

There it is—a link between all three forgeries. Unfortunately, the connection is an evasive lawyer and a dead man. But what if Lockhart didn't die in the crash? Could someone else have been in the car? Why hide all these years? And what role does Sutton play?

He types up a search warrant. It takes some convincing, but the judge approves Whitney's request to inspect Andrew Sutton's home for evidence connecting him to the forged paintings, as well as any corroboration of an accomplice—possibly Henry Lockhart.

The police arrive at the Sea View condominium complex. The two-bedroom penthouse is so generic-looking that Whitney double-checks the condo number, confirming they entered the right residence and not a display unit used to show prospective buyers.

There's nothing personal about the space—no photos, or trinkets, not even magazines on the table. If Sutton is involved with the painting thefts, it's not to display them in his home. The walls are devoid of any decoration.

The place hardly suggests Sutton lives there—let alone a partner. Only the clothes in the master bedroom hint at occupancy. Whitney inspects the suits and shirts hanging in the walk-in closet. They're organized by brand rather than by color or season: Richard Anderson, Brooks Brothers, Brunello Cucinelli, and Ralph Lauren lined up in alphabetical order.

Whitney opens the top drawer of the built-in dresser; it contains ties, again organized by label. The index card at the front of the row says,

"Brooks Brothers." He cocks his head to one side, recognizing the pattern on one tie: navy blue with turquoise origami animals. He picks it up to check—Hermès, not Brooks Brothers. Isadora gave him the same one for Christmas when they were married.

A leather-bound book lies on top of the dresser. The first page has "Richard Anderson" written at the top, with a list of names underneath. Whitney recognizes the names of prominent Old Brookville families. As he flips through the book, he spots "C. Vos" under Brooks Brothers and "B. Curtis" under Ralph Lauren. Sutton's method of matching his wardrobe to his clients is either obsessive-compulsive or calculating.

His cell phone buzzes. "Lieutenant Whitney."

"I just received a call from the manager. What the hell are you doing in my home?"

"Mr. Sutton, we are executing a search warrant."

"For what?"

"Evidence of art fraud."

"This is insane. I'm with a client, or I'd be right over. Be sure to leave a receipt."

Doubt worms its way through Whitney's brain. So far, their search has been a complete bust.

"Lieutenant, here in the back bedroom," Ryan calls out.

He enters and finds Officer Ryan unfurling a large sheet of paper. "Can you hold it open? I want to take a picture; this looks familiar."

The whoosh of a message being sent fills the air. Whitney's about to comment on proper procedure and using the station's camera when, a moment later, a notification chime answers.

"I thought I recognized this. It's a sketch of John Singer Sargent's *A Garden in Florence*. We just saw this at the Lehrer Museum," Ryan says.

"We?" Whitney asks.

A sheepish expression crosses Ryan's face. "Me and Laurel."

Whitney knits his brows. "Okay." He calls out to the other officers, "anything else?"

"I found receipts for a garage rental and utility bills," Sergeant Stone says.

"Most people have utility bills."

"For a garage rental? Electric, water, and heat for a garage?"

"Add those to the receipt. Make sure we don't leave anything off."

Their search of Sutton's condo complete, Whitney and Ryan follow their one lead to the Charles and Margaret Lehrer Museum. Once the hilltop home of a shipping magnate, the building was constructed around the turn of the 20th century, and modeled after a much older European villa—with soaring ceilings, a copper mansard roof, and intricate moldings that framed tall arched windows. Charles Lehrer bequeathed the property to the town of Upper Brookville on the condition that his wife could live there for the rest of her life. Upon her death, it was to be converted into an art museum.

Whitney shows a photo of Sutton that he pulled from the attorney's website to the receptionist at the entrance.

"Has this man been here recently?" he asks.

The woman shrugs. "Lots of people come through here."

"The Sargent exhibition is on the second floor, is that right?"

"Yes, Sergeant, the Sargent display is up those stairs," she giggles.

Whitney figures she must have been waiting a long time to make that pun. Rather than spoil her fun by informing her that the bars on his uniform indicate lieutenant not sergeant, he smiles back at her and purchases two passes.

Ryan leads the way to the gallery where *A Garden in Florence* is on display. The painting is obviously the source material for the sketch they found. A museum guard stands in the threshold between rooms.

"Are you usually stationed here?" Whitney asks.

"Not to this gallery specifically—we don't have enough staff for that. I'm assigned to the east wing of the second floor."

Whitney shows him the photograph of Sutton. "Has this man been here recently?"

"Him? Yeah, I recognize him. He's come in a few times. Last time he brought a camera. I told him it's prohibited to take photographs of the art. And if he wants a picture, he has to go to the gift shop."

Whitney thanks the guard. He and Ryan head back downstairs. They wait for a group of middle school students to finish buying souvenirs before approaching the cashier. The man at the register hesitates over the picture of Sutton—it looks familiar, but he can't recall which day he was there.

Ryan places a rolled-up poster and an oversized book on the counter. "Is it possible to look up who's purchased these two items?" he asks.

"*The Paintings of John Singer Sargent* by E.T. Hoppe and a print of *A Garden in Florence*," the cashier says, reading aloud while scanning the barcodes. "These are popular items. It will be a long list."

"Do you have anything else of *A Garden in Florence*?" Whitney asks.

"Yes, we have postcards and giclée prints." The cashier points behind him.

Framed prints of various paintings on display at the museum decorate the wall behind the salesperson.

"Aren't those the same as this?" Whitney taps the rolled-up poster.

"Oh no, the giclée prints are a much finer reproduction, able to capture the detail of each brushstroke. They're printed on archival paper at the same dimensions as the original."

"Can you tell me who's purchased those?"

The list of museum attendees who purchased the art print is significantly shorter than those who bought the poster. Whitney has the salesclerk print out one receipt—GDN FLO/JSSAR GCL $439.68 A. Sutton Visa ... 2135.

CHAPTER 34

A ndrew Sutton leans back in the chair, one leg crossed over the other. He breathes in the aroma of his coffee before closing his eyes and taking a long sip. Whitney stands invisible on the opposite side of the one-way glass. The attorney appears unphased by the search of his home the previous day. He checks his wristwatch—an unnecessary gesture, given the large-faced clock mounted on the wall in front of him.

He's wearing a blue suit with a red tie, the classic power combination favored by politicians and businessmen. Did Sutton choose the outfit specifically for this meeting—or for a later one? And if the former, which designer does he associate with an appointment at the police station?

"Good morning," Whitney says as he enters and sits across from Sutton. He places a photograph of the drawing they found in front of the attorney. "We found this in your condo."

Sutton leans forward, allowing himself a glimpse at the photo, then takes another sip of coffee.

"I can assure you, Lieutenant, that is not a stolen piece of art," he says.

"Is it your cousin's? The art student?"

"Yes, that's right. It's the only piece of his I have."

"He was quite good. Was this a special place—summer home, perhaps?"

"No, something of his own making. Henry was ..." Sutton looks up at the ceiling, one corner of his mouth curling into a faint smile. "... Inspired."

"I'd have thought you'd want it framed and hung in your home."

Sutton puts down his cup and checks his watch again. "I'm a busy man, is that all?"

"What can you tell me about this invoice?" Whitney slides a photocopy across the table.

Sutton places two fingers on the paper, dragging it closer to him. He scans the page, then pushes it back toward Whitney.

"One of my clients leases an outbuilding on their property, another client rents the building. What of it?"

"Nice commission—how fortunate for you. Who are your clients?"

"Come now, Lieutenant, you know that's privileged."

"It's interesting that two of your clients were victims of forgery, and that your cousin, Henry Lockhart, worked for a third family who also had a painting replaced by an exact duplicate."

"What kind of evidence is that? Is this a sick joke? Henry's dead. How on earth did you convince a judge to sign off on your warrant?"

Two quick raps at the door interrupt them. Sergeant Stone enters without waiting for a reply. "Lieutenant, you need to see this."

Whitney gets up and follows her. A wall-mounted TV is tuned to a cable news channel. A red "Breaking News" banner scrolls across the bottom. All eyes in the squad room are watching the screen.

The commentator, an attractive woman in her late fifties, reads from a paper in her hands.

"To repeat, we've just received documentation from a confidential source that may shed light on the Margeaux Curtis murder. Apparently, a series of love letters took an ominous turn once the relationship ended."

The woman flashes a sly smile before continuing, "What drove Margeaux's secret lover to go from 'Nobody else gives me a thrill, with all your faults, I love you still,' to the savage declaration, 'Vengeance is in my heart, death in my hand. Blood and revenge are hammering in my head'? The first letter is signed 'Denny,' the latter is unsigned. However, our source claims the handwriting on both letters is identical, and that 'Denny' is Lieutenant Denis Hackett of the Old Brookville Police Department. Is this why they've struggled to catch the killer? Is Detective Hackett hiding behind the blue wall of silence?"

She stares directly at the camera, then the feed breaks to a commercial for a local restaurant.

The room goes dead silent. The assembly of officers stare at the screen in shock and disbelief. A cacophony of ringing phones erupts moments later. Calls are coming in on office lines and personal cell phones. Officers grab the closest device and issue the same response: "No comment."

"How the hell did that make it on air?" Whitney mutters. Momentarily forgetting about his meeting, he cradles a receiver between his ear and shoulder while jotting notes. Andrew Sutton approaches, a self-satisfied smirk on his face.

"Lieutenant, it looks like you have your hands full, so I'll be on my way. You'll hear from me soon regarding harassment charges." Sutton turns, smoothly navigating through the bedlam and exiting the building.

Chief Eaves pokes his head into the turmoil. He catches Whitney's eye and motions for him to come to his office.

Whitney finishes his call: "... there's no blue wall," and heads toward the chief's office. He shuts the door behind him, and the squad room's chatter becomes a muffled din.

The chief has his elbows on his desk, and his hands are clasped with his chin resting on his thumbs—his trademark thoughtful leader pose.

Hackett paces around the room, his face red with anger. He immediately lashes out at Whitney.

"This is horseshit, and you know it. I'm the one who told you about the notes." He slams his hands on the desk, leaning toward Eaves. "Whit's trying to discredit me; he's jealous of my new job as chief of Harper's Cove."

Eaves leans back, bringing his clasped hands to his ribcage. His gaze lingers on Hackett's hands before meeting his eyes. Hackett reads the look, removes his palms from the desk, and stands upright.

"Whitney isn't responsible for this mess. He already corroborated your alibi. Someone else leaked your *billet-doux* to the press."

"My what?" snaps Hackett.

"Love letters."

"Those aren't mine. Well, some are. But not the one about blood and death."

"Did you ever threaten her?" the chief asks.

"NO! Never."

"You're on administrative duty, starting immediately."

"But you just said Whit proved I'm innocent."

"I can prove where you were most of that night," Whitney says. "But the ME's report gives a broad time frame, and your poker alibi doesn't cover all of it."

Hackett snaps his head toward Whitney. His eyes narrow and his lips press into a tight line—the truth behind his saintly alibi now exposed. He opens his mouth to protest, but Eaves cuts him off. "There has to be a formal investigation. Once you're cleared, if needed, I'll speak to Harper's mayor. In the meantime, you will stay home. You will not discuss any Old Brookville matters with anyone, for any reason. If you even whisper about a parking ticket in your sleep, I'll torpedo your job at

Harper's Cove—and any other prospects. Understood?"

"Yes, sir."

"You can go, Denis."

Hackett bangs the door behind him, his frustration evident, but the force isn't enough to draw attention from the chaos in the squad room.

"What do you think, Whit? Is he lying about the second letter?" Chief Eaves asks.

"I don't think so. If someone's out there forging paintings, couldn't they just as easily forge Hackett's writing?"

"Not like you to go in for conspiracies, but this time, it might not be far-fetched. I'm not surprised he lifted a line from a Frank Sinatra song to woo a woman, but using a line from Shakespeare to threaten her? Hackett? I don't see it. He's not exactly the literary type."

"Shakespeare?" Whitney asks.

"*Titus Andronicus.* I read it in high school—benefits of a classical education. Call Troop L and set up a meeting with one of their investigators."

"The State Troopers, not Nassau Police?"

"Too many connections between us and them. The optics aren't good."

The politics of police leadership raises its ugly head again—the one part of the job that continually gives Whitney pause about seeking the chief's position. No one likes calling in outsiders to investigate their own people. Old Brookville is too small a department to have an internal affairs division. Thankfully, there hasn't been a need in the past—not that the Old Brookville officers are Boy Scouts—far from it. Just that previous instances were minor and handled in-house.

"The note left with Mrs. Curtis' body also had a quote from Shakespeare," Whitney says.

Eaves looks out his window at the traffic on Northern Boulevard. He had hoped his last couple of years as chief would be quiet and uneventful. "So, our murderer is a student of the Bard. Or maybe he's hoping to get us chasing at shadows."

He turns back to face his lieutenant. The haggard lines on the chief's forehead were never apparent to Whitney until this moment. "Set something up with Troop L right away."

"Yes, sir."

† † †

The headquarters for Troop L is a gray monolith made of concrete and dark-tinted windows. Whitney meets with the state investigator assigned to the case, Inspector Jankowski—a tall, hulking man as formidable and cheerless as the building.

In a windowless room, Whitney sits ramrod straight at the conference table; the institution deserves respect. Jankowski makes a point of slamming the case files down hard. He occasionally leans across the table to bark in the lieutenant's face.

Whitney doesn't flinch—he's on the same team and knows the playbook. He agrees that Old Brookville should have notified the State Troopers as soon as they learned Hackett was involved with the murder victim, but it wasn't his call to make. Whitney doesn't say this out loud—he doesn't need to. Jankowski understands decisions like that come from the top brass, but he's enjoying the opportunity to dress Whitney down.

He returns to find the station house still in an uproar. Jankowski was right—they were naïve to think they could keep Hackett's involvement under wraps. But who leaked it to the press? By Whitney's count, only a few people knew about the affair, and he can't imagine the chief or Hackett tipping off the community access news.

A small protest group marches in front of the station, holding signs saying, "Who Polices the Police?" and "Justice for Margeaux!" Other signs are more succinct, featuring the word "Cops" inside a red circle with a slash through it—the universal symbol for "no."

Their prompt arrival feels suspect. Had the same unnamed source tipped off local activists too? Whitney is given the unenviable task of managing the protesters, drawing yet another short stick for crappy jobs that day. He approaches the group and asks to speak to the person in charge.

"Trying to deny us our constitutional right to protest?" asks a man wearing a yellow T-shirt with "Don't Tread on Me" printed on the front.

"No, I'm here to inform you about the rules regarding a peaceful protest. You cannot block municipal building entrances, so keep this area clear. And anyone obstructing my officers from performing their duties will be arrested. You have fifteen minutes to remove any cars from the reserved spaces, or they'll be impounded."

"Hey, I fought for our country. I fought for our freedom. You can't scare us." The man leers at Whitney.

Looking each person in the eye before addressing the man in the yellow shirt, who appears to be the group's leader, Whitney says, "As one service member to another, I shouldn't have to remind you that our job was to protect the rule of law and our freedoms. Follow the law, and we won't have any problems."

Whitney goes back inside. He and the reception officer watch the group through the video monitor. A few people immediately move out of the traffic lane and onto the grass. Two women walk toward a car, while the rest appear to be in conversation.

"If they haven't cleared the entrance in ten minutes, buzz me," Whitney says.

CHAPTER 35

Four days after discovering the pencil sketch of *A Garden in Florence*, Whitney spends the night with the original painting. This is his second night at the Lehrer Museum actually—the previous night passed uneventfully. He hopes his, and Officer Ryan's, theory—that the sketch they found is a precursor to the forgery—proves true. Chief Eaves and the museum's director don't believe that one necessarily corresponds to the other.

However, the risk of losing donors is too great should the Lehrer Museum fail to protect a valuable painting. Reluctantly, the director acquiesces, allowing the Old Brookville Police department to stake out the museum for the rest of the John Singer Sargent show. Afterward, the exhibit will ship to the National Gallery of Art for the next leg of its tour, leaving any security concerns to that museum's director.

Inside, the museum is dark. The only illumination comes from low-wattage security lights mounted on the baseboards, casting a soft glow on the polished floors. Whitney waits in the gallery that houses *A Garden in Florence* along with several other landscapes and two of Sargent's most popular portraits: *Lady Agnew of Lochnaw* and *Portrait of Madame X*. The women appear disinterested in Whitney's presence—something to his left has captivated Madame X's gaze, while Lady Agnew looks right past him.

Whitney stations himself behind a large abstract sculpture. Time passes slowly in the dark and he resists the urge to check his watch. What difference will it make? The forger will show up or not. The need to stretch his aching limbs becomes harder to ignore. He makes subtle movements, alleviating the increasing stiffness, while mindful to remain silent.

Remaining focused solely on the stakeout is another challenge. Worry over Laurel's safety never leaves his thoughts. If he's right, and the forger sent the threatening note—which also means they killed Margeaux

Curtis—he'll soon face the source of his sleepless nights. His heartbeat quickens. His daughter's safety is everything. But if fatherly protection drives his decisions, this entire operation could go sideways fast. Stay calm, stay focused.

Whitney reminds himself why he's here: *A Garden in Florence.* He peeks at the serene landscape from behind the sculpture. A stray thought pops in his head: A trip to Italy would be nice, especially if he is accompanied by Nora. Suddenly, he realizes this is where Laurel will be going—the Uffizi is in Florence. Of course, the painting's subject and her trip being in the same city is just a coincidence, but the parallels are disorienting.

Out of the corner of his eye, something catches his attention. He's immediately brought back to the task at hand; all extraneous thoughts vanish. Whitney strains to see, but the hallway is a black void. He glances up at Lady Agnew and Madame X, but the women in the portraits remain aloof and offer no assistance. Was it his imagination? No, someone is definitely in the outer chamber. He's sure of it.

A dark figure with a large bundle under their arm silently creeps into the gallery. They stand for a long moment in front of *A Garden in Florence* before quietly unwrapping the quilt to reveal a sun-drenched landscape—the twin to the painting on the wall. With swift yet purposeful movements, the figure reaches up, removes the painting, replacing it with the one they brought.

Whitney steps out from behind the sculpture. "Stop what you're doing." He turns on his flashlight, pointing it at the thief. But before Whitney can focus on their face, there's a brilliant explosion—light floods his field of vision, a loud noise causes ringing in his ears. In an instant, the figure is gone.

It takes a moment for Whitney to regain his bearings; he blinks repeatedly to clear the spots from his eyes. Despite the ringing, he hears footsteps sprinting up the marble stairs. As soon as he's able, Whitney rushes after the forger.

At the top of the steps, Whitney flicks on the overhead lights—there's no point staying in the dark. A dull banging echoes through the corridor. He bolts past the "Staff Only" sign, down the hall, and turns right at the end. A figure struggles to wrench open a large double-hung window. Whitney unfastens the strap on his holster, his hand steady at his hip. He's never drawn his weapon on a suspect before; and the range is the only place he's ever fired it. But this is no ordinary suspect—someone had threatened his daughter. Someone had killed Margeaux Curtis. If it comes to it, he won't hesitate. But he'd rather not cross that line.

"There's nowhere to go," Whitney says.

The figure turns around. He's dressed in all black. The sleek running pants and slim-fit turtleneck accentuate an athletic form that is usually hidden by the suits Whitney is accustomed to seeing him wear.

"Sutton, it's over." Whitney says.

The man in black returns his attention to the window and gives another shove. The window creaks and rises an inch.

"Andrew!"

"I'm not Andrew." His fingers slide under the bottom rail, hoisting the window all the way up.

"Henry?"

Turning, the figure makes a small bow.

"Aren't you the clever one, guessing my sketch was a study of Sargent? Or was it that art student daughter of yours who figured it out? How is she, by the way? Still zipping around in that cobalt-blue Beetle? You know, there's a lot less of those on the roads these days. It'd be easy to find her." Lockhart leers at the lieutenant, daring him.

Whitney's heart beats wildly in his chest, partly from racing up the stairs and partly from his natural fight instinct surging just below the surface. He knows it was the ex-boyfriend who tampered with Laurel's car, yet Lockhart's veiled threat gets under his skin, provoking him. He suppresses the growing impulse to just shoot—he can't let the enraged-father side of himself take over. Whitney glares back at the figure.

During their standoff, Lockhart is the first to break eye contact, glancing at the lieutenant's right hand, which is dangerously close to the gun on his hip. "I'm unarmed."

Whitney's voice is low, bordering on a growl. "You came after my daughter. Did you think I'd just let that go?"

"I would never hurt a child."

He's certain Laurel would take offense to that characterization. But the slight hitch in Lockhart's voice adds sincerity to his claim. Was the threat just a mind game meant to distract him from the case? Whitney takes a deep breath, relying on his training as his tone slips back into the measured cadence of authority. "Where's Andrew?"

"There is no Andrew. He died a long time ago."

"The car crash. It was your cousin who died."

"You've been checking up on me, Lieutenant. Should I be flattered?"

Whitney assesses the situation. There's nowhere to go—they must be at least thirty feet up—so why is Lockhart at the window? He intentionally switches gears—anything to delay. "Did you always want to be an artist?" he asks.

"Artist?" He huffs. "I'm so much more than that. I create masterpieces."

Lockhart clearly doesn't suffer from impostor syndrome. Agent Smith had said art forgers often have an exaggerated ego.

"Seeing your work, there's no denying your talent," Whitney says, playing to his vanity.

"I showed a certain aptitude even at a young age. My mother used to say I was born to be an artist." Lockhart's voice trails off, his expression tightening. He turns back to the window, bracing himself against the memory he usually keeps buried—his last day with his mother. He'd won a prize in art class. To celebrate, she took him to the diner where she worked and told him to order whatever he wanted. He picked a three-scoop ice cream sundae covered in hot fudge. The next day, they left to visit his mother's sister and her family. That night, he was told his mother left for a job interview. She never returned.

Lockhart wipes his eyes on his shirtsleeve. For a moment, Whitney thinks he's about to give himself up. Static crackles through the radio. Whitney's hand slides away from the gun as he unclips the radio from his duty belt.

"Third floor," he whispers into the mouthpiece.

The sad memory that haunted Lockhart just moments ago has lost its effect. A neutral mask replaces the sorrowful expression he just wore. He maneuvers one leg outside the window, straddling the sill.

Whitney needs to keep him engaged—his mother appears to be a touchstone. "Your mother must have been very proud of your acceptance to art school."

Lockhart pauses, half in—half out the window, letting out a soft sigh. "She disappeared. The Suttons raised me, only taking me in because deserting an orphan would have reflected badly on their good name. It was made painfully clear I didn't belong in their world."

A clattering of footsteps echoes along the hallway. Lockhart leans to one side for a better view, he spots a pair of officers far behind Whitney.

"I see your friends have joined us, but unfortunately I must be going."

He picks up the painting, pulling it and his other leg through the window and disappears.

Whitney rushes after him, scrambling through the window. His foot slips out from under him as he steps out on the steeply pitched copper roof. He grabs wildly at the window casing. A tingling sensation ripples through his body, and his palms sweat.

"Careful, Lieutenant. I hope you're wearing rubber-soled shoes," Lockhart's voice calls from the darkness.

Regaining his footing and not wanting to risk another slip, Whitney continues to hold on to the window. He catches his breath and waits for his eyes to adjust before peering around the dormer.

Lockhart sits near the ridge line, knees pulled close to his chest. The Sargent painting lies flat on the roof beside him, one hand gently resting on the frame.

"Henry, how about you come down from there?"

"I quite like it up here. It's serene."

"Okay, but let's talk some more. Can you tell me what happened with the accident? Why was it reported that you died?"

Asking open-ended questions is a hostage negotiation technique— it creates time to find a peaceful solution. Whitney figures that, in this case, the Sargent painting is the hostage.

There's a long pause.

"It was spring break. I was out—took the train to the city, I think. Andrew took my car to go partying, probably swiped my driver's license in case he got a ticket. The lunkhead cops who found the body told my aunt I was dead because that was the name on the license and registration. By the time I returned home, she was drunk—not to mourn me, but to celebrate. Can you imagine? What kind of sick bitch celebrates the death of their nephew?"

Whitney ventures up the roof and adjusts his positioning, lowering his body so he's able to sit, and leans against the dormer. It feels moderately safer than standing.

"They'd left me alone in that house so often, never realizing it gave me time to discover their secrets. My uncle had a hidden safe. It took days of trying combinations until it finally popped open. Inside, I found a note saying, 'Be a stronger man than I was,' paper-clipped to my birth certificate. I was always afraid of her, and apparently wasn't the only one. The night of the accident I decided to throw it all back in her face and said, 'When you look at me, do you think about the lascivious things Russell did with your sister?' She flew at me, seething with rage, but in her drunken state, she tripped and cut her head on the table."

Lockhart's face contorts into a hideous mask as he changes the pitch of his voice, in what Whitney assumes is an imitation of his aunt. The words drip with contempt. "'You think you're so smart, you don't know shit. My sister was a temptress, a whore. The whole point of that visit was to tell me she and Russell were in love and wanted to get married, raising you and Andrew together, along with that new abomination growing in her belly. Ha! There was no way I could allow that, so I grabbed a kitchen knife and cut it out of her.'"

Whitney doesn't move, stunned by the revelation. He can only imagine the trauma it inflicted on Henry. Whitney has struggled with his own feelings of abandonment, but to learn your mother didn't leave, that your aunt murdered her, and your uncle is actually your father—that's the stuff of Shakespearean tragedies.

Lockhart draws in a long breath, then while releasing it slowly, a small sob escapes. At the sound, a wave of sympathy courses through Whitney.

"Throughout my life," Lockhart says, "I was told my mother abandoned me when really, that ... that monster killed her."

There's a long pause before he continues. "The next thing I know, my hands were around her throat squeezing. She slumped over, eyes rolling up into her head. I thought I killed her, but then she coughed and laughed, said I was weak, just like my father. I ran upstairs to clean out what I needed, including Andrew's school ID."

"Henry, I'm sorry. I can't imagine what you must have gone through that night," Whitney says, trying to connect with Lockhart. "Hating your aunt for what she did is natural. Anyone would feel the same way. I even understand your frustration with your father. I know how it feels—my father abandoned me and my mom. But weren't you and Andrew friends—the parties at college?"

"You don't have a clue what I went through. Andrew was an unremarkable snot—not my friend. He stole my car. He killed me. Me!"

Lockhart pounds his chest with his palm, his voice echoing in the darkness. He stops, taking a moment to rein in his anger. His emotions reset in the silence. When Lockhart continues, his voice is flat, dispassionate, as if he's narrating someone else's life and not his own.

"I got my things and went back downstairs. The old souse was still lying on the floor—not the first time she's blacked out from booze. For a woman who publicly prided herself on having the best of everything, in private, she lapped up the cheapest rotgut there was. I placed the bottle on the ground next to her, watching as the remaining alcohol soaked her clothes and the carpet. Aunt Patrica always enjoyed a good smoke when she drank, so I lit a cigarette and placed it between her fingers. Just as I was leaving, I saw a flame dance along her blouse and jump onto the sofa."

Whitney's stomach churns. He struggles to contain the involuntary gag reflex, sickened that Lockhart could set someone on fire. Burned flesh has a distinct odor that, once experienced, can't be forgotten. Thankfully, the darkness conceals his revulsion. He tries again to persuade Lockhart to come down.

"It's criminal how she treated you, but ..."

Lockhart cuts him off, his voice rising to a shrill, "But? But what? What about what she did? Butchering my mother—I hope she's burning in hell."

The ping-ponging between emotions concerns Whitney. Before tonight he wouldn't have thought Sutton (now Lockhart) to be suicidal. But here they are on a roof with limited options.

"Why the forgeries?" Whitney hopes that by changing the subject, he can get Lockhart to relax and talk longer. "You became Andrew, got your law degree, made a life for yourself—why the scheme? You make plenty of money, can go anywhere, do anything."

The polished, high-priced attorney version of Lockhart returns. "Oh, Lieutenant, now you disappoint me. It's never been about the money. I have a talent—I should use it. Besides, some people just don't deserve what they have."

"Did Margeaux Curtis get what she deserved? What about Hackett, you orchestrated that whole set-up didn't you?"

Lockhart sighs. "That was a shame. Margeaux was ... enchanting. If only she saw things my way. As for Lieutenant Hackett, he was just a stroke in a broader canvas."

Whitney stands, holding onto the dormer corner with one hand to steady himself. He reaches the other towards Lockhart.

"Come back inside. We can work something out."

"No, I doubt that would be in my best interest. Besides, even if charged with only depraved indifference for my aunt ..." He pauses again, lost in some unwelcome memory. "We both know that any death occurring during the commission of a felony—oh, such as grand theft—is first-degree murder. What could we possibly work out?"

One of the other officers cranes his head out the window. "Lieutenant, you okay?"

"Hold there," Whitney replies while glancing over his shoulder. As he turns his attention back to Lockhart, his weight shifts—his hand slips. He gasps, clutching at the dormer for balance.

Lockhart stands, rolls his shoulders and stretches as if preparing for a morning jog. The movement is casual, almost graceful. A tingle crawls down Whitney's spine and radiates through his arms and legs.

"This has been delightful, Lieutenant, but time to fly."

Lockhart snatches up the painting, holding it above his head, and charges.

Is he insane? Whitney dives flat against the roof. Sliding toward the edge—heart pounding, adrenaline surging—survival is his only thought.

The slick metal roof offers little resistance; his badge scrapes against it—skrrrrrt—the sound shrill in his ears. One shoe slips into open air; however, the other snags on the gutter.

Laurel's face flashes in his mind. Please hold. Please. Whitney has stopped, but he doesn't dare move. Since becoming a father, he's focused on protecting her from harm. He never considered the effect if something happened to him. He can't desert her like his father deserted him, even if it isn't his fault.

Lockhart's form hurtles toward him. Whitney braces for a kick. Instead, he leaps over Whitney's prone body.

"Goodbye, Lieutenant."

Lockhart soars from the roof. Whitney stares in disbelief. Time seems to freeze as Lockhart hangs suspended in midair before disappearing into the night. Holy shit, Whitney thinks, he's going to make it.

One October, when Laurel was still in high school, Whitney took her and Sydney to a pumpkin festival in Tarrytown, New York. The quaint little town was the setting for Washington Irving's *The Legend of Sleepy Hollow* and now hosts a popular Halloween festival. Giant, fire-breathing dragons made entirely from pumpkins greet visitors to the fairgrounds. And at night, a caped headless horseman rides through town.

The girls carved jack-o'-lanterns and sampled every pumpkin-themed food there was, including pumpkin pie, pumpkin ice cream, pumpkin bread, deep-fried pumpkin seeds, and candied pumpkin. Whitney tried the pumpkin beer.

The festival's main draw was the various pumpkin-throwing competitions, starting with children, followed by teens, then adults, culminating with the grand finale when the festival workers rolled out a trebuchet to launch obscenely huge pumpkins. A hush would descend over the audience as the giant gourds sailed through the air. Gravity eventually pulled the pumpkins back to earth with a loud, squishy splat, causing the crowd to erupt in cheers.

Moments after Lockhart jumped from the roof, a thick, wet splat echoes in the dark, triggering a memory of erupting pumpkins. Whitney's stomach lurches. He climbs through the window, then directs the second unit to the grounds behind the museum. Trotting past the other officers, he hears one of them say, "Son of a bitch jumped."

Usually the setting for elegant fundraisers, the courtyard is now the scene of a gruesome accident. As a police officer, Whitney's seen more dead bodies than he'd care to remember—some looked peaceful, as if asleep, but others not so much. With each of them, there's always an underlying thread of sadness.

A little while ago, when taunted by Lockhart, the overprotective, fatherly side of Whitney wanted to throttle the man. Now, looking at the corpse, all he feels is sadness at the loss of the person and the talent. Some might say it's justice; he got what he deserved. But Whitney wonders how things could have turned out if Henry's mother wasn't murdered all those years ago.

Lockhart's body lies on the flagstone pavers, his right leg bent at an unnatural angle, his head encircled by a large pool of blood. The broken frame of the Sargent painting lies just beyond his outstretched right hand. A screeching wail of an ambulance, faint at first, grows louder. Henry Lockhart/Andrew Sutton is pronounced dead at the scene.

CHAPTER 36

Whitney calls the museum director to report that the Sargent painting is now in police custody as evidence, and that the frame was damaged. The director's voice shifts from anger to relief as he learns the canvas survived its brief, ill-fated stint as a hang glider.

His job at the scene completed, Whitney returns to the station house. While typing his report, he notices the utility invoices taken from Sutton's apartment. Residual adrenaline is still coursing through his body from his near fall from the roof; chasing a new lead feels like a better use of his energy than sitting at a desk. After filling out the form for a search warrant, Whitney rushes out of the station and heads to the judge's home.

The judge is wearing a paisley robe, striped pajamas, and a scowl on his face when he opens the door.

"I know it's late, Your Honor, but I need to secure the location. There could be other paintings, and Sutton may have had an accomplice," Whitney says.

The last part he adds to stress urgency. It may be misleading, but it's not impossible. Just because Sutton and Lockhart were the same person doesn't mean someone else isn't involved.

The judge hands back the signed warrant, yawns, and closes the door.

It's Old Brookville, so Whitney is not surprised to find a manned guardhouse at the entrance. The property owner spends most of their time out of state, and retains a private security company to watch over their residence.

"Good evening. Does Mr. Andrew Sutton rent a garage on this property?" Whitney asks.

"Garage? Oh, you must mean the carriage house. Yeah, Mr. Sutton rents that."

"I'd like to see it," Whitney says, flashing his badge.

"Does Mr. Sutton know you're here?"

"Andrew Sutton leaped to his death earlier tonight. I have a search warrant to inspect the property."

"Oh, jeez, that's a shame. Okay, come on in."

The wrought-iron gates swing inaudibly on their electronically controlled hinges.

"Follow the driveway. You'll see a spur off to the right that leads to the carriage house," the guard says. "Here's the key. I need to call the office so they can notify the owner."

Whitney pulls up to a quaint-looking structure. From the different brickwork patterns, it's clear the building has been modified from its original use. At one time, two pairs of large double doors allowed carriages to pass through. Since then, one entryway has been bricked over, the other converted into a front door with windows on either side.

He enters and flicks on the lights. The large, open space is Lockhart's art studio. Standing in the center of the room is an easel, brushes and paints are arranged in precise rows on a nearby table. In front of the easel is a large free-standing corkboard with the museum giclée print of *A Garden in Florence* pinned to it, along with detailed sketches.

The studio is cold, in both temperature and by its minimalist decor. The carriage house mirrors his condo in that it too lacks any personal items.

A soft electric hum fills the space. Whitney closes his eyes while trying to locate the source. To his right. He looks—a staircase. As he ascends, the noise grows louder. It's late in the year to be running an air conditioner.

The upstairs is just as open as the first floor, but here paintings cover most of the wall space. Lockhart transformed the loft into an art gallery. The one item disrupting that illusion is the bed. Above it hangs a small landscape—is this a place of honor, or just segregated from the others?

Even after catching Lockhart with the Sargent painting, Whitney feels a rush of triumph as he stares at the abstract Kenneth Thorpe artwork. He recognizes two other paintings: Mark Baldwin's Vincent Mellor piece— a bright, red-hulled boat docked next to a haphazard pile of lobster traps—and Benjamin Curtis' haystack painting by Etienne Renarde. Even with the naked eye, Whitney can see a scratch in the latter's surface.

Eight other paintings decorate the walls that he doesn't have a clue about. Could they be Lockhart's own works, or other stolen originals? Whitney taps a number into his phone and leaves a message. He's counting on Agent Smith to call back soon. It's not Gardner Museum big, but finding three—maybe more—stolen paintings should merit a quick response

Between the paintings, thick charcoal-gray velvet drapes hide the windows. Whitney wonders if that's for privacy—or to protect the art from sunlight? He continues his search and locates the source of the humming: a self-draining dehumidifier unit. He notes that the thermostat is set at 63 degrees. Lockhart took great care to ensure the environment would preserve the artwork.

In the back corner of the upstairs is a small bathroom and closet. The door creaks as Whitney opens the closet and is surprised by its contents. Unlike what he found at Sutton's home—an array of tailored suits grouped by brand label—only two items hang here: a pair of white carpenter pants and a blue-striped oxford shirt. On the floor is a pair of white sneakers with a single drop of black paint on the toe. Whitney smirks, amused by the contrast between Lockhart's pristine painting clothes and the splattered mess that adorns Laurel's.

The expression fades quickly as the memory of Lockhart's broken body surfaces. His words, "I would never harm a child," linger in Whitney's mind, and he believes them—Lockhart's moral line feels all the more poignant given that there was no one to protect him.

Tucked further back on the closet floor is an old brown cardboard box, affixed with a faded orange sticker: "Cremated Remains." Why keep the ashes? Whitney shakes his head, astonished by the tangled threads of Lockhart's life.

Agent Smith returns Whitney's call in less than thirty minutes. They arrange an on-site meeting at 8:00 a.m. Whitney takes photos of all the paintings, using both the station's camera and his cell phone. Not knowing how the Art Crime Division operates, he uploads the images from his cell phone to a cloud account, just to be safe. In previous dealings with the Feds, teamwork wasn't part of the playbook.

Back downstairs, Whitney checks the kitchen: an espresso maker, a single demitasse cup, and in the fridge, a loaf of bread, cheese, and apples—a ready-to-go still life.

After finishing his search, Whitney locks the door behind him and heads back to his car. A rosy glow in the east pushes the blackness away. Whitney sets the timer on his phone, allowing himself a brief nap before Agent Smith's arrival.

A light tap on his window startles Whitney awake. Agent Smith stands there, holding a cup of coffee. Whitney grabs his phone—eight minutes remain on the timer.

"Looks like you could use this," Smith says, handing him the coffee as he exits the car.

Smith's team busies themselves unpacking bins from a nondescript, bluish-black cargo van while he and Whitney discuss the events of the previous night.

Any concerns Whitney had about being cut out of the case prove unfounded—perhaps because the Art Crimes Division is so small they welcome any outside help, or maybe Agent Smith just isn't a power-hungry jackass.

Smith explains their next steps: they'll study the paintings they know are forgeries, then, using what they learn from Lockhart's techniques, they'll examine the other pieces. He admits that the authentication process will take a long time, unfortunately. If it's determined Lockhart didn't create the unknown paintings, the next challenge will be to find the legitimate owners.

The art squad busies themselves packing each painting with care. They also confiscate Lockhart's paints and brushes for chemical analysis.

CHAPTER 37

Teddy struggles to stay awake as he rides home on the Long Island Rail Road. The gentle rocking of the train eventually lulls him into a peaceful sleep. When he wakes, he finds himself alone. Thankfully, the Oyster Bay station is the last stop; otherwise, he would have ended up somewhere in Suffolk County.

Earlier that day, he'd delivered several pieces to one of his collectors in the city. He prefers dealing with the cluttered, intimate shops of Greenwich Village over the glitzy Manhattan Art & Antiques Center. It may be riskier doing business one-on-one, but in the city's labyrinth of tiny stores, Teddy figures he's a needle hiding among haystacks.

Today's buyer is someone he's worked with a lot over the years. The shop owner always greets him with the same joke: "Hi ya, Rosie! How's your friend Sue?" When he first started, Teddy introduced himself as Theodore Roosevelt Smith, explaining that his parents were great admirers of the former president, but that everyone called him "Rosie." It's a convincing lie because it contains elements of the truth.

The idea of a man having a woman's name amused the shop owner— hence the greeting, a reference to the Johnny Cash song *A Boy Named Sue*. Teddy often wonders if the shop owner knows the song was actually written by children's author Shel Silverstein.

Teddy is in a good mood—the price of silver is high, and he got more than he hoped. He takes the long way home through Roosevelt Park and visits the Theodore Roosevelt Monument Assemblage—a collection of stones representing different moments from the former president's life. He traces his fingers along a boulder from San Juan Hill and a stone from the Adirondacks, where Roosevelt learned he'd become president— a fitting tribute to a man who loved nature and his own legend in equal measure, truly.

Teddy follows the path to the beach. Something about the smell of the sea air is spiritual. He feels closer to God here, on the shore, than he ever did in a church. He pauses, admiring the bits of orange and gold reflected on the bay's dark water, the rhythmic sound of the waves soothing his mind. Teddy closes his eyes and prays. He gave up asking forgiveness for his crimes long ago. Now he asks God for only one thing—please make Rose well.

By the time Teddy winds his way through the park and onto West End Road, the sky has turned a dark shade of purple. A few blocks later, he sees a reassuring sight—his house is aglow. The thought of a dark house, or an ambulance in front, terrifies him. He enters and hangs his coat on a peg by the door. A savory aroma of roasted chicken wafts from the kitchen to greet him.

Chandice calls out, "I have a surprise for you."

As he steps into the small kitchen, he sees Rose sitting at the table, cutting vegetables. A smile tugs at Teddy's face. He blinks hard, willing back the tears, hoping the women don't notice.

"Now what's this? If you're bringing in a sous chef to help with the cooking, that's coming out of your salary."

He crosses the well-worn linoleum flooring to where his wife is seated at the far side of the table. Teddy wraps his arms around Rose and whispers, "How are you, my love?"

Good, I feel alive," Rose answers, with more strength and conviction than he's heard in her voice in months.

"Well, in that case, let's celebrate."

Teddy releases his hold on his wife and turns to the counter behind him. He pushes the button on the old transistor radio and, after adjusting the dial, bows to his wife, holding out one hand. Rose stands unassisted, rising in a fluid, graceful motion. Teddy draws her near, and they sway to Joe Cocker's raspy *You Are So Beautiful*.

Rose looks up at Teddy, her eyes glistening. "I think the treatments are working."

"Then the prayers of this old sinner have been answered."

"In that case, we need to work on saving you next. We'll go to St. Dominick's on Sunday."

"OK, you two lovebirds, are you going to dance or help me with dinner?" Chandice interrupts.

"Dance," they reply in unison.

The next song begins, *I Don't Want to Miss a Thing* by Aerosmith.

Teddy twirls Rose in a gentle circle.

Chandice can't help but smile. "Well, all right, just keep clear of the stove."

The next morning, Teddy awakens to the smell of coffee and eggs. He ambles downstairs to the small kitchen. Chandice arrived early and is at the stove frying eggs while humming to herself. Without turning around, she asks, "You're coming with us today, right?"

Teddy looks down at his feet, feeling guilty about the many times he couldn't. "Yes, I'm coming today. I always want to be there for her, but the insurance doesn't cover it all. I'm doing the best I can."

"I know, she just misses you when you aren't here. Take these up to her." Chandice hands him a plate with eggs and toast.

Teddy lingers at the doorway of their bedroom, watching his wife sleep, as waves of love and regret wash over him. He leans close and kisses Rose on the cheek.

"Good morning, my love," Teddy murmurs.

Rose's eyes flutter open.

"Ta-da, breakfast in bed, m'lady. I wanted to take you out for a day on the town, but that shrew downstairs insists we go see some witch doctor instead."

Rose sits up. "Dr. Caslon, you mean, and you're coming with us today, right? Can we do something special afterward?"

"Of course, anything for my best girl. You just name it."

Her eyes twinkle as she flashes her husband a mischievous smile. It's the same smile that hooked him long ago when they were teenagers.

"I'm in for it now, aren't I?"

Rose nods while eating her eggs.

In the doctor's waiting room, Teddy paces in circles, occasionally stopping to pick up a magazine only to put it immediately back down. Chandice reads her textbook, unfazed by Teddy's anxiety.

Rose emerges from the exam room and reassures the pair that she is just fine—and hungry. They go to Rose's favorite restaurant for lunch.

After they place their orders for shepherd's pie, Rose is silent, folding and unfolding her napkin—her nervous tell. Teddy casts a worried glance at Chandice, who replies with a shrug.

"I have something to tell you both," Rose starts. She looks back and forth between the two people she most cherishes.

A wary silence falls over the group.

Rose takes a deep breath, then blurts, "Dr. Caslon says I'm in complete remission and won't have to see him for another year."

It takes a moment for her husband and aide to process what was said. Teddy's jaw goes slack and he leaps from his chair so fast it nearly topples. He races around the table and sweeps Rose into a hug. After keeping his emotions restrained all morning, the tears come easily. He lifts her off the floor and spins her around as Chandice breaks into applause.

"Teddy, everyone is watching," Rose says.

"Hot plate." The waiter calls as he approaches with the lunches.

Teddy releases Rose and holds her chair while she sits. He then returns to his seat, wiping his eyes on his shirtsleeve.

"Anything else?" the waiter asks.

"Yes, we're celebrating. Bring over a bottle of champagne," Teddy says.

When they finish their meal the threesome go to a nearby beach. Rose is feeling more energetic than she has in months. She and Teddy walk hand in hand along the shore. Chandice waits on a bench, allowing the couple to have some time alone. It's a clear, crisp day. The wind coming off the water stings Teddy's ears, but as long as Rose is happy, he'll walk through fire for her, or more befitting the weather, cross a tundra for her. It dawns on him that he'll no longer have to be the Squire. The weight he's carried for so long slips.

"Can we go shopping?" Rose asks. "I want to get a little present for Chandice. She's been so wonderful to me."

"Of course, my darling."

"I saw a shop near the restaurant. You'll have to distract her. I want it to be a surprise."

"Okay, I'll come up with some kind of excuse, but you'll need to be quick. She watches over you like a mother hen."

"It's sweet how she looks after me. I might not be needing her help so much now, and I want Chandice to know how much I appreciate all she's done."

As they head back to the car, Teddy claims the downstairs toilet needs a replacement ballcock and he wants to stop at the hardware store. Rose suggests she and Chandice visit O'Leary's Gifts to window shop. She winks at her husband, smiling at the shared ruse.

He parks on the street in front of the gift shop. Linking arms, Rose and Chandice head toward the storefront, its windows reflecting the colorful bouquets from the flower shop across the street. A bell jingles as they open the door. Linking arms, she and Chandice head toward the storefront, its windows reflecting the colorful bouquets from the flower shop across the street.

The women stroll around the quaint Irish import store, looking at hand-knit sweaters, Belleek figurines, and Waterford crystal. Once Teddy joins them, Rose nods and makes a swirling motion with her hands, indicating it's time to distract Chandice.

He rummages through the paper bag and pulls out the receipt. "That clerk made a mistake, this doesn't add up. Chandice, get out that fancy phone of yours and double-check this for me."

The aide makes her way through the narrow aisles to where Teddy is standing. Her handbag dangles from her elbow as she searches for her phone.

Rose signals to the shopkeeper, pointing to a gold necklace with seed pearls. He disappears briefly, returning with a small green box tied with a white ribbon, which Rose slips into her coat pocket.

Chandice checks the hardware purchase on her calculator app, then double-checks at Teddy's insistence. "This adds up fine."

"Quick, come here before Rosie sees. What do you think of this?" He points to a large Waterford crystal pineapple with gold leaves.

"It's nice, but a bit extravagant for Rose's taste, don't you think?" Chandice picks up a lap quilt with a Celtic knot pattern. "I think she'd be much happier with this."

"Okay. Will you take her to the car? I want to buy this without her knowing."

Teddy adds a smaller crystal pineapple to his purchase. He'll finally be able to keep his promise and take Rosie to Hawaii.

The mood in the car during the ride home is joyful, filled with laughter and sly glances between the different conspirators. Teddy parks the car close to the front walkway and assists Rose into the house. Chandice follows behind, carrying the bag with the quilt. She's about to say good-bye when Rose hands her the wrapped box. "Don't open this until you get home. It's a little thank you gift."

Chandice bends over to hug Rose. "Thank you, and I'll see you tomorrow."

"Take the day off. I'm spending tomorrow at home," Teddy says.

The couple snuggle together on the couch under the new quilt. He flicks on the TV and finds a Cary Grant movie marathon—*Bringing Up Baby*, followed by *Arsenic and Old Lace*. It's the best day Teddy could have hoped for. The crystal pineapple sits on top of a Hawaiian vacation brochure next to the remote control. Shortly after Cary Grant's character, Mortimer, discovers a body in the window seat, Rose falls asleep.

CHAPTER 38

The rooftop confrontation with Lockhart and the long hours inspecting his studio have left Whitney drained—physically and mentally. He's a little amazed there isn't more adrenaline keeping him awake. Within moments of lying down, he's sleeping soundly— no black voids dragging him down. Then a strange, persistent noise interrupts his well-deserved rest. As his mental fog lifts, Whitney realizes it's his phone buzzing.

"This is Whitney," he mumbles, glancing at the bedside clock. It reads 3:53 a.m.

"Hi, Lieutenant. It's Ezra Ryan. I found the cup."

"What the hell are you talking about, Ryan?"

"Miss Tierney's cup—the one the Squire stole. I think I found it."

Whitney bolts upright, his head suddenly clear. "Where are you?"

Twenty-five minutes later, with a to-go coffee cup in hand, Whitney meets Ryan at Glen Cove Hospital.

"Start from the beginning, Ryan."

"I was on overnight duty with EMS, and an emergency call came in. While preparing the woman for transport, I noticed a shell-shaped cup on a tray in the bedroom. It even has faded painted flowers on it, just as Miss Tierney described."

"You think the patient is the Squire?" Whitney asks.

"No. Her husband. The woman's been sick a long time. It's unlikely she'll make it. The husband is with her now and hasn't left her side since we brought her in."

"Give me the address. I'll get a warrant and check it out. Stay here and monitor him."

After rousing the striped-pajamaed judge for yet another warrant, Whitney makes the short drive to the address in Oyster Bay. It's a small, two-story home with a front porch that wraps around one side.

He enters the house and proceeds upstairs to the bedroom. Whitney finds the Belleek cup on the tray, just where Ryan said it would be. He lifts the cup by sticking a pen through the delicate handle, and brings it to eye level. It definitely has faded daisy-like flowers painted on it. He places the cup into an evidence bag.

Whitney scans the room—no silver in sight. In fact, there's very little in the room at all. He makes his way through the rest of the spartan house. If this is where the Squire lives, he's not selling his spoils to achieve a luxury lifestyle. It's curious how two thieves, Lockhart and now the Squire, both targeted the Gold Coast Brookvilles, yet they themselves live in such austere dwellings. At least this home is cozy.

He heads outside to look over the single-car garage in the backyard. The judge had narrowed the scope of the warrant to include only the main house, since that was where Officer Ryan saw the cup. The garage door is locked. Whitney peers through the small window, raising his hand to block the glare of the rising sun. The garage is uncluttered: Hand tools hang from a pegboard, and small jars line the work shelf. Of course, a stockpile of silver left out in the open would have been too much to hope for.

Once the evidence is logged and the DA consulted, Whitney submits an arrest warrant electronically. He prefers the old paper method—it's how he was trained—but for speed, he files through his tablet. Two lesser reasons also guide his choice: staying current with technological advances—always a good thing—and avoiding a third off-hour visit to the same judge—a definite bad thing.

Driving back to the hospital, Whitney thinks how small things—a sketch, an old teacup—can crack open a case. As he reaches the emergency department, raised voices emanate from inside the room Ryan is guarding. They rush inside.

The husband shouts at the doctor, "They said she was better, that she was in remission!"

The doctor places his hand on the man's shoulder and leans close to whisper. The man falls to his knees, sobbing.

Whitney shows the doctor his badge and tells Ryan to get a glass of water as they move the man to a chair. The doctor explains that Mrs. Seaman has just died—cancer.

"She told me it was gone for good this time," Teddy says to no one in particular.

Ryan arrives with the water. "Here, drink this," he says, handing the man a paper cup.

Teddy looks up, meeting Whitney's eyes. "You a cop?"

Whitney nods.

"He's one too?" Teddy asks, jerking his head in Ryan's direction. "I suppose you want to talk to me."

"I'm sorry for your loss, but yes, we do need to talk. After you take care of the final paperwork for your wife, I'll drive you to the Old Brookville station house."

Teddy draws a slow breath. The air feels heavier, his clothes heavier still, and he's not sure he can stay upright under the weight. His mind grasps at the happy memories from only the day before—walking the beach with Rose, making plans for the future—but the images keep slipping away.

A hospital representative hands him a clipboard with forms. He signs without reading. The rest happens in a blur. The officers escort him from the hospital. One tells him he's under arrest while the other gently brings his arms behind his back and fastens the handcuffs. Someone reads him his Miranda rights, the voice distant and muffled. He says nothing for the entire ride to the station.

Whitney places him in an interview room with Sergeant Stone, then heads to the kitchenette to get coffee for the widower. As the microwave reheats hours-old coffee, Whitney places a quick call to Chief Eaves.

Looking through the conference room window, Whitney watches as Sergeant Stone consoles their suspect. He feels conflicted—it doesn't feel right bringing in a man so soon after his wife passed away. But the Squire has been elusive for years; Whitney isn't about to let him disappear on his watch.

Teddy's face bears the heavy burden of grief, making him look older than his age. The overhead fluorescent lighting makes him look older still. Whitney enters and sits across the table from the enigmatic Squire.

"Are you Ernest Seaman?" he asks, placing the coffee cup before him. The man ignores both the question and the offering.

Whitney tries again.

"Mr. Seaman, you've been through quite a shock, and I'm sorry for your loss. Did you understand the rights I read to you earlier? Are you ready to talk to us?"

The man's head hangs low. Without looking up he says, "I did, I do. I just think maybe I should wait to bury Rose first."

Whitney places a plastic evidence bag containing the seashell teacup on the table. "What can you tell me about this?"

Seaman lifts his head slightly, enabling him to glimpse the bag.

"That's my wife's. It belonged to her mother."

"Has she had it long?"

"Since she was a young girl. Her mother died when she was a child."

"And she's had it all this time?"

The man murmurs, "Uh-huh."

"Now, the funny thing is, I have a report of this same item being stolen during the past year."

"It's just a teacup," Seaman replies under his breath, turning away.

"Is it? It looks unique to me—a seashell cup with little seashell feet. It's Belleek, that's an Irish pottery brand. Why, you could drink in the Irish Sea with a cup like that."

Seaman's eyes grow wide as he snaps his head back, meeting Whitney's gaze. A flash of panic crosses his face, then disappears just as quickly.

Whitney continues, "What makes it even more unique are the painted flowers on the sides. The woman who owned this cup treasured it because it belonged to her mother. She and her sister painted the flowers."

"Sisters," Seaman croaks, his eyes welling up. "Never considered it. Rose was small when her mother died. She only remembered a teacup with some flowers—I figured some other kid had painted one like it."

Sergeant Stone leaves the conference room, returning with a box of tissues. She places them on the table. Teddy yanks one out, dabs at his eyes and blows his nose.

"Mr. Seaman, the teacup wasn't the only thing you took from that home. Do you have more to tell us?"

He looks around the room. His reason for being—Rose—his reason for everything, is gone. Whatever happens now doesn't matter. He lets out a deep sigh. "It's from Glenwood. I took the cup and a pair of silver tastevins. I'm the one you call the Squire."

They'd barely tied him to the stolen cups. Yet after all these years, the Squire just confessed.

Stunned by the revelation, it takes Whitney a moment to focus back on the investigation. "How'd this start?" he asks.

"It was supposed to be a short-term solution. Rose was sick. The little insurance we had barely covered her treatments. At first, I borrowed just to get us through the first round of chemo. Those people have so much. I thought if I just took something small—something they wouldn't notice—we could get by. And once Rose got better, I would return what I took. My plan worked in the beginning, before you and the press even knew about me. But the cancer kept coming back, always worse than before. I couldn't keep up."

A half-hearted chuckle escapes as he continues, "People are funny. Some clients actually seemed glad I stole from them."

Whitney passes a pen and pad across to Seaman.

"Write it down, with as much detail as you can."

He spends a few minutes scribbling, then passes the pad back to Whitney. The now-familiar handwriting lists a few homes and the items taken from them.

Seaman admits to taking the Belleek cup and the two silver tastevins from Glenwood, as well as taking Alice Madison's picture frames years ago. It would have been helpful to speak with Mrs. Madison, despite the extensive coverage the theft received. Unfortunately, the actress passed away not long after the frames' mysterious return. Included on his list are three other items he claims to have taken and since returned. His confession acknowledges only a small number of thefts compared to all the cases on file. But Whitney knows the chief will want to press charges for as many burglaries as possible against the Squire.

Needing more information, Whitney takes a different approach. "Where are the tastevins?"

"I'd rather not get anyone in trouble or ruin someone's reputation. I brought them to a collector to appraise. That person had no reason to question my ownership."

"We'd like to talk to them just the same and return the cups to the Voses."

"I like you, Lieutenant Whitney, I really do. But I'm tired. Today's been ..." Seaman closes his eyes and swallows hard. "... the worst day of my life. I don't want to talk anymore, especially without legal representation. I'd also like to call Chandice—Rose's nurse."

"Mr. Seaman, Sergeant Stone is going to take you downstairs to be booked. You can make your call after that."

Seaman stands, he looks like a broken man, nothing like the dashing romantic figure so many people imagine the Squire to be. It's obvious the loss of his wife devastated him. Whitney sympathizes, so he adds, "Are you hungry? I can order some food for you."

"That's most kind, but no thanks." He shuffles out of the room.

Whitney returns to his desk. Following up on the details of the Squire's confession is not straightforward. First, he has to research the locations, since Seaman identified the homes by building name, like Glenwood. A visit to the Wolver Hollow Historical Society provides him the information he needs.

Computers work great if someone has already input the data, but there's nothing like asking an old-timer when you need obscure town history. Now with the addresses in hand, Whitney runs a reverse lookup to get the names and phone numbers of the homeowners.

His first call is to Mrs. Grayson, who sounds offended that the Squire didn't leave behind his trademark note card—a status symbol among his victims.

"I don't even know what a sugar caster is, or where to begin looking for it. Are you sure he took it from my house?" Mrs. Grayson asks.

"It's listed in our suspect's statement," Whitney replies.

"Say, since you have the Squire in custody, can you get him to write a note for me? Bitsy Monroe has hers framed in her living room."

Unbelievable, Whitney thinks—victims wanting mementos.

The second number rings for an inordinate time without an answer. Whitney circles the name Moorefield, adding a question mark to remind himself to dig deeper.

A personal secretary answers his third call, takes a detailed message, and says they'll relay it as soon as it's a decent hour to call Berlin.

Chief Eaves arrives, along with the county prosecutor in tow, for an update regarding the Squire and to determine the strength of the evidence against him. Whitney shows them Mr. Seaman's written confession.

"That's it?" Eaves asks. "What about the recent robberies?"

"That's all the information he's willing to share. He's asked to have an attorney present from now on," Whitney replies.

"Confessing to five burglaries—that should be plenty, right?" Chief Eaves directs his question at the prosecutor.

"Four of which were supposedly returned," the prosecutor points out. "Not that it matters legally. But his attorney could argue he didn't actually steal those items—he's just distraught over the loss of his wife and seeking attention. From what I understand, the Glenwood case is the only one with physical evidence. Charge him with that for now. He's a sympathetic character, practically adored by the public. If we go after him too hard, it'll backfire. Let's wait and see what else comes to light."

Over the next few hours, Whitney fields calls from the public defender's office, all five mayors, reporters from The New York Times, Newsday, The Daily News, and The New York Post, as well as radio and TV producers. He briefly fantasizes about his first order as chief: hiring a public relations officer. It seems like for every call he finishes, two more queue up. Finally, he's through—almost—one last call and then he can go home. He dials the number for Miss Tierney.

On his way out, Whitney checks the holding cell. Theodore Seaman is asleep on the cot.

At home, Laurel is busy typing on her laptop. She looks up when she hears her father enter. "Sooooo, what's new, Dad? Anything interesting happen today?"

"No, not really, sweetheart. Same old, same old," he says, hanging up his jacket.

"What?! Come on, it's all over the news—you caught the Squire."

"Oh, that? Well, yes, that happened. Actually, it was your friend Ryan who identified him."

Her eyes grow wide. "Really? How'd he figure it out? What's the Squire like?"

"I'll tell you what I can over dinner."

Laurel is too excited to cook, and Whitney doesn't want to go out, dreading questions from curious diners. The pair finally settles on grilled cheese sandwiches and salad. Whitney gives a quick synopsis of how they identified and caught the Squire.

"Why'd he take silver? Did he say?" Laurel asks.

"He used to make deliveries to the estates when he was young. He remembered watching the staff polish the silver while preparing for formal dinners. Life has gotten a lot more casual since then; he figured the silver sets were just sitting there neglected. His plan was that when his wife got better, he'd pick up extra work and buy the items back. But with her increasing medical needs, the entire scheme snowballed out of control."

"Let me get this straight," she says. "He's stealing antique silver, with the intent to buy it back and return the pieces—and incredibly, it's working. But then why does he leave notes calling attention to himself?"

"Good question, my junior detective. I'm not sure he fully knows himself. My guess is part guilt, part ego."

"He won't go to prison, will he? He didn't hurt anyone."

"He still broke the law, sweetheart. That's something we can't ignore."

"But he had his reasons."

"Ask anyone in prison, and they'll tell you they had their reasons."

"Not good reasons, I'll bet," Laurel mutters.

The hypocrisy gnaws at him, and Whitney loses interest in his sandwich. If it were him, wouldn't he do anything to save Laurel?

Whitney eyes his daughter. Like most women on the North Shore— and probably a good number of the men, too—she already imagines the Squire as a swashbuckling figure. When they hear his justification— a husband's desperate attempt to care for his ailing wife—the Squire's legend will only grow.

At first, he's relieved that Laurel isn't as interested in Henry Lockhart as she is in the Squire, perhaps because Lockhart's motives weren't altruistic like Seaman's, or perhaps the ghastly ends spoil the intrigue. Still, Whitney wants to make it clear the danger is gone.

"We found a stationery box in Henry Lockhart's studio. It contained Smythson note cards, the same as the one I received. Also in the box was a fountain pen and Montblanc gray ink, matching the ink on the card."

Laurel doesn't respond.

"I bring this up because I want you to know you're safe."

"Why'd he want to hurt me?" Laurel asks, her voice slightly quivering.

"He didn't, at least that's what he said. His objective was to frighten me, throw me off balance—which it accomplished, by the way.

"But he killed Mrs. Curtis and messed with my car. I'm still kinda freaked out by that. How'd he know where to find me?"

Whitney sighs. He'll have to tell her the entire story.

"Sutton, or rather Lockhart, didn't touch your car. It was Sculptor Boy, Birk. He saw you with Ryan and let the air out of your tires. He didn't know about the note. It was just a coincidence. I didn't tell you right away because until we identified who really sent the threat, you were still at risk. If you knew it was that dopey ex of yours who tampered with the car, you'd have let your guard down and not taken the situation seriously. And I needed you to take what happened very seriously."

Laurel sits for a moment, staring at the uneaten half of her grilled cheese sandwich.

"Birk's a jerk," she says, then giggles. "That rhymes, and it's perfect. Birk is a jerk."

Whitney can't agree more.

CHAPTER 39

The following morning, Katherine Tierney arrives at the station house precisely at 9:00, escorted by Caleb Vos. Whitney leads them into the conference room. On the tabletop rest three mugs, several plates, a stack of napkins, a coffee carafe, and a white bakery box. It's a gesture of respect to Miss Tierney. The station's typical welcoming offerings include weak or burned coffee in a paper cup.

"Coffee?" Whitney asks.

"Aye, thank you," Miss Tierney replies.

Caleb nods.

Whitney pours the coffee into the three mugs and passes them around. Opening the box, he offers its contents. "Danish? They're not as good as the madeleines, but they're fresh from a local bakery."

To be polite, Miss Tierney reaches for an apricot danish. She takes a small bite and places it on a plate in front of her. Mr. Vos declines the pastry.

"We've heard you caught the Squire. Is that true?" Vos asks.

"It appears so. Miss Tierney, can you identify this?"

Whitney sets the evidence bag with the teacup on the table. She lifts it, hesitant at first, then turns it over several times in her hands. He sees her eyes well up, but not a single tear falls.

Finally, she says, "Yes, this is mine."

Whitney explains how Officer Ryan discovered the cup and Mr. Seaman's confession to being the Squire. He tells the story of Seaman's wife, an orphan from Ireland adopted by an American couple, who had very few memories of her original home, except for painting a teacup with her sister. When she became sick, Mr. Seaman resorted to stealing to pay her medical bills. Finding a cup similar to the one his wife described, he felt compelled to take it.

Throughout Whitney's recap, Miss Tierney folds and unfolds her napkin—her movements deliberate, methodical. She's so engrossed in the process that Whitney wonders if she's listening at all.

He finishes. No one responds at first. The wall clock ticks away several seconds before Miss Tierney asks, "What about the Tiffany tastevins?"

At that moment, Whitney understands how she earned her nickname, "the General." Miss Tierney's composure never wavers. Even after learning that she and her long-lost sister were separated not by an ocean but by a short drive—and that truth only revealed after her sister's death—her concern remains for her employer's property.

"The Squire—Mr. Seaman, that is—isn't willing to divulge who he sold the pieces to. He claims the buyers believe he owned the silver, and he doesn't want to make trouble for anyone."

"He was Maeve's husband, and he did all of this to take care of her?" she asks.

"It appears that way, though records show her name was Rosemary."

"She was born Maeve Roisin. Her adoptive parents must have changed it to Rosemary to sound more American. I'd like to have my cup back."

"Of course. Once the indictment is in place and the court case concluded. For now, it remains evidence."

"Oh, come on, Lieutenant, is that necessary?" Vos asks.

"It is. Miss Tierney's cup, being so unique, was how our officer made the identification that enabled us to catch the Squire."

"I understand," Miss Tierney says. "I'd like to meet Mr. Seaman. He's my sister's husband, after all."

"Yes, of course. Follow me, please."

Both Tierney and Vos stand.

"Mr. Vos, if you wouldn't mind waiting here, I'd like to update you on your missing Thorpe painting."

"You'll be okay, Katherine?" Vos asks.

She nods and follows Whitney out of the conference room and downstairs to the holding cell, where Ernest Seaman is reading a newspaper.

Whitney apologizes for the limited accommodations as he brings over one of the cushioned office chairs for Miss Tierney, rather than have her sit on a metal folding chair. He tells Officer Byrne to get Miss Tierney anything she needs.

Whitney then returns to Vos, informing him that they recovered his Thorpe painting, along with the details of the crime. Vos is stunned to learn that Andrew Sutton was Henry Lockhart.

"When he first approached me looking for work, I only agreed because I vaguely remembered there was a family tragedy. My memories of Andrew from Cornell are hazy and unimpressive. Honestly, based on just the few times I met him, I liked Henry better. Andrew—the real Andrew—was cocky and careless. Out of sympathy, I threw a little work his way. Over time, he proved himself to be an excellent attorney. I considered him a friend. Now, I don't know what to think," Vos says, a trace of sadness in his voice.

There's an electronic ping. Vos takes out his phone, presses some buttons and returns the device to his jacket pocket.

"I have another appointment. We should check on Katherine."

They head downstairs. At the bottom, Vos freezes—his jaw tightens, eyes narrow. "What's the meaning of this?" he demands, gesturing sharply toward the cell. Seaman sits inside, head down, forearms resting on his knees. Beside him, to Vos' astonishment, sits Katherine Tierney.

"'Tis all right, Caleb," she says, calm but firm. "Clearly, Ernest must remain in here, so I asked the officer to let me join him."

Whitney grabs the keys from Byrne.

"She insisted, Lieutenant. What was I supposed to do?" the officer asks apologetically.

Whitney opens the cell door, and Miss Tierney and Ernest stand up.

"I have to go now, Ernest. I'll be back soon. But before I do—may I ask, did my sister have a happy life?"

"I tried my very best to see to that. From the moment we met, I loved Rose with all my heart. I'll keep loving her until the end of time. And please, call me Teddy."

"I believe you, Teddy. And thank you."

She steps out of the cell. "Caleb, I'll need your best recommendation for an attorney to represent my brother-in-law."

A guilty plea is unlikely, but the prosecutor hopes for a nolo contendere plea, meaning no contest, which would avoid a trial. The Squire has a sympathetic backstory, and the prosecutor doesn't want to risk a not-guilty verdict. He assumes the case will be assigned to an overworked public defender, who will be just as happy to avoid a trial. However, the district attorney sees his easy victory slipping away when it's revealed that Ernest Seaman is being represented by one of Manhattan's top criminal law firms.

At the arraignment, the prosecutor reads aloud the formal declaration of charges. Grand larceny in the third degree is the top charge—a class D felony. It's also noted he's a person of interest in several other burglaries still under investigation. A team of lawyers sit with Mr. Seaman at the counsel table. The most distinguished member of the team whispers to their client. Mr. Seaman stands and pleads not guilty. Flustered by this turn of events, the prosecuting attorney asks for $100,000 bail.

The judge looks over the top rim of her glasses. "That seems a tad excessive, given this is a first offense, and it wasn't a violent act. What does the defense say?"

"We respectfully request zero bond. Mr. Seaman is grieving the recent loss of his wife and is currently in the process of planning her funeral."

"Zero bond. So be it," the judge says.

"Your Honor, at least have him surrender his passport," the flustered prosecutor sputters.

The Squire tugs at his lawyer's sleeve, whispering something before the attorney can object. A moment later, Seaman's attorney addresses the judge, "My client does not have a passport, Your Honor."

"That was easy," the judge says, banging her gavel. "Next case."

CHAPTER 40

The funeral service for Rose Seaman is subdued and sparsely attended. Rose had no surviving family except for Katherine Tierney. Among the other attendees are Caleb and Jordan Vos, Chandice, a couple of people who had worked with Rose during her time as a maid, the staff from Fleischer's butcher shop, and, of course, Teddy. To ease Katherine's concerns about the press and curious onlookers eager to glimpse the Squire, Caleb arranges for extra security at the church and cemetery.

Old Brookville police cruisers escort the small procession of cars from the Brookville church to the Old Brookville cemetery. A winding fieldstone path leads from the parking area up a hill, past old-growth rhododendrons, to the burial site.

Presiding over the Vos ancestors is a massive granite memorial— a life-size figure of a woman wearing a flowing Greek-style robe and a wreath of flowers on her head, emerging from the stone. Her outstretched arms hold a banner declaring *Gloria in Excelsis Deo*—Glory in the highest to God.

A dozen ledger monuments covering the graves of the Vos family encircle the statue. The large, casket-size stones lie half-buried in the ground. The markers all look the same: carved granite with the deceased's name, birth and death dates, and the family crest—a shield divided diagonally with a fox on one side and tulips on the other. Rose's marker bears a Celtic knot instead of the Vos family crest.

Katherine and Teddy stand arm in arm as the minister reads a prayer. Each person in attendance places a violet nosegay on the mahogany casket. Caleb Vos, on behalf of Katherine, invites the attendees to a private luncheon at Glenwood. The mourners meander to their cars, giving the husband and sister of Rose Seaman some time alone for their last goodbyes.

"All this time, she was so close," Katherine whispers, and then convulses in sobs.

Teddy wraps his arm around Katherine's shoulders. "She never forgot you."

The pair stand in silence, each lost in their own grief. Katherine pulls a tissue from her purse to blot her eyes and takes a moment to compose herself before heading back down the fieldstone path.

She climbs into the limousine, joining Caleb and Jordan, the weight of the day settling on her shoulders.

"Is Ernest coming?" Caleb asks.

"He says he needs a bit more time and will meet us later."

CHAPTER 41

A t 11:30 a.m. the following Monday, after failing to show up for his hearing, court officers issue an arrest warrant for Ernest Seaman. While investigating his whereabouts, they learn the last time anyone remembers seeing him was during the funeral for his wife, Rose.

The previous week, Whitney had been part of the team escorting the funeral procession. He watched the graveside service from a respectful distance. The police presence remained until Mr. Seaman left the cemetery; they assumed he left for the reception at Glenwood, and had no reason to follow him.

But Seaman never arrived at the luncheon. Instead, he left a voicemail for Miss Tierney, saying that he wasn't up to socializing and was going straight home. In the message, he also asked her to convey his gratitude to the Voses for all they'd done.

A search of the house on Duck Pond Lane yields no clues. Mr. Seaman's car, an older light green Ford sedan, is not at the Oyster Bay home. However, a sealed envelope addressed to Lieutenant Whitney is found on the kitchen table. Inside is a handwritten note.

Lieutenant,
If it were my fate to spend the rest of my days in your cell, with
occasional visits from Katherine, I would have happily stayed. But
we both know that's not how it would be. It's not my intention to
cause you any more trouble, but I could not bear the thought of her
visiting me at the type of facility the state would surely provide.
Besides, I have unfinished business and promises to keep.
Sincerely, Teddy Seaman

Whitney closes his eyes and sighs. Why would he take off? The larceny charge for the tastevins is minor, a D-class felony—barely more than a slap on the wrist. Even if the prosecutor tied every suspected Squire burglary to Seaman, the Voses' high-powered attorneys would make sure he served little, if any, time. And what promises?

A Be On the Lookout (BOLO) is issued with the description of Seaman and his vehicle. His car is finally located that night at a nearby beach. The officer who first spots the vehicle assumes it belongs to teenagers making out—typical nighttime beach-goer activity. But as he nears the car, the windows are un-fogged, allowing him a clear view into the empty interior. A small bouquet of violets rests on the passenger seat with a handwritten note: "'Til we dance again, my love."

Video from the camera at the concession stand disproves any theories the police initially had regarding suicide. Despite the grainy footage, Seaman is identifiable as he takes a backpack from the car and walks toward town. Whitney is relieved he doesn't need to call Nassau County Police for a team of divers—combing through freezing waters for a body is not a fun job.

The volume of the chief's voice increases with each word. "The Squire got away? What are you doing about it?"

"I've spoken to Chandice, the woman who worked for the Seamans. She claims not to know where he is. The last time she saw, or even spoke to him, was during the funeral," Whitney says.

"Do you think she's covering for him?" Chief Eaves asks.

"No, she seems legitimately worried about Mr. Seaman and shocked at the turn of events."

"Who else could have information about him? Who had contact with him?"

"Besides his attorney, the only other visitor he had was Katherine Tierney."

"From Glenwood?"

Whitney nods. "She came every day when we were holding him downstairs. I called earlier to set up an appointment to talk with her later."

"Tread carefully, Whit."

Whitney returns to his office and settles at his desk. But before he has a chance to prioritize his work for the day, Lois knocks on the doorjamb. "Mrs. Vos is here to see you, Lieutenant," she says.

"Okay, please send her in."

Jordan Vos enters and sits in the chair opposite Whitney. Even with heavy boots and a puffy winter coat, Mrs. Vos still looks fashionable.

"Good morning, Mrs. Vos. How can I help you today?"

"First, Katherine has nothing to do with Mr. Seaman's disappearance. I want that very clear."

"It's procedure—we need to interview her, she was the last person to speak with him."

"Procedure, right. You should know, Caleb and I are prepared to do everything—and I mean everything—in our power to ensure she does not become a scapegoat."

"As I said, my meeting with her is a formality."

Jordan Vos narrows her eyes as she weighs the lieutenant's words. "We both know how much politics plays a role in this town. If someone's not connected, they're treated differently." She clasps her hands in her lap and leans forward. "Katherine and my mother-in-law had ... a history. A connection that goes much deeper than the public knows—she saved Eliza's life when she was pregnant with Caleb. So, you see, she saved my husband's life as well."

The phone on Whitney's desk rings, interrupting her story. Whitney waves his hand, dismissing the noise. She waits until it stops, her eyes never leaving Whitney's.

"I have my own personal connection with Katherine, beyond marrying into the Vos family. Pardon the pun, but I wasn't born with a silver spoon in my mouth. While in college, I worked at Glenwood—yes, under 'The General' herself. After graduating, I applied for an internship at Vos Technologies. Whenever papers needed delivering to the estate, Katherine insisted it be me. That's how Caleb and I met." A small smile tugs at her lips as memories of their first encounter surface.

"Years later, on my wedding day, my father-in-law Jonah pulled me aside. He told me a secret regarding my internship. Since I had included my Glenwood employment on the application, he asked Katherine to confirm. He was surprised when she said she needed to check her records—the General was known for recalling every employee's name and service dates. When she returned, she handed Jonah this."

Mrs. Vos passes a folded piece of paper to Whitney. He notices the embossed initials 'KT' at the top, with 'GLENWOOD' printed just beneath. He opens it carefully. The neat, formal handwriting inside reads:

If you don't hire this young woman immediately, you're a damn fool.

Whitney folds the paper back and hands it to Mrs. Vos. "I don't know Miss Tierney very well, but somehow, this note doesn't surprise me," he says. "You must have made quite an impression on her."

Jordan Vos lowers her gaze, a faint flush coloring her cheeks. She lifts her head and meets Whitney's eyes again, her expression is softer but unmistakably resolute. "Katherine Tierney is more than just the secretary for Glenwood. She's family—and we'll protect her as such."

He notes the quiet strength in her stance and is impressed that the loyalty Miss Tierney has for the Voses goes both ways.

"No one's above the law, Mrs. Vos. However, if it puts your mind at rest, nothing leads me to believe Miss Tierney has any involvement in Mr. Seaman's disappearance. I have a few follow-up questions to ask her, but barring any surprises, my report will state that Ernest Seaman acted alone."

"Thank you for that." Mrs. Vos leans back, visibly relieved. She then pivots to her next order of business.

"Now, I'd like to inquire about our Thorpe and the Tiffany tastevins."

Whitney is mindful not to smile, but Jordan Vos' technique of confessing a personal confidence followed by a professional inquiry mirrors similar conversations he's had with Miss Tierney. Is she even aware of the similarities?

"The provenance documents you supplied prove the Thorpe painting belongs to you and Mr. Vos. And I'm pleased to report that Agent Smith from the Art Crime Division of the FBI anticipates the return of your art soon. Regarding the tastevins, Mr. Seaman never divulged where he sold any of the silver. Unfortunately, with his disappearance, the return of your family heirlooms may take quite a while—if they're ever recovered at all."

CHAPTER 42

A beautiful early June evening settles over the Cantor Roof Garden of the Metropolitan Museum of Art, Laurel feels a flutter of apprehension at being the center of attention. Isadora arranged for the extravagant graduation/bon voyage party in her daughter's honor. The usual city noises are drowned out by the clinking of glasses and calls of "Laurel, over here."

Laurel spots her friend Sydney and rushes over, relieved to see a friendly face among a swarm of her mother's acquaintances. The young women stand together at the railing, gazing out at the city skyline.

"I'm so jealous of you!" Sydney says. "Living in Florence sounds like a dream come true. And, wow, this party—after my graduation, my dad just grilled burgers in the backyard."

"I loved your party, even if your dad barely let the patties warm up. I think I was a vegetarian for the rest of that summer."

Laurel grins then glances back at the guests, spots her mother, and offers a small wave. "This is bigger than I wanted, but ... it's nice— thoughtful, even."

"So, all's good between you and Izzy then?" Sydney asks.

Laurel bites her lip and looks down at her feet. "Life with Izzy is ..." she lifts her head and forces a smile. "... complicated. She said she didn't know Birk was anyone important to me. You'd think a guy coming to the apartment looking for me would be someone she shouldn't ..."

She tips her face toward the sky. Sydney places her hand gently on Laurel's shoulder. "Are you okay?"

Laurel looks at her friend. "She's never been a normal mom. But she's trying, and I'm trying not to dwell on it. She might not have known who he was, but he certainly knew who she was. I figure by the time she visits me in Italy, any lingering desire to yell at her will be completely gone. Besides, I have so many good things happening now.

"Speaking of your good things," Sydney shifts her gaze and says, "Hi Ezra!"

"You two look thirsty." He hands each woman a tall, fluted glass. Laurel's heart races as Ezra's fingers lightly brush the back of her hand. The warmth of his touch spreads through her body and into her cheeks; she hopes her face isn't as scarlet as the ruby-colored cocktail.

"What's this?" Laurel asks.

"Campari, sweet vermouth, and Prosecco—it's called a *Negroni Sbagliato*," Ezra replies.

"Fan-cy," Sydney says.

The young women clink their glasses and toast "to good things," an unrestrained burst of schoolgirl giggles follows.

Isadora presided over every detail of the party with meticulous care, insisting on perfection from the food to the venue—even if her plans didn't fully reflect Laurel's desires. A week before the event, Laurel had begun to feel nervous.

"I said a small party, Mom, family, a few friends. Your condo would have been fine."

"Pfft, you'll be working at the Uffizi. What's a better locale for your bon voyage than another museum? It'll be a small group, plus a few friends of mine who can help with your career. You'll thank me for this."

Sipping her cocktail and gazing out over Manhattan, with the setting sun bathing the city in gold, Laurel realizes that, despite everything, she is thankful for her mother's party.

The celebration's theme is Italy and art. Isadora's requirements: The food has to be delicious, beautiful, and practical—meaning easily managed by people standing with a drink in one hand. Isadora had visions of meatballs rolling off plates and raining down onto 79th Street.

True to her word, Isadora invited only a handful of her friends, each with strong ties to the art world. The guests include the Met's director, who Isadora photographed for *New York Magazine*. He is so impressed by Laurel and her internship at the Uffizi that he offers her a personal tour of the Met's facilities the following week.

Whitney and Nora step out onto the Garden balcony. He places his hand on the small of her back, the satin gliding under his fingertips, mindful not to let his hand drift lower. He was hesitant about bringing Nora, it being hosted by Isadora, but Laurel insisted. The two women would have to meet eventually—he just hoped it could be delayed a decade or two.

They head to the bar. Whitney orders a glass of Prosecco for Nora, and a glass of beer for himself. He scans the crowd until he spies Laurel talking with Sydney.

Laurel had cut her hair into a chic bob, saying she wants to focus on her internship not her hair. An added benefit of the recent cut—most of the pink-streak is gone, the little that remains is tucked behind her ear. She's wearing an orange-and-gold summer wrap dress—very European.

Whitney watches his daughter move about, chatting effortlessly with the diverse party guests. He marvels at her transformation into a young woman fully capable of taking care of herself. Hell, she'd even helped him crack a forgery case. But he's also going to miss the little girl who lived in her Tinkerbell T-shirt and mismatched socks. A smile tugs at the corners of his mouth.

"What are you grinning about?"

Isadora interrupts his thoughts. He never even noticed her approaching. Whitney introduces Nora to her. He never would have predicted that, minutes later, they'd be nattering like old friends.

She kisses Whitney on each cheek, Isadora's standard method of greeting. His previous dates found Isadora intimidating because she's both his ex-wife and a former model. Her flirtatious nature didn't help. Whether knowingly or not, Nora diffuses the situation by saying, "That looks fun," and kisses both of Isadora's cheeks.

"Oh, I like this one, Ricky," Isadora coos.

Whitney, Nora, and Isadora spend a few minutes on small talk before delving into who will visit Laurel and when. Thankfully, it's an easy conversation—Isadora will go in November, and he and Nora will visit over Christmas.

"She's a remarkable young woman," Nora says.

"We did pretty good with that one, didn't we?" Isadora says, appearing to have slipped into the skin of 'proud mama' as if it were a new dress.

"Let's just hope she sticks this thing out," Whitney mumbles.

"Relax, it's not like you're paying for this. Besides, it seems like she's serious about this conservation thing—well, mostly," Isadora says nodding toward Laurel.

The threesome glance across the rooftop, where Laurel is deep in conversation with Ezra. He hands her a small wrapped package.

Laurel holds the box in her hands, her pulse quickening. Is it a ring? Her mind races—he's not on one knee, so it can't be. Still, what if he is proposing?

Afraid she's the center of attention, Laurel darts her eyes around the balcony, checking to see if everyone is staring at her. It feels like an eternity has passed since he handed her the present.

"Open it."

Did he say that? Or was it just in my head?

She looks up; Ezra has a lopsided grin on his face, and a lock of hair hangs over one eye. She reaches up, brushing it to one side. Turning her focus back to the gift, she realizes he wrapped it himself. The paper is a map, with a heart drawn around the town of Florence. Laurel smiles at him before tearing into the wrapping. She opens the package, revealing a small silver box. Her finger traces the etched wreath on the lid.

Laurel throws her arms around Ezra's neck, holding him in a long embrace. The discarded wrapping paper blows away like a colorful tumbleweed until it's picked up by a waiter.

"Thank you," Laurel whispers into his ear, then breaks free and chases after the waiter to retrieve the wrapping paper. She holds the paper against her stomach, flattening it with her other hand as she walks back to Ezra.

Whitney harrumphs. While she's no longer a child, he's not sure he's ready for all the changes that a young man bearing gifts can bring. Nora smooths the furrow from his brow with a gentle finger.

"I wouldn't worry about that," she says. "She's too focused on the Uffizi to let anything stand between her and this opportunity. Besides, it's good to make a man wait—makes him more appreciative."

Nora flashes a knowing smile at Whitney.

"It does, does it?" he asks, pulling Nora close to him. Isadora melts away into the background as he dips Nora with a flourish and kisses her.

The week before Christmas, Whitney is sitting at his desk, finishing paperwork on his last day before flying overseas to visit Laurel. Sergeant Stone steps into his office.

"All set for Italy, Lieu?" she asks.

"Just about. Our flight's at 6:09 tomorrow morning. We arrive in Rome, then take the train to Florence, where Laurel will meet us."

"Does she like it there?"

"Says she does. I think it was a bumpy start at first—new country, new language, new people—but she sounds great now. I'm just hoping she doesn't decide to stay permanently."

"I think Officer Ryan feels the same way," Stone says.

Whitney grumbles, "Is that still a thing?"

"Would you rather she meet an Italian count and decide to stay?"

"Don't you have work you should be doing instead of bothering me, Sergeant?" he says with a smirk.

Officer Byrne enters with the day's mail. He places a few bright red envelopes on the desk—obviously holiday cards—along with a package. He then hands an official-looking envelope directly to the lieutenant.

Whitney stares at the box for a moment, but first he slices open the letter out of habit. At the top is the insignia for the Harper's Cove Police Department—underneath set in gold-embossed letters: CHIEF DENIS HACKETT. The letter itself is handwritten and succinct.

Best decision ever.
PS. thanks.

Whitney brushes the letter aside, his attention drawn back to the package. It's wrapped in brown paper with a postmark saying New York, NY. A flash of the last box he received at the station races through his mind. A queasy feeling grows from deep within his stomach. Eileen Stone notices some color has drained from Whitney's face.

"Lockhart's dead," she says.

He blows out a long breath, weighing the package in his hands. His fingers hesitate for a moment before cutting into the wrapping with his letter opener. Taped to the top of the box is a note. Whitney recognizes the half-script, half-print handwriting.

Kindly return these to Katherine's family. I know it's part of
their holiday tradition. And tell her Nollaig Shona Dhuit.

Before handing the note to Stone, he types the phrase into his phone. It takes the search engine a nanosecond to answer his question. Whitney holds up the screen so Sergeant Stone can read:

"*Nollaig Shona Dhuit* is Irish Gaelic for 'Happy Christmas.'"

Inside, nestled safely in white tissue paper, is a pair of silver tastevins.

AUTHOR'S NOTES

This is a work of fiction. While many characters, places, and events are products of the author's imagination, this story also references historical figures, as well as actual events and locations—including President Theodore Roosevelt, David Berkowitz (the "Son of Sam"), Wolfgang Beltracchi, Mark Landis, Michelangelo, Giorgio de Chirico, and Steve Martin—as part of its narrative backdrop. These references are based on public knowledge and historical record, though in some cases, creative liberties have been taken for the sake of storytelling. No representation is intended beyond that.

The Old Brookville Police Department is real, and while this tale is set in the present day, the depiction of the building and the areas it patrols is inspired by my memories from when my father, Charles Kenneth Smith, served as sergeant, lieutenant, and ultimately chief of the department. Whenever he could, he shared intriguing cases, some of which became seeds for this novel—most notably, the thief who left notes at the crime scene. I remember no other details from that case, and by now it has become a familiar cinematic device.

I grew up in East Norwich, NY—a small town that, despite having its own zip code, is tied to Oyster Bay through the schools. Most people outside the area know Oyster Bay better, thanks to its rich history, and that hamlet plays a secondary but important role in the narrative. Both places are part of my roots, and I wanted to honor them here.

All of the artists my forger, Henry Lockhart, copied are fictional— except for John Singer Sargent, whom I singled out to ground the forgeries and because I admire his work. The painting *A Garden in Florence*, however, is entirely my invention. I also couldn't resist the

Sergeant/Sargent pun, and it wasn't until I began writing these notes that I realized I'd accidentally wandered into *Catch-22* territory. Louis Comfort Tiffany is another actual artist I chose to incorporate into the story because of his ties to the Oyster Bay area. He did design silver tastevins, but the one described in this novel is made up.

My debut as a writer has brought both hurdles and successes. I've had to navigate critiques and strike the right balance with research—enough to add realism, but not so much that it bogs down the reader. I'm grateful to my family and friends, who encouraged me through those creative challenges and gently pulled me back when I got overly absorbed in the details. People have called me a nerd for getting excited about odd things, like the history of a specific paint pigment or an obscure silversmith— but some of those nerdy finds made it into the story (and some—okay, most—did not). I also learned how to sprinkle clues so the ending isn't obvious, yet still lands with a satisfying (I hope) jolt. Regardless, I've thoroughly enjoyed every rabbit hole I've ventured down along the way, and I'm thrilled to have the chance to share this adventure with you.

Thank you for joining me on this ride. Whether you're a fellow mystery lover, a Long Island local, or just someone who picked up the book on a whim—I'm honored you came along. I hope you enjoyed the twists, turns, and maybe even a few of the interesting tangents as much as I did. It's been a long road bringing this story to life, and I truly appreciate you chose to spend your time with it. While this is my first novel, it may not be my last—Whitney, Laurel, and a few other familiar voices have already started whispering in my ear.

ACKNOWLEDGMENTS

While writing this book, my three biggest champions were Connor, Cooper, and Samantha—my littles that became bigs. Their unwavering belief in my ability to step out of my comfort zone and into a new creative realm provided the daily motivation I needed.

I am incredibly fortunate to have had the support of many wonderful people throughout this journey. First and foremost, I want to thank my very patient husband, Greg, for his countless readings of my manuscript and for always offering insightful feedback with kindness and humor.

A special thank you goes to my dear friend and editor, Chris Nicholson. Chris, your expertise, attention to detail, and ability to push me to be my best have made all the difference.

I had the privilege of benefiting from the expertise of several dedicated police officers as I wrote this book. I am deeply grateful to Det. Jerry Aylward (ret.) of the Nassau County Police Department for his early reading of the manuscript and for generously sharing his time, knowledge, and friendship. My sincere thanks go to Sgt. John Ferriso (ret.) of the New York Police Department, whose guidance and invaluable insights into police procedure helped shape my story. Thank you to Detective Jason Takacs of the Fairfield Police Department for his participation in an "Ask the Detective" event hosted by the Fairfield County Writers' Studio and the Sisters in Crime Connecticut chapter. The dedication of these officers to law enforcement and their willingness to share their expertise has been an indispensable resource.

Any liberties taken with police procedure are entirely my own and should not be attributed to these decorated professionals.

I am also grateful to the Sisters in Crime writing association and the Guppies group. Through their classes, guest speakers, critique groups, and support, I was able to craft a much better story than I could have on my own.

To my cousin Jessica Durand, who bravely took on the role of beta reader—thank you for your invaluable perspective. Your insights helped me clarify scenes and strengthen the narrative.

Throughout my career as a graphic designer, I've been fortunate to work alongside incredibly talented individuals. At different points along the way, I've found creative kindred spirits whose support has meant the world to me. To Susan Lampe-Wilson, Beth St. James, Jennifer Thermes, and Lori Wendin: I am in awe of your many talents and treasure the friendships we've built over the years.

Thank you to Peter Francesconi for giving me my first writing assignment. Even though my original 250 words were trimmed to less than half that, your belief that I could take on something beyond my usual skill set sparked a desire to keep writing.

And of course, there's my mom, Paige Dawson.

Finally, there are two people who, even though they are no longer with us, have had a profound influence on me: my father, Ken Smith, and my best friend, Eileen Aylward.

COLOPHON

This book is set in *Questa*,
a typeface designed by Martin Majoor
and Jos Buivenga for the Questa Project.
Questa has its roots in traditional rational
serif faces but features a larger x-height and
reduced stroke contrast, making it well-suited for text.

Chapter headings are set in *Calder Dark* by
Mariya Lish of InHouse Type Foundry.

A customized version of *Bellfort Rough*
by Bartek Nowak of GRIN3 was used
for the book's title.

Kirsten Smith Navin is a graphic designer, debut novelist, and unapologetic type nerd. After years of making other people's words look pretty, she finally decided to write some of her own. Originally from Long Island, N.Y., she moved across the Sound and now lives in Connecticut with her family. When she's not designing page layouts, illustrating, or admiring the swoony curves of a good Bodoni typeface, she can usually be found reading or binge-watching mysteries.

www.ingramcontent.com/pod-product-compliance
Lightning Source LLC
Chambersburg PA
CBHW020418110726
47899CB00006B/2045